ALONE

Alone

**ERIC
KRUGER**

Space Monkey Press

The Benjamin Drake Adventure Series

Hauler

Bounty

Trapped

Alone

| one |

'This is bullshit,' Lieutenant Lily Wells blurted and stomped out of the room. There wasn't much space in the living unit to stomp around in, so he waited for her inevitable return.

'He's untouchable. Doesn't matter how much evidence I have against him. I can't use it.' She set off again but stopped short. The look he was currently receiving did not mean *fix this*. Instead, the look meant *agree with me and sympathize*.

'Uh, that sucks,' he ventured.

'It does. So much,' she said and flopped down on the worn-out couch next to him, her curly brown hair falling into her eyes.

I know, but have you tried to— his brain started but he quickly strangled that thought and buried it deep, deep down. Practical solutions would have to wait till later.

A sound in the adjacent room alerted them to their white box meals being ready.

'I'll get 'em,' he said and quickly returned with two identical white boxes. He handed one over and took his spot on the old couch.

He was burning to tell her about his day and the crazy woman who tried to kiss him and then stab him. Better wait, he knew there was more venting to be done first.

'And he knows it too,' she said through a mouthful of food. 'The way he talks to me. He knows he holds all the power.'

Instead of answering, he nodded and took a bite of food. Best to keep his mouth full and occupied.

'It's like he forgot what happened to his predecessor. As if he is any different.'

They both sat in silence for a while. Outside, the normal nighttime noises drifted in. Living in a higher-numbered sector meant the noises included some screaming, security drones, and the occasional crackle of a distant pulse rifle. The war was too far away from New Franco to disturb anyone's daily life.

'I hate that slimy bastard,' Lt. Lily Wells hissed.

Drake quickly stuffed more food in his mouth, narrowly beating his foot to it.

Briefly touching her chest, as she always did when talking about Sammy Sanders, she mentioned something Drake didn't catch. He decided to let it slide.

Wells finished her meal and tossed the empty container on the small table in front of them. She had the access codes to all the appliances in the living unit and swiped her Human Interface Console to access the Data Display Unit on the wall. Penta considered HICs as a necessity for security personnel, so while Lt. Wells served her two-week suspension, she underwent the procedure to have her busted-up HIC removed and replaced by a brand new, state-of-the-art model.

She accessed the news channel on the DDU and increased the volume.

A computer-generated image of what people perceived as a trustworthy human sat behind a desk, also computer-generated, with a DDU behind them displaying images of explosions and chaotic scenes. Those were not computer-generated.

'As the war continues, Penta issued a statement to its citizens promising them they had nothing to fear. Penta has been able to resist the Shangcorp forces trying to invade our borders. They added that the recruitment bonus had increased to ten thousand credits. Penta believes—'

The DDU went silent, and the screen turned black.

'Same story every night,' Wells said.

His crazy kiss and stab lady story would have to wait for another night.

'Where's Jimmy tonight?' she asked.

'Not sure,' Drake said and glanced at his HIC. Unlike Wells' new one, his was outdated and getting harder to read. 'No messages either. Who knows with him, right?'

Lt. Wells shrugged.

'I need to go. Another long day ahead of giving crims the stink eye and watching them go about their business.'

Drake hated to see Wells so frustrated.

'They could have arrested you instead of probation. At least you're still working and free.'

Wells turned her head and made eye contact. *Agree with me and sympathize.*

'What I'm saying,' Drake kept digging his grave, 'is that we could have had this conversation sitting in a detention center instead of this beautiful palace.' Drake swept his hand across the small room.

The tiniest hint of a smile appeared on Wells' lips. 'I know.'

'So tomorrow when you see a bad guy and you have to restrain yourself from making even the smallest mistake and giving Penta the opportunity to lock you away, just remember, it could have been worse. You could have been working minimum wage and sharing a tiny living unit with the world's loudest snorer.'

The smile increased a fraction.

'I'll try to remember how lucky I am.'

'Good.'

Wells stood up and walked to the door. Drake followed and pressed the DDU to open the door.

Hugging Drake, Wells said, 'Good night. And thanks.'

'Anytime,' Drake replied, and reluctantly let go.

* * *

'Here. It's already warmed up. We're going to be late, ya know?' Jimmy Something warned, as he handed Drake the white box meal. Drake only had one eye open but managed to grab hold of the box.

'Thanks.'

'Better eat it quickly, ya know?' Jimmy said again and left Drake's room.

Sitting up, Drake opened the other eye and breathed in the aroma of the white box meal. It smelled like hot steam, and Drake reluctantly took a bite. He tried to ignore the texture as he swallowed a few mouthfuls down. Being on the road all day, you never knew when the next meal would be available, so he consumed all of it before swinging his legs off the bed and into his trousers. He found his boots, slipped on a shirt that looked clean enough, and grabbed his jacket. A quick look in the mirror told him what he already knew. He was getting older. A few grey hairs had showed up in his stubble lately. He was losing track of the new wrinkles popping up. Running a hand through his shortish dark hair, he felt relief to feel it as full as ever. At least he had that going for him. Opening his door, he found Jimmy standing outside, waiting.

'Where were you last night?' Drake asked as he squeezed past him into the hallway.

'Out, drinking, ya know.'

Jimmy upped his pace and put some distance between them. Unlike Drake, he still looked exactly the same as when they met. A mop of unruly red hair sitting on top of a wiry ball of nervous energy.

'Drinking? With whom?'

Jimmy shuffled quickly around the corner, towards the elevator, ignoring Drake.

By the time Drake caught up, Jimmy was already waiting inside the elevator car with two other people.

'Ground floor, please,' an elderly lady instructed Drake.

He obliged and all four occupants disembarked on the ground floor and made their way towards the building's front exit. Drake and Jimmy made their way to the Hyperloop terminal. It was a quiet five-minute walk, as they dodged other pedestrians and hustled as quick as they could to catch the early Loop.

With seconds to spare, Drake and Jimmy ran through the terminal entrance. The Hyperloop was approaching. It slowed down and stopped right in front of them on the platform. The doors slid open, and people peeled out of it. Once the red light above the doors turned green, everyone on the platform rushed into the white tube and looked for a seat.

Seconds after stopping, the Hyperloop took off, and soon it was back up to speed.

Unlike the Hyperloops outside of cities, the inner-city loops ran underground, not on piles in the sky. Soon after departure, the Hyperloop went down into the ground, and the view through the windows changed to a blur of white cement. Bright LEDs lit up the cabin, and Drake squinted as they scorched his pupils. Their destination was clear across town from their living unit, but it only took five minutes to get there, as they took the non-stop express loop. Before Drake could even get comfortable in his chair, the Loop stopped, and everyone disembarked.

'So, who was drinks with?' Drake tried again.

Jimmy didn't try to outrun him this time.

'Just some old friends, ya know. Not really your crowd.'

They walked in silence. The sidewalks were practically empty in this sector, as it was a manufacturing and business sector. Enormous gray buildings lined the wide roads which carried Hydrocomets and other types of hydrogen-powered trucks. A few hydrocars also passed by. A sign reading *NF55 Haulage* hung over an open gate and signaled their destination.

Drake and Jimmy entered the premises and went straight to a large warehouse filled with Hydrocomets. The place was buzzing with activity, with trucks coming and going. Drake walked straight to a Hydrocomet showing the number fifty-seven. After a quick swipe on his Human Interface Console, he entered the truck and sat in the driver's seat. The passenger door opened, and Jimmy joined him.

'Why would they number it fifty-seven if there are less than twenty trucks here?' Drake asked.

'I don't know. To appear bigger than they are, ya know?'

Jimmy's answer made sense.

'You good to go? Let's get out of here before you-know-who sees us.'

'Almost,' Jimmy replied as he downloaded the day's itinerary to his HIC and finished typing the coordinates into the truck's Data Display Unit. 'Good to go.'

Drake had already run his pre-drive checks and the Hydrocomet awaited his input. DDU screens filled the cabin; he could switch most tasks to automated mode. Having two people operating it was unheard of and overkill, and in fact, the company only employed Drake. They merely tolerated Jimmy at Drake's request. Drake never liked Hydrocomets, and every day that feeling grew stronger. He felt like a passenger, not a hauler in them. He always switched off as many of the automated processes as he could to combat that feeling.

'Let's do this,' Drake said, grabbing the yoke.

Jimmy grabbed Drake's arm. 'Shit.'

Drake glanced at Jimmy before looking straight ahead again. 'Shit,' he echoed.

'Get out of my truck, asshole!'

Letting out a deep breath, Drake said, 'Wait here.'

After putting the Hydrocomet in idle, Drake jumped out of the cabin and walked over to the woman who was yelling at him. Drake was one of the bigger guys in any room and standing in front of the yelling woman made him appear even larger. Her voice being the only thing big about her. As she looked up at Drake with her permanent scowl, she had to crane her neck.

'Forgot to sign in. Again!' A portable DDU waved in front of his face. Or rather, his chest.

Calmly and with no force, he pushed it aside. 'Please don't do that.'

'I wouldn't have to if you signed in every morning like everyone else.'

The joys of hauling for someone else in a truck owned by them and a destination decided by them. It was one of the last industries that survived automation, yet he felt like a robot going through the motions every day.

And now he had to deal with this, too.

'You see me walk in here every day, log into the truck, and drive away. If that's not good enough for you, fire me.'

Drake knew she had no authority to do that. Daddy only gave her the job because *women shouldn't haul.* Everyone knew Kieran Bund treated his daughter like shit for one reason only: she wasn't a man. She was barely more than an employee to him. Drake, and everyone else working at NF55 Haulage, would have had sympathy for her and would have had her back if it wasn't for one tiny thing.

'Seems you came in ten minutes late with yesterday's load. And since we work by the hour, that'll be one hour's worth of penalties applied to your pay this week.'

She was a total dick.

'I'll have to see who had to unload the cargo, and who checked it in and so forth to see how far-reaching your error was. How many people might have been affected. But I have to be honest, Drake, it's looking pretty expensive.'

'Do what you have to do, Jack.'

'It's Jackie! And you bloody well know it.'

'Why is Jack yelling at you?' Jimmy yelled out from the truck.

'Get the fuck out of my warehouse!'

Smiling, Drake turned and walked to the Hydrocomet. He opened the door and, as he sat down, he noticed Jackie was long gone.

'That woman needs to relax a bit, ya know?'

'I thought today was the day that vein on her head was finally gonna pop,' Drake laughed.

'That would be so cool, ya know?'

'Right?'

Drake brought the Hydrocomet back to life.

The green arrow superimposed on his screen guided him along the short drive to the highway. Once they entered the traffic, Jimmy scanned the DDU in front of him searching for a speeding caravan. Latching on to a train of Hydrocomets helped everyone and made everyone's journey quicker and more efficient. The law limited caravans to five trucks, and Drake had to wait for one to appear with a slot for them.

'Okay, get ready. I have a live one,' Jimmy announced a few minutes later.

Drake saw the caravan approach on the superimposed image on the windscreen and switched on Autodrive. As much as he liked to be hands-on, he had to give up control as the lock-on procedure was a completely automated process with no manual override. The caravan flew past them, making the Hydrocomet rock side to side. Once past them, the Hydrocomet fell in behind the caravan, sped up in the slipstream, and locked onto the last truck in line.

A message on the screen confirmed the process was completed.

Having not much to do, Drake turned to Jimmy.

'So, where are we going?'

Jimmy consulted his HIC.

'Um, looks like we're picking up cargo in sector thirty-four and taking it to,' Jimmy swiped around on his HIC, 'a place called Walker.'

'Walker? You are kidding me, right?'

'I'm pretty sure that's how you pronounce it, ya know?'

'It is, Jimmy. I mean, have you ever been to Walker?'

Jimmy shook his head.

'Until I met you, I never left New Franco, ya know, so unless we've been there together, then no.'

An alarm let them know a truck leaving the caravan, and Drake focused back on the controls of the Hydrocomet. A truck, two in front of them, moved to the right and dropped behind them as it lost the momentum of being part of the caravan. Drake's Hydrocomet automatically picked up speed as the trucks behind and the one in front pushed hard to reengage with the caravan. Once everyone had locked back into position again, Drake dismissed the alarm.

'It's a shit town full of shitheads. Hopefully, we can drop and go.'

| two |

Sector thirty-four was right on the cusp of where livable met dangerous. As the sector numbers wound their way down to one, everything became better. Better living units, cleaner streets, less crime. If you went the other way, and the numbers increased, so did things like crime, burned-out hydros, and vacant buildings. Thirty-four was the gateway to both worlds of New Franco. The living units were small and stacked upon each other, but clean and safe. Being a lower-numbered sector meant the housing units shared the area with factories and warehouses. Their windows were intact and had minimal graffiti on them. A few drones buzzed overhead, making sure everyone behaved themselves.

This was one of the last sectors to still have drones patrolling. In the past, Penta had a bigger presence in the higher-numbered sectors. Although they let them run themselves, they kept up their patrol numbers as a show of force. But, since the war with Shangcorp broke out, they moved most of their security personnel and equipment to the newly-found military division. The higher-numbered sectors were left unpatrolled.

Over the years, Penta had let the local crime bosses run their own sectors which turned out to be a stroke of genius. Once Penta withdrew its security forces from the outlying sectors, the crime bosses cemented and enforced their authority, and each sector ran like a small, independent territory. The withdrawal of its forces from the governing corporation led to more stability.

It was not all sunshine and roses. The crime bosses and gang leaders ruled with unchallenged authority and justice was swift and brutal. Still, since Penta's withdrawal from the outer regions, a natural order had befallen the sectors.

'Should be close now, ya know?'

Once they detached from the caravan, Drake took control of the Hydrocomet. Shortly after they turned off the highway and entered sector thirty-four.

Tiny living units lined the streets, and soon gave way to more industrial-looking buildings. Drake followed the green line dissecting the road until it ended in a red inverted teardrop in front of a gray building. Not that the color made it unique as all the buildings looked the same. Seeing a large, open door in the building, Drake slowly turned the truck around and backed it up towards it. It was a slow process as they had an empty cargo trailer hitched to the Hydrocomet. As he approached the opening, he stopped the Hydrocomet and switched it off. After years of being a hauler, Drake had the sense to know which pick-ups were going to be easy, and which ones complicated.

This was going to be a slow one.

'Looks low tech, ya know?'

Drake smiled at Jimmy's observation.

'Sure does, buddy. This might take a while.'

They exited the cabin and walked into the gray building.

'Whoo-hoo! Over here!'

Both turned their heads to find the voice.

'There,' Drake pointed with his chin.

The interior of the building was cavernous and dimly lit but a small brightly lit office stood out in a corner. It also contained the source of the voice.

'That's it! Come on over.'

'They sound friendly, ya know?'

'Seems that way,' Drake mumbled, bracing himself for a personality type best avoided this early in the day.

Crates littered the floor, and they walked in a zig-zag pattern around them toward the guiding voice.

'There we go,' the voice announced.

'I'm Drake and this is Jimmy. We're from NF55 Haulage.'

A smile spread across the already friendly face. More creases in his skin, combined with the white curly hair, Drake guessed he would be a grandfather or even a great-grandfather.

'Well, how do you do, Mr. Drake and Mr. Jimmy?'

'Just Drake and Jimmy will be fine.'

'Well, all right then. Drake and Jimmy. I'm Mr. John Simons but I guess you'll have to call me John?'

Mr. Simons was the opposite of Jimmy— - dark skin, white hair, and about fifty years older— but Jimmy stared back at him like he was looking in a mirror. Big smile from ear to ear, nodding his head along with Mr. Simons.

'John, if you could point—'

Mr. Simons had already turned around and was walking back into his office.

'What the — ?' Drake looked at Jimmy, a beaming opposite of the old man.

'I wish he was my grandpa, ya know?'

'Huh? What are you talking about, Jimmy? You just met the guy!'

'I know. I know, Drake. I never had any grandparents, but if I had, I wished they looked like Mr. Simons, ya know?'

'You mean completely opposite to you?'

Jimmy gave him a puzzled look.

'He seems like a lovely man, Jimmy. How about we see where grandpa disappeared to?'

The door to the office stood open, and Drake and Jimmy entered. Mr. Simons sat behind a desk, swiping through an old portable DDU. Drake couldn't see any other chairs so they remained standing.

'Not to rush you, Mr. Simons, but would you arrange for your staff to load the cargo, please?'

Carefully placing the Data Display Unit down, and wiping the surface, as if to pat it, Mr. Simons looked up at Drake, still smiling.

'There is no staff here, Drake. It's just me.'

Drake turned around and surveyed the cargo containers scattered around the massive warehouse space.

'Just you?'

'Yes, sir. Has only been me, for forty years.'

'Wow,' Jimmy whispered.

None of the containers had any logos or words on them about their contents, and the walls did not have company posters or any clues.

Drake was curious about what Mr. Simons had in those boxes. He was also curious as to what he had been doing alone for forty years hauling for someone. It meant that time was much more important than his curiosity.

'Fine. So, I take it we are loading it ourselves?'

'There is an exolifter in the corner, Drake. Feel free to use it. Oh dear, did I charge it?' Mr. Simons' smile faded into a frown.

'Thanks, I'm sure it will work fine. Jimmy, can you help Mr. Simons with the admin, and I'll load the truck?' Drake couldn't call the older man by his first name, and it didn't bother Mr. Simons either, as he didn't correct him.

'All over it, ya know!'

Drake went over to the exolifter, leaving Jimmy to spend time with his surrogate grandfather.

He was right. This was going to be a slow job. The exolifter must have been one of Mr. Simons' first purchases, forty years ago. Most of the paint on the exoskeletal suit had been worn off, leaving only a few yellow spots hinting at the original color. Multiple wires hung exposed and showed signs of previous repair. Most of them had some tape or silicone sleeves around them. Unlike the units they used at NF55, the frame consisted of metal, not carbon fiber, and the straps were leather, not recycled plastics.

Fearing the worst, Drake located a tiny DDU on the back of the suit and checked the battery level. Thirty percent.

Laughter erupted from the small office as Jimmy's imaginary reunion blossomed.

Drake let out a sigh, and stepped towards the exolifter, hanging in its charging dock. He grabbed one of the leather straps that hung in a loop and shoved his arm through. Twisting himself, he grabbed the other leather strap and maneuvered his other arm through it. Both straps had adjusters on them, and Drake yanked on them to fit the unit securely on his back. Stepping away from the charging dock, He was surprised by the weight of the unit and as he took his first step, he almost fell over. Drake had only ever used carbon-made models which weighed a fraction of this museum piece. After finding his balance and linking his HIC to the exolifter's DDU, he engaged the leg supports. Simultaneously, two braces deployed from the unit on his back and took up position next to his legs. Being an older model, Drake had to strap them manually to his legs. Once done, he activated the arm braces via his HIC and once again, he strapped them on manually. A process that usually took a few seconds, took him almost five minutes, but in the end, he managed it.

It was time to make some calculations and decisions. The exolifter only had thirty percent charge left. Checking his HIC, at full power, the unit would run out of juice in ten minutes. For this unit, full power meant roughly eighty percent lifting power, leaving Drake to lift the remaining twenty percent. Thirty boxes sat waiting for him to load. No way could he do that in ten minutes, even with an exolifter doing eighty percent of the work. Drake dialed the power back to seventy percent, and the time left on the battery went up to twenty minutes. Tight, but doable. With no time to waste, Drake started work, lifting the boxes and placing them in the cargo trailer behind the Hydrocomet. Soon he was sweating, as even with the exolifter's help, he still had to lift thirty percent of the cargo's weight and carry it to the truck. He kept an eye on the power reading, knowing he was cutting it awfully close. Drake also tried to ignore the continued laughter coming from the office. Just for once, he would love to be the one sitting in the office and watching Jimmy do the heavy lifting. As soon as he imagined Jimmy struggling to lift anything, even at the newer model's ninety percent capability, he chuckled. They both had their strengths and their parts to play. He knew it but a man could dream, couldn't he?

'You almost done?' Jimmy's timing was impeccable, as always. Drake turned to face him as he lowered the last box.

'Why? You about to offer some help?'

Jimmy scrunched up his face in confusion.

'No. Just thought you might want to hurry up, ya know? Time to get on the road if we want to stay on schedule.'

A glance at his HIC showed the exolifter had four percent charge left. Just enough to lift Jimmy up and throw him over the building and onto the highway. Instead, Drake used the remaining power to ease his walk back to the charging dock.

'Here's some water,' Jimmy said as Drake came back from returning the exolifter.

'Thanks.'

'Thank you so much for your help, Drake.'

'No problem, Mr. Simons,' Drake replied. 'We got everything we need, Jimmy?'

'Oh yes, we finished ages ago, ya know? Just waited on you.'

Drake forced a smile. 'Okay, time to go.'

'Good luck gentlemen, and remember Jimmy, at least it wasn't red.'

Jimmy's eyes teared up as he doubled over from laughing. 'At least it wasn't red!'

Drake had no intention of getting involved in their little inside joke and climbed into the cabin, ran the pre-drive checks, and waited for Jimmy to get in.

'What a character, ya know,' Jimmy said, climbing aboard and strapping himself in. Shaking his head, he programmed Yolanda, Drake's nickname for the truck's AI and operating system, with the coordinates for the drop-off.

'At least it wasn't red.'

| three |

The drive to Walker was long and monotonous, and soon Jimmy was asleep in the cot in the small living area behind the front seats. Leaving the truck on manual, Drake asked Yolanda to make a call. Three white dots appeared on the windshield, randomly swirling around and then moving together, merging, and taking the shape of a face. A face he quite liked. As he was still in manual driving mode, the face promptly popped to the side, leaving him with an unobstructed view of the road.

'Hey,' Lt. Wells said from the corner of the screen.

From the scene behind her, she was still at work. Since returning from Shangcorp, Lt. Wells had been on probation and placed back on general duties. She had a small cubicle to work from, surrounded by the other security officers and all their noise. Her caseload had taken a dive, as Penta assigned her to minor crimes and civilian grievances only. No major or complicated cases allowed. Penta miraculously decided to let her keep her rank, and she knew, everything considered, she came off light.

'Happy to see you're taking the night off and relaxing.'

'Ha, ha, hilarious. No point sitting in my unit by myself. Might as well be working.'

There was no need to ask what she was working on, especially being after hours and off the clock. He knew there was only one thing she did when not working or hanging out with him and Jimmy. One thing that gave her a purpose and fueled the fire he saw in her eyes.

Sammy Sanders.

The slimy bastard that stabbed her in the chest, left her to die and now sat on the throne of the sector fifty-nine crime cartel. He ruled with Penta's blessing, which made him untouchable.

'Still on the road to Walker?'

'Yup,' Drake said and scanned the telemetry next to Wells' face. 'Still a few hours to go.'

'Jimmy in the back?'

'Uh-huh. Doing what he does best. Sleep.'

'Have you noticed a pattern lately? Whenever I call or come around, he's missing. Am I being paranoid?'

The last few months have been some of the most peaceful times in Drake's life. Since escaping Shangcorp and finding the hauler job at NF55, his life had settled into a predictable pattern. Jimmy and he would haul cargo, and when they returned from the road, they would spend their nights hanging out with Lt. Wells. After the drama of the last few years, it suited him just fine. Sure, it was a tad boring at times, repeating the same pattern over and over again, but how could he complain? He was back on the road hauling. He shared a living unit with his best friend and Lt. Lily Wells had become a permanent fixture in his life.

'What do you mean? He's just tired.'

'So, you haven't noticed how every time I come over, he has some errand to run, or an old friend to catch up with?'

Drake had noticed it, but years of living and working alone didn't prepare him for the minefield of emotions and expectations that came with having a best friend. Maybe Jimmy just needed some space? Maybe he missed his old life and wanted to keep in touch with it?

'I'm sure it's nothing. Just coincidences.'

'I'm telling you, it's not. Can you have a chat with him? Make sure he and I are good? Maybe I said something? You know, he can be very sensitive.'

'I promise, I will. There's nothing I want to do more than explore Jimmy's feelings with him.'

'Great! I'm so glad to hear that, Drake.'

'I was being sarcastic, Lily.'

'I know.'

'You ever been to Walker before?' Drake changed the subject.

'Um,' Lt. Wells frowned. 'Don't think so. It's quite far away from New Franco, and I can't recall chasing anyone that far. Except for you, of course.'

'So, that's all I am to you? A record?'

'No, but it's the defining thing.'

Risking his life, staying in Shangcorp, and finding her again, was the best decision he ever made.

'You'd remember if you had. Walker is a dump. Bunch of outcasts living in the desert and doing who knows what.'

Lt. Wells let out a small chuckle.

'Now I'm intrigued. What's the cargo then? What does a bunch of misfits in the middle of nowhere need from New Franco?'

A valid question and one Drake never thought of asking. Haulers had a very flimsy, adaptable code of honor. One rule was to never ask any questions about the cargo. Chances were, you'd be better off not knowing.

'No idea. Let me check the manifest.'

Accessing the DDU integrated into the dashboard, Drake pulled up the manifest for the pickup from Mr. Simons and displayed it on the windshield, next to the Lieutenant's face.

'Okay, here we go,' Drake said as he started reading it. It was a quick read. 'Doesn't say.'

'It would kill me not to know. Why don't you ever ask questions? Anyway, I have to go, Drake. It's getting late, even for me. Be safe.'

'You, too. We're almost there. I guess we'll stay overnight and leave in the morning.'

Lt. Wells' face dissolved, leaving an empty space on the screen.

* * *

A few lights were still burning in Walker by the time Drake and Jimmy rolled into town. The town was mostly asleep. It was always going to be an overnight haul, and Drake followed the green line on the road to the only truck stop available. Calling it a truck stop was a bit of a stretch. A single hydrogen refueling station, with a tiny building next to it, sat in the middle of an open lot. Located in a semi-arid region, there were hardly any plants or greenery and only a few trees scattered around. Sand swirled around the parking lot of the truck stop, as there was nothing to block the wind. Drake pulled the Hydrocomet into the lot and parked in the furthest corner. He doubted anyone was in the small office, so he decided to sleep and refuel in the morning.

After checking all the systems and making sure the truck was secure, Drake squeezed through the two seats and made his way to the bunk beds behind them. The drive to Walker was a long one, and Drake looked forward to some sleep. Jimmy claimed the bottom bunk and was peacefully snoring away. As Drake readied himself to jump up into his bed, something stopped him.

A shape on his bed.

An orange shape.

Seymour.

Suppressing the urge to wake Jimmy and tell him to keep his toy on his own bed, Drake picked up the orange Automated Service Robot and placed it on the ground. It weighed more than Drake expected and he wondered how on earth Jimmy carried it up there.

At last, Drake stretched out in bed and soon joined Jimmy's snoring chorus.

* * *

'Oi! You awake in there? Oi!'

Opening his eyes, it took Drake a second to figure out where he was and what was happening. Loud banging on the door, focused his attention.

'Open the door!'

The words 'morning person' and 'Benjamin Drake' had never been used in the same sentence. The yelling and banging continued outside, and Drake tried his best to keep his eyes open.

'You up, Jimmy?'

'Uh-huh. Who's at the door?'

'How should I know?'

'You want me to go ask, ya know?'

If they weren't parked on a lot in Walker with a cargo unit full of whatever the locals needed, Drake might have taken Jimmy up on his offer. But considering they were parked on a lot in Walker, in the middle of nowhere, and someone was clearly keen for a chat, Drake gave in and swung his legs off the bed. He let them dangle over the edge for a second before jumping down. Jimmy was sitting on his bed with Seymour.

'They sound a bit angry, ya know?'

'It's because they have to live in this shithole.'

Drake grabbed his clothes, put them on, and squeezed back through the front seats. He opened the door and jumped down from the cabin.

'Who are you?' a leathery-faced man demanded.

In any other town, they would have scanned the Hydrocomet's registration plates and seen who it belonged to. They would also recognize it is a commercial vehicle, and as per the law, it would show them the place of origin as well as its destination. In any other town, they would make the necessary arrangements to unload or accept the cargo, if appropriate. Drake would be able to sign off on a job completed and head home. In any other town.

But this was Walker.

A shit town full of shitheads.

'We're from New Franco with a delivery. Parked here last night because we mistook this truck stop for a truck stop.'

The man ran his hands through the three strands of hair on his head.

'You being smart with me?'

'Unintentionally, I promise.'

'Eh?'

'Never mind. So, this is a truck stop, then?'

The man glared at Drake. 'You didn't tell me you had company.'

Drake turned and saw Jimmy standing behind him.

'Don't see it being any of your business, but yeah. How about you make yourself useful and fill the truck?'

'Why would I do that?'

'Didn't we just go through this? This is a truck stop, right?'

'Yea, so?'

'So do the one thing you are here to do.'

'I'm not here to do shit,' the man said, spat on the ground and walked away. He crossed the road and disappeared into a living unit.

'Who was that?' Jimmy asked.

Drake shook his head. 'Just a typical Walker resident being a dick, I guess.'

A light shone in the only building on the lot, and Drake motioned towards it. Jimmy joined him and they walked over to it. An automated door slid open as they approached, and they entered the small building. Another weather-worn face stared them down from behind the counter.

'Did Frank give you grief?' the woman behind the counter asked as they approached.

'Frank, huh? I take it he doesn't actually work here?' Drake replied.

'Frank? Hell no! Hasn't worked a day in his life. Claims Basic Income like every other idiot in Walker. So, you here from New Franco?'

'Yes ma'am. Was hoping to fill up and then drop the cargo.'

'Well, best get at it, then. Your truck is taking up valuable space.'

Drake smiled and nodded. Good old Walker hospitality.

'Let's go,' Drake said as he pushed Jimmy out the door.

'You pull her up, and I'll connect the hoses.'

'Thanks, Jimmy.'

The hydrogen station only had one pump, and the lot it was on was quite small. Drake had to maneuver the Hydrocomet a few times to get it aligned so that Jimmy could connect the hoses to the truck. Finally, after a few attempts, Drake received the all-clear from Yolanda, the truck's AI, that everything was good to go. He put the truck in hold and joined Jimmy outside.

'So, you gonna tell me what's been going on?'

'Huh? What are talking about? Nothing's going on, ya know?'

Jimmy walked away from Drake and assumed a new position, leaning up against the wall of the small building. It was still close enough for Drake to talk to him.

'Something's up, Jimmy. Whenever we're home, you're never there. I only see you in the truck and even then, you sleep most of the time.'

Drake glanced over at the hydrogen pump and saw it was almost done refueling the truck.

'I'm not going to push this, Jimmy, but even Lily mentioned it.'

'Pfft, figures, ya know,' Jimmy mumbled.

'What does that mean?'

Jimmy started an intense study of his feet and the surrounding dirt.

'Nothing.'

A loud buzzing alerted Drake that the truck's hydrogen tank was full. Ignoring Jimmy, he decoupled the hoses and placed them back into their cradle. Next, he accessed his Augmented Retinal Projector and scanned the code on the pump's screen. Drake's HIC vibrated. He entered his NF55 login details and paid for the hydrogen with NF55's credits. A confirmation message concluded their business.

'Let's go, sunshine,' Drake said, poking fun at Jimmy's sullen demeanor.

| four |

Situated in a semi-desert, in the middle of nowhere, Walker wasn't much of a town. Some would call it nothing more than a settlement. The drive from the refueling station to the drop-off only took a few minutes. The destination turned out to be a typical Walker-style building. A big, unpainted, concrete square with no distinguishing features. Except for the inverted red teardrop on the Hydrocomets screen, Drake would not have identified it from the surrounding identical buildings.

Drake spotted a driveway leading up next to the building and steered the truck towards it. Rounding the corner, a sign appeared on the Hydrocomet's screen.

AUTHORIZED PEOPLE ONLY

FORCE WILL BE USED

'Better make sure our credentials are in order.'

A camera mounted high on the building came to life as they neared it. Next to it, a mounted pulse gun slid out of a slot in the building and turned to face them. Drake brought the truck to a halt.

The sign on the screen made way for another miserable Walker face.

'Who are you? What do you want?'

Drake was astounded that no one in this town could scan things.

'Just scan the bloody truck and let us in.'

He could feel Jimmy reeling next to him, but chances were this miserable lot would lodge a complaint about the delivery, regardless of his attitude.

The man on screen, like most Walkers, was obnoxious but harmless. All noise and no action. Which made Drake hate them even more. The mounted pulse weapon retracted into the building and the man's face disappeared from their screen. Driving slowly, Drake made his way to the back of the building. There, four slack-jawed men awaited them. He recognized one as the man he had spoken to.

After turning the truck around and backing it up to the massive door in the back of the building, Drake shut the Hydro-comet down.

'Let's get this done, so we can get the hell out of here,' he said as he disembarked.

The door to the cargo bay was already open, but as Drake walked around the truck, he found all four men still standing there, arms crossed.

'Do you need an invitation? Everything in there is yours. Just go on and get busy unloading.'

Their arms remained crossed.

The man who appeared on their screen earlier spat on the ground and stepped closer to Drake.

'New Franco fell to the Shangcorp fuckers yet?'

'Uh no. If it did, how would we get this stuff to you?'

'Heard it's gonna happen. Real soon, too.'

'Best hurry then, so we can be back in time for the invasion.'

'Not gonna happen here, though. Ain't that right?'

Three heads nodded agreement in unison.

'Glad to hear it.'

Drake recalled Lily's words. *Why don't you ever ask questions?*

'Why is that?' He regretted it at once.

The man nodded his head at the three men, and it surprised Drake to see them move. They entered the cargo unit attached to the Hydrocomet and came back out, carrying one of the boxes. The men didn't bother with exolifters, and being on the larger side, they didn't struggle too much. They placed the box down between Drake and the man, doing all the talking. The man smiled at Drake, then accessed the HIC in his arm, before he typed in a code on the tiny Data Display Unit mounted on the cargo box. A clicking sound told Drake the box was open.

The man didn't open the lid but instead addressed Drake.

'The reason we won't fall to Shangcorp is because they won't stand a chance.'

Dramatically, he kicked the lid of the box to expose the cargo within.

Pulse guns.

Neatly stacked, fresh from the production line.

That's why he never asked questions. It kept him uninvolved.

Now he was involved.

Transporting weapons was not a big deal and in the past Drake had done his fair share. Since war had broken out between Penta and Shangcorp, all trade in weapons had been outlawed. The newly formed Penta Military Division needed all the weapons they could get. And since Penta made all the weapons, only they had the authority to transport weapons.

Especially to trigger happy idiots out in the desert.

The man stood beaming with more pride than teeth.

'That is a lot of weapons, ya know?' Jimmy broke the silence.

'Yup, and it's none of my business. So how about you three keep unloading, and we'll be out of here?'

Drake motioned to Jimmy, and they walked to the front of the Hydrocomet.

'Did grandpa tell you what the cargo was?'

'Um, not really, ya know?'

'Not really, or no? Big bloody difference, Jimmy.'

'Um, not sure?'

It didn't matter. Regardless if Jimmy knew, or Jackie or anyone at NF55, if Penta Security pulled them over, found the weapons, they would lock them up at once. The faster they could empty their truck and get back on the road, the better.

'Jump back in the truck and make sure everything is up and running. We're leaving as soon as they're done.'

* * *

As the lid to the cargo bay closed, Drake sped off. He didn't want to waste another minute in Walker. He also wanted to put as much distance between him and those weapons.

'Yolanda, call Lily Wells,' he instructed the truck's AI as soon as they hit the highway.

The three dots merged almost at once.

'Hey. I was about to call you and see how things are going in Walker. Hi Jimmy.'

'Hey Lily,' Jimmy replied flatly.

'Are you in your office? Can we speak?'

'It's not an office, it's a desk with no privacy. And no, I'm not there, I'm on my way to a job. Break-and-enter.' Lt. Wells rolled her eyes.

'So, you're alone?'

'Yes Drake, I'm alone!'

'So, remember how you told me to ask more questions?'

'Mmm, I guess? Why?'

'Well, I did, Lily. I asked a question that I knew I didn't want the answer to.'

'You all right Drake? What's going on?'

Drake glanced at Jimmy, who looked ready to flee.

'I asked them what the cargo was.'

'Asked who?' An irritation had crept into Lt. Wells' voice.

'The clients. In Walker. I asked them what the cargo was.'

'Oh. And?' Curiosity replaced irritation.

Drake realized he made a mistake calling Lt. Wells. In true Benjamin Drake fashion, he acted before thinking it through. Jump in headfirst and deal with the consequences later. He had her attention now, but what he had to tell her would only upset her. He had wanted to share his discovery but hadn't thought about how it would affect her.

Jump, then think.

'Drake, what was it? You called me so it had to be important. C'mon, spit it out.'

Jimmy slowly shook his head.

Drake jumped again.

'Penta pulse weapons. Crates, full of them. Straight from the assembly line.'

Lt. Wells' face froze on the screen. If not for the slight movement of the vehicle she was traveling in, Drake would have reset the communication line. The silence filled the distance between them.

'I'm sorry. I shouldn't have asked them, and I shouldn't have called you.'

More than one demon fed the fire inside of Lt. Wells. One demon was Sammy Sanders, newly crowned boss of sector fifty-nine. The man who stabbed her in the chest and left her to die. This demon was pure payback. He had no hidden agenda or personal reasons for what he did. She was in the way, and he removed her. Still, what he did to her was unforgivable, and changed her life. She had vowed to exorcise him.

Demon two was personal. He hadn't succeeded in hurting her, but he tried to destroy her. Although he failed, he would never stop trying. He was a parasite and needed to be exterminated.

He was also part of the leadership of the newly-formed Penta Military Division, a position and rank he achieved by double-crossing his biggest asset. The man who stole Mars, Captain Raymond Santo. Making deals and selling out friends had always been his modus operandi and newly promoted, Colonel Eugene Davis found himself placed high in the hierarchy and protected from his past.

A past that included Lt. Wells.

'Davis is behind it,' she finally spat out the words.

'That's what I thought. That's why I called you.'

'If I... ugh... that man... fuck!'

Lily's knuckles tried to break out of their skin, and Drake wondered if she was about to fracture her vehicle's yoke.

'I'm sorry, Lily, I shouldn't have told you.'

'It's fine, Drake. Not your fault. It's good, actually. He believes he's untouchable. I might be powerless right now, but I'll never forget. I'll never give up.'

He was scared, seeing Lily so determined to exact revenge on Davis.

'You okay?'

One blink and her entire face softened.

'Yes. Got to go. I'm almost at the scene. Bye, Drake. Nice seeing you again, Jimmy.'

Jimmy mumbled a reply to her.

Drake smiled at her face before it disappeared off the screen. She had taken on a more familiar look. A more comforting one.

Except the eyes.

They were still on fire.

| five |

A long black strip divided the landscape into two symmetrical parts. Both were dry and almost void of plant life. There were no hills or landmarks, just vast empty spaces. A green line on the black strip ran straight and disappeared into the distance. No deviations. No changes. Only a straight line surrounded by nothingness.

Drake loved it. The vast open spaces allowed him to breathe deeper, filling his lungs in a way he could never do in New Franco or any other city. Being out here, he felt at peace. Although he was born and raised in New Franco, it was here where he felt most at home.

Next to Drake, Jimmy was swiping away on his HIC, completely immersed in it, not caring about the outside world streaking past them. Drake flicked the Autodrive on and the audible confirmation from Yolanda startled Jimmy.

'You tired? I can watch things if you want a rest, ya know?'

'No, I'm good, thanks, buddy. Just thought it might be a good time to have a chat.'

Jimmy had one eye back on his HIC. Was it a lack of focus or Jimmy trying to avoid what was coming?

'What do you say you switch off your HIC and we talk?'

Jimmy gave him a suspicious glance before abandoning his HIC.

'What do you want to talk about?'

'I think you know.' Jimmy's face was frozen. 'You and the Lieutenant.'

Jimmy squirmed and looked at his arm, hoping his HIC would somehow save him.

'Did something happen that I missed?'

'No.'

'I know she can be a bit blunt sometimes. Did she say something that hurt your feelings?'

'No.'

'Then how about you tell me, instead of me guessing and you grunting at me?'

Jimmy's lips moved; a clear indicator of an internal dialogue taking place.

Drake waited it out. A quick glance at the truck's screen showed everything to be running smoothly. The estimated time of arrival back at NF55 was also still in the green. He turned back to Jimmy and waited.

Finally, Jimmy said, 'I wish we were back in Lan-noi smashing rocks, ya know?'

This was not the answer Drake was expecting.

'Huh? What do you mean? That place sucked. We lived in a car and worked our asses off and I almost died there!' Drake grabbed his rib cage and ran his hand over it to remind Jimmy of their narrow escape stealing a hydro and Drake taking the beating of his life. Even after they arrived back in New Franco,

Drake still had to wear the graphene sleeve for weeks to help his ribs heal.

'Yea, but it was fun. Just us, ya know?' He said the last part so quietly, Drake had to lean in to make sure he caught it.

'What are you talking about! Look at us. Hauling together, living together. It's the same.'

'Till we get back home, ya know.'

Drake didn't want to say it out loud and put it out in the world, but he knew what the problem was. It was clear.

Lily.

'You are jealous of the lieutenant.'

Jimmy looked like he smelled one of his own farts.

'No! I'm not jealous, ya know? But yes, her. Why does she always have to be there? And why are you always trying to please her, ya know?'

'Please her?'

'Yes. That's why you took this job, isn't it? It pays shit and you are hauling for someone else. You're only doing it because it's legit and you want to impress her, ya know. Don't tell me you like this job?'

'Jimmy, this job is great.'

No one in the cabin believed that.

'I thought you liked Lily?'

'I do, ya know, but you spend all your time with her, and because of her, you took this job. And, ya know, it's *your* job. I don't even get paid for this. But I went along, because—' Jimmy shrugged, as if that would explain it.

'Because I forced you?'

'No, because I wanted to. I love being partners with you, Drake. But it feels like I've become a burden, ya know? You can do this job alone. You have more fun when I'm not home. Maybe I—'

Drake didn't want him to finish his sentence. 'Is that why you're always going out when Lily is there? What do you think we get up to?' Drake laughed.

'I don't know.'

'Nothing. Just talking. About you, half the time. We're just friends, Jimmy. And you are a friend. You know Lily is crazy about you. There is no need to feel like this.'

'But I do.'

Drake had not seen Jimmy this sad since they met. He was staring off into the distance, his mind somewhere else.

'I'm sorry, Jimmy. I guess I have been a bit preoccupied with the Lieutenant lately. How about, tonight, just you and I go for a drink? Maybe you can introduce me to some of your old friends, huh?'

Jimmy still had a sullen look on his face, but Drake saw a little sparkle in his eyes.

Punching Jimmy in the shoulder, Drake said, 'C'mon! It'll be great! You can even pretend we're back in Lan-noi!'

Although his eyes were a little watery, the smile on Jimmy's face was real.

'No thanks. Last time we drank there, those Slavor girls almost killed me!'

* * *

Advertisements started to clutter the windscreen announcing their arrival in New Franco. Jimmy did his best to get rid of them, but every time he closed an ad, another one popped up. Drake merged into the traffic on the superhighway – a massive multi-lane road that ran in a gigantic circle around New Franco. Regardless of the time of day, the highway was always packed with vehicles.

The sun was about to set, and Drake and Jimmy could feel the tiredness of a day spent sitting in the truck seep in.

'Ready for that beer?' Drake asked.

'Oh yeah. But we don't have to go with my friends, ya know. It could just be us.'

Drake wondered if there were actual friends but didn't ask.

'Your call, buddy.'

'I think just us, ya know.'

Drake nodded and smiled.

Approaching their turn-off, Drake moved over a lane and took the exit. It took them into an industrial area, Sector 56. A few more minutes and they would be at the depot. Drake glanced at the ETA on the screen and saw green numbers. Traffic was light and soon they arrived back at the depot, well ahead of time. Drake parked the Hydrocomet, and together they did the final checks before disembarking.

'Cutting it pretty close, pretty boy.'

Jackie.

Greeting her with his biggest smile, Drake said, 'If you mean bringing her home two hours early as cutting it close, then yeah, I guess so.'

'Have you completed all your sign-offs?'

Drake kept smiling.

'Yup. Everything is done. No issues to report.'

'Hmmm,' Jackie breathed out and searched for something on her HIC. 'Not according to this report. What I'm seeing here is that the client wasn't too happy.'

'Really?' Drake rolled his eyes at Jimmy. He knew this was coming.

'Said you were insulting and rude.'

Drake almost laughed out loud.

'Yeah. So was he. Have you ever been to Walker, Jackie?' A silent stare served as an answer. 'Well, they're all dickheads out there. Trust me. I just spoke his language.'

Assuming they were done, Drake turned to grab his bag and get out of there.

'A complaint is a complaint, so there will be a five percent fine on your paycheck this week.'

When Drake turned back, Jackie was already scurrying away.

'Fuck you, Jack,' Drake mumbled.

Jimmy hopped out of the cabin and joined him.

'Let's go, Jimmy. I really need that beer now.'

* * *

Jimmy came back to the table carrying two glasses of beer. From the unmarked tap, as usual. Like most unmarked beer, it satisfied the only two criteria: it was cold and cheap. Drake took a big gulp and felt the cold liquid run through his body, calming him down. The sooner he could drown out Jackie the faster he could get to enjoying the night with Jimmy.

'So, this is the place you go every night?'

Most of the tables were taken and only a few spots remained empty at the counter. The crowd were working people and some still had their dirty uniforms on. Not the classiest joint Drake had ever been in, but far from the seediest. His glass was clean and the beer cold. Not a bad place.

'Some nights, ya know. Not always. Depends.'

Drake hoped letting Jimmy decide the location for tonight's beers and putting him in his environment would ease this tension between them, but Jimmy was still all nerves.

'You okay, buddy?'

Jimmy glanced at his HIC before answering. 'Yea, you know, just tired.'

The drive out and back to Walker had been long, and Drake didn't blame him.

'We don't have to stay if you don't want to?'

Another glance at his HIC.

'No, it's not like that, ya know.'

A minute passed before Drake spoke again.

'Wonder what we're hauling tomorrow?'

Drake saw Jimmy's eyes involuntarily shoot down to his HIC. It was like a tic. Every time Drake spoke, Jimmy's attention went to his HIC.

'Are you supposed to meet up with someone, or be somewhere else?'

Another glance.

'No, it's just—' Jimmy shuffled his feet nervously. .

'Buddy, what the hell? Just spit it out.'

'I want to contribute more. I want to be a partner, not a seat warmer, ya know.'

'Jimmy, you're—'

'It's fine. I don't mind. Didn't mind. But now I want to be more again, ya know.'

Drake could see he had more to say, so he waited for Jimmy to gather his thoughts.

'I have a contract, a good one, ya know. Major credits. A contract we can do by ourselves and get away from NF55. You and me, ya know.'

The more he talked, the more animated Jimmy became.

'Uh-huh? Last time you had a contract for me, we ended up putting Santo on Mars.'

It was a half-truth and a slight exaggeration. Jimmy did hire Drake to haul Bismuth, which ended up in Jacob McKenna's new shuttles, which in turn transported Santo and his team to Mars, where they did in fact occupy Mars. But when the dust settled, Penta exonerated both of them, as they were merely puppets in everything going down.

'This time it's different.'

'Sure it is,' Drake laughed. 'Tell me how this is different.'

Jimmy swiped the artificial skin on his arm, which turned into a screen. He read something on his Human Interface Console as if getting his facts in order.

'There is almost no risk involved, although the number of credits would suggest otherwise,' Jimmy recited.

'There is no such thing as a high-paying job that doesn't involve risk! Not for a hauler, anyway. I think you're getting scammed, buddy.'

'I'm not, ya know! This is legit.'

'Okay, settle down. If it's so legit, where did you get it from?'

Rotating his beer glass a few times, Jimmy pondered his answer. It took five rotations to find the correct one.

'The old man.'

'What old man? Who are you talking about?'

'From the Walker job.'

The old man. The one who had Drake load illegal firearms into his truck and haul it across the country to a bunch of dickheads who were going to shoot and kill who knows who. That old man.

'Fuck no.'

Jimmy stopped playing with his empty beer glass, but his eyes were still looking down at his hands.

'Drake, I'm doing this job. With or without you, but I'm hoping with, ya know.'

'Jimmy, I think you're making a mistake. Running firearms, illegally in a time of war? Seriously, buddy? That's crazy!'

'So is working your whole life for someone else, ya know, and waking up one day realizing it's all over, and you've been running in circles.'

Drake opened his mouth but closed it again. He had no answer.

* * *

Staring at the two rings, he slowly lifted the glass and placed it in the middle and above them, making a Venn diagram with the new condensation ring. Drake wondered what he'd have to write in the circles to make the middle one happiness. Or even, content. He thought putting Jimmy, Lily, and Drake down would do it, but he knew that was not true. Hauling, friends, and stability was also a lie. It didn't matter what words he used, things weren't connecting and overlapping to form the perfect middle.

'Is it more pulse weapons?'

Jimmy was mesmerized by Drake's condensation art and snapped out of it when he spoke up.

'I guess, I mean, yes, that's what he does, ya know.'

'And you know all this from your little meeting while I loaded the truck by myself?'

'Uh-huh. He's a very straightforward guy, ya know. He told me what the cargo was and if we ever wanted to make serious credits, to give him a call.'

'What? You knew the whole time we were hauling weapons?'

'Uh-huh.'

'And you never thought to tell me?'

'It never came up, ya know?'

'Jimmy, I specifically asked—'

If not for the look of innocence on Jimmy's face, Drake would not have let this go.

'That's not a contract, Jimmy. That's an empty promise with no guarantees.'

Jimmy ran his fingers over his arm to activate his HIC. 'But this is,' he said holding up his arm. Drake leaned forward to read the text displayed on Jimmy's HIC.

...so, as discussed, I have an opportunity coming up. A simple collection. Due to the nature and location, it needs to be handled privately and discreetly. Which made me think of you, Jimmy. Talk to your partner, but please hurry. I need to know ASAP.

'It's still not a contract,' Drake insisted.

Jimmy swiped his fingers toward Drake, who felt his arm buzz slightly. Looking down, Drake saw a file-received notification. He opened the file and read it.

'Okay, I stand corrected. It is a contract. But the credits on offer imply risk, even if he denies it. Besides, we'll need a truck, so it's not possible.'

'Say we had a truck, ya know. Would you do it then?'

They didn't, and even an older Hydrostar would be way more than they could afford. This thing was dead before it even started.

'Sure, Jimmy, in the impossible and highly unlikely event that we ended up with a truck, I'd consider it.'

Jimmy's look caught Drake off guard. His eyes were filled with hope and his smile was confident.

'So, if I can get us a truck, you'd do it?'

'That's not what I said, Jimmy.'

'But you'd consider it?'

Drake didn't want to answer.

'Hang on, I need to piss,' Jimmy said and left the table.

Drake looked at the three wet circles on the table.

Contract + Jimmy + Own Truck = Happiness.

| six |

'Even if we found a cheap truck, an old Hydrostar, it would take far more credits than we have. Or could get hold of in time. He said to hurry which means it has to happen quickly, and I can't see how we could do this quickly. Or slowly, to be honest.'

A few drops of rain started to fall, but the walk back to home was relatively short, so they pushed on.

'You're thinking about this all wrong, ya know?'

Drake pulled his collar up higher.

'How so?'

Jimmy rubbed his hands together for warmth, but it made him look comically mischievous.

'I know you're against stealing, ya know,' Jimmy looked at Drake to confirm he hadn't changed his mind or morals in the last few meters. 'So, we'll have to do this operation by the book.'

'If we do it.'

'Yes. So, the only way is to buy or borrow or, ya know, rent a truck.'

Drake had never heard of anyone lending out their truck, and renting one was not an option. Contractors would haul cargo for you, but no one was going to rent you their truck and allow you to drive it yourself. Just not gonna happen. Which only left buying.

'So, we're back to square one. Buying a truck. And like I said, we don't have the credits.' Drake realized Jimmy had not thought it through. The lure of a large sum of credits blinded him.

'But there is a way, ya know,' Jimmy said rubbing his hands again. This time Drake was convinced it was done on purpose.

'Jimmy, just tell me. I'm too scared to ask.'

Grinning, Jimmy said, 'We borrow the credits. With all the credits we'll make, ya know, we can pay it off and keep the truck when we're done. We'll be set!'

He made it sound so easy.

'Borrow from whom?'

The only places to borrow credits from in a Penta territory were from the centralized bank or loan sharks. They were both equally ruthless and vindictive. One claimed to be legal, but the differences were negligible. Dealing with either was a sure way to sign your life away. Once you owed them, they owned you.

'I know a guy,' Jimmy said, brimming with confidence.

'You know a guy?' Drake mocked him.

Their living unit block was around the corner. It was still raining but had dwindled to a drizzle.

'Yea, ya know, a guy who does these things.'

They rounded the corner and Drake saw their building.

'And by *these things* you mean illegal loans?'

Drake waved his HIC across the DDU next to the door leading into the block of living units. A computerized voice welcomed him, and Jimmy copied his movements and received his own welcome. The door slid open, and they entered the small lobby. The elevator was already waiting for them and programmed to take them to their floor. They entered and within seconds exited again.

Lt. Wells stood waiting in the hallway in front of their unit.

'Great,' Jimmy mumbled.

'Hey!' Lilly greeted them as they walked up to her.

'Why are you standing outside?' Drake asked.

Lt. Wells had an authorized code to enter the building and their unit, something Drake gave her, so he found it strange seeing her standing there outside of their unit.

'Oh, I just arrived, and I was finishing a call anyway, so—' She locked eyes with Jimmy. 'Haven't seen you in a while? How are you?'

Drake saw Jimmy relax as she spoke to him. He always did have a soft spot for her. Whatever this thing was between them, it could be fixed. It had to.

'I'm fine, just tired, ya know. Good to see you too.' Jimmy made his way past her and entered the unit.

Wells looked at Drake and shrugged.

'How was Walker?'

'All I can say is, be glad you haven't had to go there. Just a bunch of dickheads being miserable in the middle of nowhere. Coming in?'

Wells nodded and followed Drake into the living unit. Jimmy was nowhere to be seen and the DDU next to his room's door had a yellow light: do not disturb.

'I'm just going to get rid of these boots quickly. Have you eaten yet?' Drake was already walking to his room to get changed.

'No, I'm starving. Mind if I grab a meal?'

'Go ahead. You bought half of 'em.'

'You want one?' Wells asked.

'Nah, I'm good. Almost done.'

Wells was already sitting on the couch watching the news when he came out of his room.

'What's the score?' Drake asked sitting down. Images of soldiers served as a background to tonight's war data. The screen was filled with numbers and the computer-generated AI host tried to explain it to the masses. Drake preferred to listen to Wells's interpretation.

'Well,' she shifted a leg underneath her and leaned forward. 'It seems there's a lull at the moment. Neither side is pushing that hard to make any gains. It's a standoff. I think, and I've heard rumors that both sides are trying to see what other weapons the opposition might be holding back on.'

'You mean nuclear?' Drake heard his voice go a pitch higher.

'No, I don't think so. They both know that would be suicide. More likely long-range hypersonic missiles and drones. Things they can send over so quickly we wouldn't have time to react.'

'But aren't those already around?'

'Yup, but we're talking bigger scale. More devastation. The current ones we have and they have are quite small. Big enough to cause serious damage, but nothing to scale. But I've heard the term 'city-eraser' thrown about.'

All because he took a contract that ended up putting Captain Raymond Santo on the moon.

'This would have happened anyway, Drake. Shangcorp and Penta have been waiting to have a pissing contest for decades.' It's like she read his mind. 'Besides, McKenna and Santo would have done this with or without you. You just happened to be in the wrong place at the wrong time.'

'I know. It's just—'

'Looked like you and Jimmy had a good night out?'

Wells had finished her white box meal and placed it on the small table in front of them. She licked her lips and wiped her mouth with the back of her hands.

Before the Lieutenant, Drake would never have imagined how much he could enjoy watching someone finish a meal.

'Yea. Jimmy reckons he might have a side hustle for us. But I'm not so sure.' Telling her a half-truth now would help when it became less of a truth later on.

'Hauling?'

'Uh-huh. But we'll need a truck and stuff, so I don't see how it will even happen. Besides, I don't want to risk my job at NF55.'

'I thought the plan was to get your own truck again?'

'Yes, but it will take time. This thing with Jimmy is a short cut, with short cut drawbacks.'

Wells uncurled her leg and swapped it around with the other one.

'What drawbacks?'

'Like a business loan to buy a truck. That's a drawback because we'll have to start paying the moment they give us the loan and we'll only receive the credits after the contract is done.'

'Can't you ask for some credits in advance?'

'Maybe. We'll see. Anyway, it's something to think about, I guess.'

Drake saw Well's arm light up and she glanced at her HIC.

'Work?'

'Yes,' she said as she scanned the message. 'Not really.' Her turn for a half-truth. 'It's the Lieutenant in charge of overseeing Sammy Sanders.' Her hand went to her chest. 'We have a long history together and they have been keeping me in the loop on Sammy's dealings and movements.'

'Is that good for you? I mean, you can't touch him, so is this healthy for you?'

Wells rubbed her chest.

'Maybe not. But one day it's going to be very unhealthy for him.'

| seven |

Like most mornings, the smell of a white box meal woke Drake. It must have drifted underneath his door, as he was alone in his room and could not see a meal next to his bed. Jimmy was usually up before him, and Drake was used to the sight and aroma of a white box meal next to his bed in the mornings. Today Jimmy was still prepping the meal. Drake rolled out of bed, grabbed some pants, and sauntered into the living area. Jimmy sat at the small table, two meals in front of him, immersed in his HIC.

'Hey,' Drake announced himself.

'I think I've got us the credits, ya know?'

Jimmy was all smiles and positive energy.

Drake still needed some time to wake up.

'Is that right?' He said, taking a seat and starting his meal.

'Oh yes. Last night, when you and the Lieutenant were up to whatever, ya know, I contacted some old friends and put the word out that we're after a loan.'

Drake glared at him, as Jimmy took a bite of his breakfast. He kept the glare until Jimmy stopped chewing.

'Don't you think you're jumping the gun there, buddy?'

'No, it's like you said, ya know, time is of the essence.'

'Hold on, partner! I was merely quoting what the old man had said.'

'Yes! Exactly. So, I put the word out, ya know, and I've found a very promising lead.'

The energy and smile never waned.

Drake took a bite of his breakfast, giving himself time to brace for the half-assed plan that he was about to hear and also to make Jimmy wait a bit longer. He looked like he might explode with energy and excitement.

'All right. . Who is—'

'His name is Steven Ward, but everyone calls him Numbers, ya know?'

'Very original. Why him?'

'He kinda works as an intermediary for people who have credits but don't want to loan it out directly, ya know. He's sort of a facilitator. Maybe that should have been his name, ya know? The Facilitator. Sounds pretty bad ass.'

'The Washing Machine would have been more accurate.'

'Huh?'

'Seriously? The man launders credits for criminals. Hence Washing Machine.'

'Yeah, I guess.' Jimmy sounded unconvinced.

Drake pushed on. 'So, you want us to borrow credits from a loan shark who we know for sure works with high-ranking criminals?'

'Actually, he's an accountant, ya know. Numbers, remember?'

'Okay, an accountant who works for dangerous people. That's our best bet?'

'Drake, as long as we complete the contract and pay them back, ya know, it doesn't matter. Look at the contract. It's a simple pick up and deliver job, ya know.'

Some jobs were simple. You showed up, loaded the cargo, and left. Then you unload it again at another place and you are done. Most contracts and jobs were like this. Clean and easy. But haulers attracted attention, especially from people from whom you didn't want attention. Bandits, small-time criminals, and even other haulers. There was always a chance the cargo was valuable which made people curious. It also made hauling inherently dangerous. Most jobs were fine, but the ones that weren't usually involved blood.

Drake had a feeling this one was the latter. The sooner Jimmy realized he was way over his head, the better.

'Nothing is ever that simple, Jimmy. But I'll tell you what. How about we go and see this Numbers guy and take it from there?'

Jimmy leaped to his feet. 'Now?'

'We have the day off, so I guess if he's available.'

'He's available!' Jimmy yelled.

'What?'

'I picked up a bit of an *I'm in* vibe from you earlier, ya know, so I sent him a message.'

Reflecting on the conversation, Drake failed to see when he might have given off such a vibe.

'Where does Mr. Numbers do his dodgy deals?'

'Just Numbers, ya know. No mister. And he works out of sector twenty-five.'

That surprised Drake. He expected to hear a high number, in fact, a very high number, but sector twenty-five. Never. The hush-hush dealings Drake had been privy to had happened in sectors with numbers closer to sixty, not twenty. Twenty was getting close to the wall which kept people like Jimmy and him away from the elite. The one percent who had all the credits and left everyone else in the higher numbers to fend for themselves. Penta protected them day and night and even with the war, they didn't pull out any of their security resources.

Numbers wasn't quite in the protected zone, but he was damn close.

'There will still be drones patrolling in that sector,' Drake informed Jimmy.

'I guess.'

'So, the moment we go there, Penta will have a record of us visiting his place.'

'Uh-huh.'

'Which means Lily will know.'

Jimmy opened his mouth, but no words were forthcoming. Drake waited for a beat, but still nothing came out.

'It's not so much what she'll say. It's just that she's under a microscope, Jimmy. Any wrong move and they'll kick her out, or worse, detain her.'

'So, we just stop living, ya know, until she gives us the green light?'

All Jimmy's frustrations and behavior of late were summed up in that phrase.

Drake looked at his friend, maybe the only real friend he had ever had, and saw the disappointment on his face. More than that. The defeat. It had been months, maybe more, since Drake had seen that look on Jimmy.

And he caused it.

'Fuck it, let's go.'

Jimmy's face lit up as the bottom fell out of Drake's stomach.

* * *

A walk, two Hyperloop rides, and another short walk later, Jimmy, Drake, and Seymour arrived at sector twenty-five. Here the living and commercial units were clearly separated, unlike the higher numbers where they mixed and often were on top of each other. This low in the numbers, the sectors had neat little clusters of commercial units, surrounded by organized groups of living units, each with a little yard. The units were much smaller than the ones beyond the wall, and roughly the same size as the ones Drake was used to, but they were free-standing and well maintained.

Jimmy and Drake stood in front of one of these well-kept living units, staring across the street at a small complex of commercial units. Seymour was sitting next to Jimmy, programmed to alert them to the presence of any drone or Automated Security Vehicle. Jimmy had also recently upgraded Seymour with an Electrical Pulse, or EMP for short, module, but that was for emergencies only. Drake hoped they wouldn't need it today, but made sure Jimmy had it at the ready, nonetheless.

A small white box diner, a Citro outlet, a general store, and a beauty salon caught Drake's eye. He assumed there would be more shops around the corner.

'Maybe you should pop in and upgrade that crappy HIC of yours, ya know?' Jimmy said, pointing to the Citro shop.

'Maybe next time. Let's get this over with first.'

Jimmy consulted his HIC and led the way across the street towards the commercial buildings. He led them past the beauty salon and the Citro outlet store before stopping. A door was nestled between the Citro outlet and the white box diner. It had no numbers or logos on it, or a DDU to open it with.

'Now what?' Drake asked.

Jimmy rummaged through his HIC again.

'Hang on,' he said, and Drake saw him access his ARP.

Visible only to Jimmy, instructions of some sort must have come up on his ARP, as he was swiping away on the door and pressing seemingly non-connected areas on its surface. He must have followed the correct sequence, as the door slid open and revealed a small space behind it.

'Let's go,' Jimmy said and entered without the slightest hesitation.

Drake quickly followed and found himself shoulder-to-shoulder with Jimmy in a tiny elevator. The door closed, and the carriage started its descent.

'I feel a bit trapped here. Who knows what will happen when the doors open?' Drake said.

'I don't think we have anything to worry about, ya know? Why would they go through this trouble just to shoot us?'

Before Drake could respond, the elevator stopped, and the doors slid open. A narrow walkway led to a door. Drake motioned for Jimmy to lead. This time there were no more virtual locks, and the door slid open as they approached it. Drake followed Jimmy through the doorway and into a brightly lit room.

In the middle of the room stood a desk, flanked by two androids. Although a common sight in factories, they were rarely seen outside of them. Most commercial Automated Service Robots did not resemble humanoids and were built with practicality, not aesthetics in mind. ASRs like Seymour bucked the trend slightly, resembling a four-legged animal, but they were more of an exception than a rule.

The two androids standing next to the desk definitely resembled a human. They stood upright on two legs, had a cylindrical head stacked with asymmetrical sensors, and two arms hanging down their sides. What made them unique were the pulse rifles in their hands.

Behind the desk sat a slightly androgynous person, with short hair and a round face. Nothing about them gave Drake a clue to their gender, age, or birthplace. The only clue was the name Steven, but that was not enough to form any conclusions.

'Which one is Jimmy?' they asked, eyes darting from one to the other.

'He is,' Drake said, tilting his head towards Jimmy, but pointing a finger to one of the androids. 'Why is that thing holding a weapon?'

One of the oldest and most well-known laws pertaining to any ASR or synthetic being was that they were forbidden from operating any weapon or device that could harm a human. Of course, Penta had always stretched the interpretation of that law as much as they could, building automated weapons and weaponized Automated Security Vehicles, but no one has ever built a human-like android capable of carrying a weapon. None that Drake was aware of.

'Are you stupid? Do you know who I am? Do you know why you are here? What services I offer? Because if you did, you would understand that someone like me, someone who does what I do, needs some protection. Oh boy.'

'I'm not stupid,' Drake snapped back. 'But as far as I know, those things aren't supposed to handle weapons. Even to protect people like you.'

'People like me, huh? If you're done insulting and lecturing me, maybe you can tell me what you want?'

The androids never moved. Drake wondered if Seymour's EMP would be enough to take them both down.

'You are Numbers, right?' Jimmy asked.

Numbers nodded.

'Oh, okay, ya know, I got your number from a friend who told me you are the person to see about securing loans for business ventures, ya know? That's what we are here for. Securing credits for a business idea. A foolproof one.'

Numbers gave Drake a look – *Got anything to add?*

'Guaranteed credits, ya know.'

Drake answered, not because Numbers was staring him down, but because Jimmy wouldn't stop rambling. 'Like he said, we need to borrow credits.'

Numbers pushed his chair back and looked at the two teal-colored ASRs, holding the pulse rifles.

'To be honest, I don't even know if they are on half the time. They just stand there. At least with humans, even dumb muscly ones, you know they are alive. But these things? Who knows, right?'

Numbers raised his eyebrows and a mischievous smile pushed out fat cheeks.

'Watch this. Goons! Hold!'

Both androids dropped onto one knee, lifted their pulse weapons, and aimed at the door that was behind Jimmy and Drake. No lights came on or anything to indicate they were on. They just went from one statuesque pose to another.

Numbers looked a bit surprised.

'See! You don't know with these fuckers.'

Drake's heart was beating faster than it did ten seconds ago and he waited a beat to make sure they didn't turn their weapons on them.

'Man, Shangcorp are going to shit themselves when they see these bad boys,' Numbers laughed.

'You mean these are Penta droids? Military Penta droids?'

'Yeah, so what? Some dipshit official couldn't make a payment, so they gave me these instead. Reckon they have thousands and thousands of them on standby, ready to go to war.'

Drake knew Penta had been struggling to recruit people to go fight in this war, but he never imagined they would break all the laws and treaties and send in automated soldiers.

'Cool!' Jimmy said next to him.

Numbers nodded in agreement.

'Credits. We need to borrow some,' Drake brought the conversation back on track.

'Well, that's what I do,' Numbers moved back, closer to the desk. 'But I need to clarify some things, seeing it is the first time we are doing business.'

Still aiming their pulse weapons at the entrance, the androids kept silent guard.

'I'm not a loan shark like those cretins in the fifties and sixties,' Numbers said, referring to the higher-numbered sectors. 'I'm a businessperson. An entrepreneur, some might say. I'm here to make a business arrangement, not give you a handout.'

Drake half expected the androids to subtly change their aim to them. They didn't.

'Handing over money and getting it back again never ap-pealed to me. Where's the risk? The fun? No, what interests me, is ideas. Dreams. So, tell me, Jimmy, what is your dream?'

'We have—'

'Jimmy,' Numbers cut Drake off. 'What is your dream?'

Drake waited for the androids to shift their aim, but even now, they remained still.

'To haul cargo with Drake. Just him and me, in our own truck, ya know?'

'I think—' Drake stopped himself.

'That's good Jimmy, I like that. Now, how am I going to help you achieve that dream?'

'By giving us enough credits, ya know, to buy a truck.'

'I can do that, Jimmy. Easily. I can make that dream come true.'

Jimmy smiled at Drake. 'See?'

'If I may,' Drake said. He waited for Numbers to acknowledge him. 'You already told us you don't like to hand over money. So, what's the fine print here?'

Numbers winked at Jimmy.

'Someone's not a dreamer.'

Jimmy let out a small chuckle.

'There is no fine print, Drake, but as you pointed out, this is a business deal, not a loan. So here it is. I'll invest the amount you need for a truck and whatever other costs. That is my part of the deal. Your part is to repay me in full, plus an extra five percent. If you don't repay me within a month, it goes up to seven and a half. The month after ten. And so forth. In addition, you'll pay me two percent of all future contracts you receive for the next ten years. Those are my terms, and they are non-negotiable.'

'Forget it,' Drake said and stood up. 'I'll pay back the loan and whatever interest seems fair, but two percent for the next ten years? No thanks. Jimmy, let's go.'

Drake walked towards the door.

'Fine,' Jimmy said but stayed seated.

'Let's go then.'

'No. I mean, fine, I accept the conditions of the loan, ya know. I told you, Drake, I'm doing this.'

Numbers smiled at Drake.

Drake walked back to Jimmy and kneeled in front of him.

'Buddy, not like this. He'll have his hooks into you for a decade. Two percent sounds small, but it's the idea. It's the principal. We won't be free. We'll be working for him.'

'That's not how I see it, ya know?'

'Huh? But—'

'I'm doing this contract, Drake, and I'm taking this deal, ya know.'

'Jimmy—'

'It's your choice, Drake. But I hope you join me.'

Drake could feel Number's smugness burning into the back of his head. Looking into Jimmy's eyes, he tried one last time.

'Please. There has to be a better way.'

'I do have other clients to see, so if we could wrap this up, gentleman.'

Drake shook his head.

'Jimmy, let's go. We'll figure something else out.'

'I'm doing this, Drake. I told you, ya know.'

Drake stood up and flopped back down into his chair.

'I'll need location access on your HICs, of course, and I'm sure there is no need to emphasize the point that crossing me or failing to pay me will have consequences that are unfortunately not very business-like.'

Now would have been a good time for the androids to move and intimate them, but still they remained motionless. Drake was slightly disappointed.

'This is a bad idea, Jimmy.'

This was the wrong tactic. A look of defiance came over Jimmy.

'Where do I sign?'

| eight |

Gray concrete flashed past them in a blur as the Hyperloop went underground. Neither one of them said a word on the walk to the Hyperloop, or even when sitting down. Soon they would get off at a terminal and board another Loop. Instead of confronting Jimmy, Drake kept watching the concrete streak past them.

Gray gave way to bright sunlight, and the Hyperloop came to a standstill. It was an end-of-line stop, so everyone disembarked the cabin. Drake waited until the crowd thinned out and they weren't walking shoulder to shoulder with the other passengers before speaking.

'Jimmy, what happened back there?'

They reached the platform for the next Loop. In seconds, the crowd would surge forward and funnel themselves into the Hyperloop. Drake would have to wait until they were moving again before taking up the conversation as Jimmy was staring at Seymour and not showing any signs of engaging him. Even before the Hyperloop arrived, the crowd condensed and moved forward as one organism, anxiously waiting. When the Hyperloop arrived, the organism spilled into the white tube. Drake saw Jimmy grab a seat next to an elderly woman, leaving him fending for himself. He found a vacant seat a few rows behind and settled in for the brief journey.

Once Jimmy agreed to Number's terms, the process was quick and uneventful. Jimmy gave Numbers access to his HIC and Numbers transferred the credits over to Jimmy. He reminded Jimmy of the condition of the transaction and then they left.

Once again, bright sunlight announced their arrival at the next terminal. Not being a last-of-line stop meant only a few people disembarked. Drake squeezed past the person sitting next to him and exited the Loop just behind Jimmy.

'Hold up, buddy!'

Jimmy stopped and Seymour sat down next to him. The walk home was only a few minutes from the terminal, but Drake couldn't wait.

'I think you've made a huge mistake, Jimmy.'

'I didn't, ya know. I know what I'm doing, Drake. I've been making deals and looking after myself long before you came along, ya know?'

Drake realized Jimmy was right, but before he could answer, Jimmy spoke again.

'You are the one that's wrong, ya know. Not being able to see a good contract when it's right in front of your eyes.'

'It's just,' Drake waited for the right words to come. They didn't.

'My whole life, people have underestimated me, ya know, but here I am. Still kicking.'

Drake had so many replies, so many things he wanted to say, but he couldn't do it.

'I'm done sitting next to you, not earning my seat, ya know? I want to be your partner, Drake, not your charity case.'

They had met because Jimmy had a crazy contract. One that made them semi-famous for a while. Then they started to follow Drake's ideas and plans, which almost killed them and left them creditless. Now they were doing a job Drake wanted to do, hauling for NF55, with the dream of hauling for themselves again one day. Except, it wasn't their dream. It was Drake's dream.

They weren't partners. Jimmy was right.

'I'm sorry, Jimmy.'

Jimmy's shoulders dropped.

'That's okay, ya know. I expected you to bail. But I'm still going through with this deal.'

Drake chuckled.

'No, Jimmy. I'm sorry I've been so selfish. Since I've met you, my life has been turned upside down and half the time I don't even know what territory we're in or who's chasing us. And since we've been back in New Franco, I've only been thinking about myself. I've not been a good partner. I haven't really been a partner. So, I'm sorry, buddy.'

Tears rolled down Jimmy's cheeks.

'It's all good, ya know.' He quickly wiped the tears away.

'It's not, but I promise it will be.?'

Jimmy nodded, shaking some more tears out of his eyes.

'Since Grandpa is in such a rush, I suggest we start looking for a truck. What do you say?'

Another wipe took care of the remaining tears.

'So, you're in?'

'Of course, I'm in!' Drake imagined Jackie yelling at him to make things easier. 'Why would I let you go off on an adventure and have all the fun?'

'Because you said it was a dumb idea, ya know?'

'Yes, well, let's just say that you've convinced me, okay?'

Balling his hand into a fist, Jimmy pumped his arm and mumbled something.

'I've already lined up a truck for us, ya know. Should we go check it out?'

Drake was happy for Jimmy to make decisions and pick contracts for them. They were partners, after all. But picking a truck? No way.

'Sure, buddy, let's go and have a look,' he said through gritted teeth.

* * *

Unsurprisingly, the sector they were travelling to was in the lower fifties. Not that it bothered either of them, as this was roughly where they met as it was the area where they both hung out. Unlike the sector where they had their meeting with Numbers, this sector had no drones flying around, and no clear demarcation of living and commercial units. The buildings looked the same and the only difference was some had neon signs hanging from them. Another difference was the armed gang members walking around. They weren't threatening, just patrolling. Even before Penta pulled its security officers from the streets and turned them into soldiers, the higher-numbered sectors took care of themselves. Penta was always more of an overseer in these sectors.

Jimmy bumped Drake with his elbow and pointed to an open lot across the street, filled with old hydrocars and a few trucks. It looked more like a scrapyard than a sales yard to Drake, but nevertheless, he smiled and nodded back at Jimmy.

'Is Seymour on surveillance mode?'

Jimmy nodded.

'Good. A place like this will definitely have pulse weapons mounted up somewhere. Just have him monitor for anything going online.'

Jimmy nodded again.

After crossing the street, Jimmy instructed Seymour to sit at the entrance and gave him instructions to monitor their surroundings. Once he was done, Jimmy and Drake entered the lot and a prompt appeared on their Augmented Retinal Projectors, informing them they had entered a commercial area with ARP enhancements. They could accept or decline. They both accepted. Model-specific information, a brief history of the vehicle, and the price displayed above each vehicle they looked at. Drake knew this information was subjective and curated by the salespeople.

Smaller hydrocars filled the front of the lot, and in the back, a couple of trucks loomed over them. They made their way over to them, as the details of the trucks appeared on their ARPs. Before Drake could criticize each one in detail and on its own merits, a weasel, hair slicked back, made its way up to them. The weasel smiled, making him look even less trustworthy, and opened his mouth to squash any suspicion that he was a decent person.

'She's a beauty, ain't she?' he said and patted the wheel arch of the derelict truck in front of them. 'Still plenty of life left in her.'

She didn't.

'Is that a guarantee?' Drake asked.

The weasel took his hand off the truck.

'Now, that there was just a figure of speech, sir,' the weasel replied, flashing his unnaturally symmetrical white teeth.

'So, it doesn't have much life left?'

The salesperson kept smiling, his eyes darting around, trying to come up with another angle.

'Well, how about you guys tell me what you are looking for and I'll make sure you leave here satisfied.'

Drake looked at Jimmy and motioned to the trucks with his head.

'So, which one did you have in mind, Jimmy?'

Shifting his weight from leg to leg, the weasel was ready to pounce.

'Well, ya know, they all look the same to me. Besides, I reckon this is your area of expertise, ya know.'

Right answer, Jimmy.

'May I show you—'

'No,' Drake stopped the salesperson. 'You may not. I'm not interested in anything you have to say. Unlock the three Hydrostar models and give my friend over here full access to their logs. All I want is the numbers. What they've done, where they've done it, and for how long. Then we'll test drive them, and then if we are interested, we'll buy one. When that happens, we'll call you back over. Got it?'

Drake knew he was being a dick, but everything about this salesperson put him off, and if there was one thing Drake hated, it was fake people.

'Yes, of course. Sounds like you know exactly what you're after. Let me get those codes for you.' The sincerity was as believable as his teeth.

Drake turned his attention back to the vehicles in front of him. It didn't surprise him that there were no newer Hydrocomet models for sale, as this was clearly not a late-model establishment. What did surprise him was to see three Hydrostars sitting next to each other. Hydrocomets and other lesser-known brands had replaced Hydrostars years, almost decades, ago. Seeing a Hydrostar on the road was becoming a rarity. Seeing three next to each other was almost an impossibility. An impossibility that made Drake happy. He loved the way they looked and how they handled, how easy it was to take over manual control of them, and how connected he felt to them. Sure, the fact they were getting on in age and reliability was an issue, but he didn't care. For him to haul meant doing it in a Hydrostar.

Walking around the trucks, he inspected them for any outward signs of neglect, whether they had received little servicing or care. He looked for signs like cracked light lenses that were never replaced, a scratch in the paint that was left to rust, or tires that were worn beyond their minimum thread depth. He ran his hand over each truck, just feeling it and getting a sense of it. The weasel would provide him with the raw data, but for now, he wanted his gut to lead him.

As Drake came around to the front of one of the Hydrostars, he found the salesperson making small talk with Jimmy.

'So,' the weasel interrupted his own conversation. 'Made a decision?'

Nice try.

'Not until I see the data.'

'Now before I do that, um, it seems there were a few mistakes made when we entered the trucks into our system.' On cue, there was the fake smile. 'Some of the information you would have seen already might have been incorrect. We'll be fixing that ASAP.'

Drake felt less guilty for being a dick.

'So, here goes.' The salesperson swiped his HIC in Jimmy's direction.

'Got it,' Jimmy confirmed a second later.

Jimmy went from one Hydrostar to the next, running an algorithm that Drake did not want to know the origin of, and gathered the telemetry, data, and history of each truck. When he finished, he made his way back to Drake.

Drake stepped up to Jimmy, who had the information ready on his HIC. Together they went through the data, crunching the numbers to pick the least worn-down truck. Drake already had a feeling about which one he wanted, but he kept it to himself. Hopefully, the facts and his gut would coincide. One truck fell out of contention at once. It must have been operated by the stingiest person alive, as it ran incredibly long distances with the minimum servicing done to it. In fact, barely any servicing at all. Chances were, it would seize up or even blow up on them. It was down to two.

Going off the data of the remaining two, it was clear they came from the same operator or company. Both trucks had seen better days and were quite old, but they had both been meticulously serviced and had traveled almost the same distance. There was nothing to choose between them. Drake looked at the two trucks and knew which one he was leaving with. The only problem was the amount. If they paid the asking price, they would leave with almost no extra credits. Jimmy had already assured him that they were the cheapest Hydrostars on the market, so hunting down another truck would be a waste of time.

'Okay, so, as you said, there were a few *mistakes* made when entering the numbers into your system, and by the looks of it, it seems most of the mistakes are about twenty percent or so off the mark. Does that sound about right, Jimmy?'

'As high as forty on some, but yes, twenty sounds about right, ya know.'

'Let's say thirty, then. So, I assume the price would have the same margin of error?'

'I assure you,' the fake smile reappeared, 'that *those* numbers are very accurate indeed.'

'Buddy, let's cut to the chase, okay? We both know you are lying through your perfect teeth. You entered that data incorrectly on purpose because you thought that no one would look at the logs in detail. And frankly, I don't care. If someone is dumb enough to buy a truck at the full price from you, that's their problem. But I'm not one of those guys, because I know that's not what they are worth.'

The salesperson kept up appearances, and the smile never wavered.

'You got me! How about I do a five percent discount for you guys, huh?'

Drake laughed.

'I'm not trying to haggle here, buddy. You committed fraud and I'm just trying to pay you what these wrecks are worth. And what they are worth is thirty percent less than the mistaken price you advertised.'

Proving fraud in the corrupt Penta justice system was an oxymoron and not a process Drake was ever going to take on. But the threat of the possibility that the sales yard would be closed until the hearing was concluded and the accompanied loss in income could be enough to persuade the weasel.

'Fifteen percent,' the salesperson persisted in negotiating.

Drake had no intention of spending the rest of the day going back and forth.

He let the silence settle around them and never broke eye contact.

'Twenty percent. That's as low as I can go. That means no commission for me. I'm afraid that's a take it or leave it number.' The smile was finally waning.

'Jimmy, pay the man,' he said.

Turning his back to them, Drake walked off to the truck.

He opened the door to the Hydrostar. At once everything felt right in the world.

| nine |

Lily looked at Drake, then Jimmy, and Drake again, before settling her gaze on the Hydrostar.

For once, Drake knew this was a bite-your-tongue moment.

He knew it, but that didn't stop him.

'You wouldn't believe the deal we got on her.'

The gaze returned to him.

'I think we did good, right Jimmy?' He couldn't stop himself.

Jimmy's survival instinct proved to be much stronger, and he nodded his head ever so slightly.

Lily let out a slow and deliberate breath.

'Are you an idiot?'

'I'm not, ya know?'

'Not you, Jimmy! Although I assume he didn't buy this by himself?'

Jimmy's survival instinct was bulletproof today. He nodded again but kept his mouth shut.

Nothing could sour Drake's mood. On the drive home the previous night, he fell in love with the Hydrostar. It was as cumbersome and outdated as he remembered Hydrostars to be, and he loved it. It was in worse shape than his old Hydrostar that he bought from Bob Turner, but he knew its potential. A little bit of time and work and she would be as good as new.

'I'm a hauler, Lily,' Drake said, assuming his statement would clarify everything.

'So? Does that automatically imply you make poor decisions, too?'

'My bad decision-making has nothing to do with me being a hauler. That's genetics.'

'Don't be smart with me, Drake. I'm really worried here.'

'Why? You know, the plan has always been for me and Jimmy to haul independently again. We've just bumped up the time frame.'

Lily shook her head.

'By taking a shortcut and taking money from a criminal.'

Drake shot a look at Jimmy whose eyes were looking everywhere but at him.

'Yeah, sure, we made a business deal with someone with a less-than-stellar past, but that was the only way we could close on this contract.'

'I can't be associated with anything or anyone remotely criminal, Drake. You know this.'

'Half of Penta are criminals,' Drake shot back.

'Maybe, but that doesn't change my situation.'

'I'm sorry. I didn't want to go off on a contract and hide things from you.'

'I appreciate that, Drake, but it doesn't change the fact that you are dealing with criminals.'

'Alleged. Numbers has never been prosecuted.'

Lily laughed.

'That doesn't mean shit! As you said, half of Penta are criminals or corrupt. It wouldn't be hard for someone like Numbers to avoid detention. Half the sector bosses in Penta have had dealings with him before.'

Hearing Lily talk about the reality of Numbers put a slight dent in his enthusiasm.

'Lily, it was a calculated risk. After this contract, we'll be set to work legitimately.'

'You are betting a lot on this contract, Drake.'

'It's solid, ya know?'

'I believe you guys think so, Jimmy, but you've already started on the back foot by borrowing money from a criminal.'

'It wasn't a loan, ya know? Numbers don't lend credits. It was a business deal, ya know.'

'Either way,' Wells addressed Drake again. 'Until this contract is done, and your debts repaid, you can't be in contact with me. Is that clear?'

The euphoria and enthusiasm Drake felt earlier evaporated. He understood why, and he knew it made sense. It still stung hearing her say it.

'Yeah, I hear you.'

Lily walked over to Jimmy and hugged him before turning to Drake.

'Please be careful,' she said before hugging him, too.

Reluctantly, Drake let go when he felt Lily pulling away. Smiling at both, she turned around, and Drake watched her as she walked away.

* * *

'I need a drink,' Drake said after Lily disappeared from sight.

Jimmy had set up a meeting for the next morning with Mr. Simons, the old man who trafficked weapons to Walker, and offered Jimmy the lucrative contract. The night was theirs and after Lily's departure, Drake wanted nothing more than to drown his sorrows.

Finding a drinking spot in the higher numbers of New Franco was easier than punching yourself in the face. Something that was also likely to happen. It took Jimmy and Drake only two blocks before they found a suitable spot. Suitable being anything that was open. As they walked in, and the door attendant scanned their HICs for any outstanding violations, Drake noticed many familiar faces. Situated close to the highway, it should not have come as a surprise to see so many haulers. He was not in the mood for company, though, so he steered Jimmy straight to the counter.

'Two cold ones, please,' he said before they sat down.

Not having specified which beer they were after, the bartender poured two glasses from an unmarked tap. He placed them down in front of them and Jimmy held his arm out for his HIC to be scanned.

'To a successful adventure!' Jimmy lifted his glass.

Drake was not in a toasting and clinking glasses mood yet, but he lifted his glass towards Jimmy, anyway. They tipped their heads back and drank their beers.

'So, what are we celebrating then, boys?' A voice bellowed right next to Drake's ear, and a hand slapped him too hard on the back. Drake's hand shot down to his side, instinctively reaching for his pulse pistol, but all he found was his empty hip. *Life had become too easy.*

'Heard you two had become an official couple.'

Drake jumped to his feet and turned, fists ready, to see who he was about to punch in the face.

Lyle Miller stood a foot away from Drake, a smug smile on his face.

'Whoa, you about to kiss me in front of your boyfriend?'

Drake almost did. He hadn't seen Lyle since the whole Jacob McKenna fiasco, and he never thanked him face-to-face for helping him out. Well, for not turning him in, but for a hauler that back-up was huge.

'Even for a million credits, I wouldn't kiss that face,' Drake replied.

'Oh, so we're negotiating the price now?'

'This isn't your mom's workplace, Lyle. Pay the full price or get out.'

'There it is. Can always count on Benjamin Drake to drag my mother into it.'

'Pretty easy to drag her into anything, considering she never kicks or screams.'

Lyle looked ready to say something but shook his head.

'I reckon the least you can do is buy me a beer. And not that crap you and your date are drinking. Something good.'

Drake couldn't argue with that.

Lyle made himself at home between Jimmy and Drake as Drake ordered Lyle a brand-name beer. The bartender poured the beer and placed it in front of Drake, who slid it over to Lyle.

'Seriously though, thanks Lyle. Putting that truck in your name allowed us to stay ahead of Penta. If it wasn't for your help, we'd be stuck in a dark detention cell right now.' Drake lifted his glass and took a long draught.

'Ah hell, if I knew it would keep you out of detention, I would never have agreed!'

Lyle returned the gesture by raising his glass and taking a big gulp. With that, the matter was closed.

'So, you rather hang out with low lifes than haulers these days?'

Sticks and stones, but Drake saw the hurt on Jimmy's face.

'Jimmy and I are partners now, Lyle. We've been through a lot.'

The hurt on Jimmy's face turned to pride.

'If you say so.' Lyle took another long swallow of beer. 'Damn, this tastes good.'

'What happened to Burt and Sara?'

'Oh, they might show up later. Or not. Who knows? They're still hauling for that mining company. Same thing day in and day out. Making good credits, but boy, is it soul-crushing.'

'I take it you're not?'

Lyle tipped his glass beer up, almost finishing it. Drake wondered how many beers Lyle reckoned he owed him.

'Nah, like I said, that gig was soul-destroying. Couldn't do it. Needed to get out on the road, a different road, if you catch my drift.'

Drake did.

'So, who do you work for now?'

Lyle finished the beer and gestured to the bartender for another one. As the bartender reached for the branded beer, Lyle said, 'No, the usual stuff will do. My friend's debt has been paid.'

Drake appreciated the gesture, although he knew Lyle would never really forget. And Drake knew he would forever feel like he was still in his debt.

'Semi-retired. Unlike those two idiots, I saved up my credits from the mining contracts, so I only do the occasional contract if it's something easy or someplace I haven't been yet.'

It sounded like the dream to Drake.

'What about you two?'

Discretion around haulers was always advised. Contracts were never set in stone, and on more than one occasion, haulers swooped in and undercut another hauler to steal a contract away from them. Playing your cards as tightly against your chest as possible was always the wisest choice. Even if that someone had helped you stay out of detention.

'Smuggling weapons, ya know, to Bulanalke.'

Both Drake's and Lyle's eyes grew wide.

'Jimmy—'

'What?'

Jimmy stared back at both.

'Lyle asked what we were up to, and seeing as you just took a sip of beer, ya know, I thought I'd answer his question.'

'Are you an idiot?' Lyle asked.

For the second time today, someone asked Drake that question.

'Maybe, but if I don't do this contract now, I'll be stuck at a job, just like Burt and Sara. Just like you were. And you know what that feels like.'

'Yeah, I do, but smuggling weapons to another territory in a time of war? C'mon Drake, where's the logic in that? This is a stupid idea. Even for you.'

There wasn't any logic to it. Nothing he could say would change the fact that Lyle was right. It was a stupid idea.

'Because it's a stupid idea, Lyle. Because I'm going to be out on the road, free, making my own choices. Because it's an adventure. Because living day to day, just going through the motions, is not living at all. Because, Lyle, I want to.'

Before he met Jimmy Something, Drake was happy to live contract to contract, truck stop to truck stop, bar to bar. Nothing pleased him more than its monotony. Then he met a dodgy criminal, caused a war, and almost died in a foreign territory. What he wanted was to see more and do more. For the first time in his life, he wanted to live, not just exist.

But lately, he had fallen back into the merely-existing grind of life in New Franco.

'It's still a stupid idea.'

'I know.'

'Have you ever been to Bulanalke?' Lyle asked.

Drake had traveled to most of the Penta territories, some smaller independent ones, and the occasional Shangcorp town or two. Jimmy and he found themselves stuck in the major Shangcorp territory for quite a while and traveled through most of it to get back home. But Bulanalke was the one place he had never been.

'No, I haven't. Have you?'

Lyle sipped his beer, pulled a face of disgust, and took another sip. He inspected the glass for a second before replying.

'Yes. Once. It's not like here, or even most Shangcorp territories, Drake. It's lawless. No corporations. Just people doing whatever they feel like.'

'Sounds amazing, ya know?'

'It's not,' Lyle turned to Jimmy, who was sitting next to him. 'Shangcorp and some tiny independents ripped everything they could out of there. Bismuth, lithium, cobalt, titanium, platinum, you name it, Bulanalke had it. The corporations who went there spent billions of credits on infrastructure, not to help the people, but to make it easier for them to grab everything they wanted. Then, once it was less profitable, they moved on, leaving the people of Bulanalke to fend for themselves.'

Lyle motioned for another beer, before continuing.

'Now, warlords and gangs are rampant and control the whole territory. Shangcorp is still the rightful owner, but they had turned their back on them. It's anarchy, Jimmy. No one is in charge. Every town has its own petty dictator. War is part of life, there. It might sound romantic, being free from corporations, but believe me when I tell you, it's not.'

'Can you maybe paint me a bleaker picture?' Drake quipped behind him.

Lyle turned back to face Drake.

'I'm telling you, Drake, it's not worth going there.'

'I get it. Bulanalke is dangerous. It's not like I've been living under a rock, Lyle. I've seen the news. I know what goes on over there. Besides, since when are you so cautious? I can remember a few times when you were on the other end of these conversations getting told off for the contracts you chose to take.'

'Unlike you, I've learned from my mistakes. Something you seem incapable of.'

Drake finished the last of his beer. It was decision time. Grab another beer and continue being lectured by Lyle or go home and get some sleep. Drake watched as Jimmy placed his empty glass down on the counter, too.

'Another round, please.'

| ten |

'Come in, come in,' Mr. Simons smiled and waved Drake and Jimmy into his office.

They entered the room and sat down in the two chairs facing the old wooden desk. Mr. Simons closed the door and joined them on the opposite side of the desk. Still smiling at them, he remained silent.

Drake recalled a typical sleazy salesperson once telling him the first one to speak in a negotiation was the loser, but Drake had never paid too much attention to salespeople or pseudo in-sights into the human mind. He preferred to just be himself. For better or worse.

'Here we are, Mr. Simons. Against all advice, we still showed up. So, let's talk business.'

The old man made a small triangle with his hands and rested them on the desk.

'Drake, I have been importing and exporting goods for a very, very long time. I'm not here to waste anyone's time or put anyone in danger. This is business, and business is about making a profit. Isn't that right Jimmy?'

Jimmy looked confused but nodded.

'Put anyone in danger? I would say going to Bulanalke is pretty much the definition of danger, Mr. Simons.'

'I prefer the word risk, Drake. Something that's unavoidable in business, but something I have accounted for. Which is why the contract is such a lucrative proposition.'

Most hauling contracts were signed over the hauler network and seldom was there a need for a face-to-face meeting with the client. The hauler's opinion or input is never needed or frankly, wanted. Their job is to grab whatever the client has and take it to wherever the client wants. But Drake wanted to look the old man in the eye and make sure they weren't being played. As the old man said, the contract was very lucrative, and he admitted it was high risk, but Drake already knew these things. What he wanted to see was his eyes when he told him so. Not a scan with his ARP to watch for spikes in the old man's heart rate, or body temperature, but to look into his eyes and see his true self.

'If you have been doing this for so long, why haven't you set yourself up with a permanent hauler by now?'

Something changed in his eyes, but only for a second.

'I have, but as you know, Drake, haulers can be quite, um, unpredictable.'

'So I've heard.'

'Besides, I've preferred to keep my operation small, as you can see.'

Drake was sure that what he could see was not all there was to see.

'So, are we signing then, ya know, the contract?'

It looked like a small operation. A warehouse filled with some boxes. Outdated exolifters. A modest office, with old furniture.

Everything pointed to a small business run by a small man. Yet Drake knew that the gleam he saw in those eyes reflected the reality. A cunning old man, running weapons underneath everyone's noses, and doing it for a very long time. He was not someone to underestimate.

'That's why we're here, isn't it Jimmy?'

Drake turned back to Mr. Simons.

'Have you worked with the people in Bulanalke before?'

For a split second, Drake thought he saw the old man flinch.

'No, I'll be honest with you, Drake. This is the first time I'm dealing with them professionally.'

'I appreciate the honesty,' Drake said. 'Not having been there before, I was hoping you might have some insight or knowledge to pass along to us.'

'I'm afraid I don't, but I assure you, I wouldn't have taken this contract if I didn't think it was viable. I'm sure someone of your character and history will find this contract to be a walk in the park.'

Drake was not sure what the old man meant by that.

'I guess if there's nothing else, then it's time to sign the contract and load the cargo.'

Drake motioned for Jimmy to come over.

'What?'

'Well, this is your contract, isn't it?'

'Yeah, I guess, ya know?'

'So, it's time for you to sign it, then.'

Fear and pride fought for a place on Jimmy's face.

With a shaky hand, Jimmy took the DDU offered by Mr. Simons and showed the screen to Drake.

'That's a contract, all right,' Drake said.

Jimmy slowly and deliberately scrolled through the contract until he reached the end. Drake doubted he read any of it, but to be fair, no hauler worth their salt ever did. When he reached the bottom, he scanned his thumbprint and a green tick came up on the screen of the DDU. It was done.

Jimmy handed the DDU back to Mr. Simons and sat down in his chair again. Sweat made his forehead shine and his eyes were wide and scared. Drake had a hard time trying not to laugh.

'How about I leave you two to it, and I'll start loading the truck,' Drake excused himself.

The only response from Jimmy was a slight nod of the head.

* * *

After a few minutes, Jimmy showed up.

'Sorry for freaking out back there, ya know. It just hit me all at once, ya know?'

'Give me a sec, buddy.'

Jimmy arrived just as Drake lifted a crate and aimed for the Hydrostar. Using Mr. Simon's outdated exolifter, he was working harder than he should have and sweat was pouring down his face and back. He had no intention of putting the crate down and chatting to Jimmy, only to have to pick it up again. Approaching the Hydrostar, Drake strained to lift the crate higher and have it level with the cargo bay floor. Once he had it in position, he pushed it along until it sat snugly next to the crates he already loaded. He looked back at the warehouse where Jimmy stood waiting. He had another ten crates to load. Slowly, he made his way back inside.

'Everything squared away? We good to go once this is loaded?'

Jimmy was still frazzled.

'You okay, buddy?'

Drake positioned himself to pick up another crate. This time the exolifter was fully charged when he picked it up but it was down to thirty percent charge. He did not want to be stuck without it.

'Yeah, just a big moment for me, ya know? Never signed a contract or anything with that many zeros in the credits, ya know?'

'It's not a small amount, but most of it will go to pay off Numbers and other expenses. Like hydrogen. So don't overthink it. It's all relative. I need to finish this loading before the suit is out of juice.'

Drake grabbed the crate in front of him and started the slow walk back to the Hydrostar. As he passed Jimmy, he was glad to see a more relaxed look on his face. Jimmy fell into step next to him.

'There's something else, Drake.'

Drake kept walking, slowly. The exo-lifter was built to help with heavy objects, not speed.

'What is it, Jimmy?' He slid the crate into the cargo hold.

'It's just,' he paused as Drake wobbled from leg to leg and turned around. 'Remember when we crossed over into Shang-corp?'

Drake did. How could he forget? It was right after they incapacitated Lt. Wells and left her locked up in a room. He still couldn't believe he did that to her, or that she forgave him for it.

'And, ya know, the boat ride we took.'

Drake nodded.

Jimmy walked next to him, head down.

'What about—'

An image of Jimmy hanging over the side of the boat, throwing up, popped into Drake's head. Drake recalled Jimmy lying on the deck, unable to move, just groaning. That voyage only lasted minutes.

For them to reach Bulanalke, they would have to travel by land for two days and then board a massive ship that would take them across the ocean to Bulanalke. A trip that would take three days. Drake had completely forgotten about Jimmy's motion sickness. Had Jimmy also forgotten about it in the excitement of scoring a lucrative contract, as he hadn't brought it up until now?

'I've heard it's better on bigger ships. Way lower chance of getting sick.' Drake couldn't recall if he heard that or not, but it sounded good. He picked up another crate and Jimmy danced around him again to allow him space to maneuver.

'Really? That's good, ya know. Because I'm in charge of this contract I would hate to not be always in control, ya know?'

Instead of replying, Drake focused his energy on moving the crates.

Jimmy seemed satisfied that the medical issue had been addressed and made himself comfortable, sitting on the ledge of the cargo bay, watching Drake.

'Best pick up the pace a bit, ya know. Would be good to get a few clicks under the belt tonight.'

Drake placed the crate next to Jimmy and slid it into place. The urge to pick him up and throw him returned but the low battery charge saved Jimmy.

'Sure thing, boss.'

'You can still call me Jimmy, ya know?'

Shaking his head, Drake trundled off to fetch another crate.

* * *

Finally the time had come to hit the road. After loading the truck, Drake took a quick shower in the Hydrostar's cramped bathroom, whilst Jimmy heated some white box meals. The highway was only minutes away, and soon after they merged onto it, Drake switched on the Autodrive. Unlocking the seats so they could face each other, Jimmy and Drake got stuck into their dinner.

'Aren't you scared, ya know?'

Drake shook his head.

'Of what?'

Jimmy took a bite, giving himself some time to gather his thoughts.

'Everything.? Bulanalke. Transporting weapons. The whole contract, ya know?'

Drake swallowed his food and ran his tongue over his teeth to dislodge any loose pieces.

'Wasn't this your idea?'

'Um, yes, but ya know, I'm more of an ideas man. A facilitator. Doing the planning and taking care of shit, that's more you, ya know?'

Jimmy looked more relaxed, having figured out a way to shift all the responsibility back onto Drake.

'Is that so,' Drake replied.

'I mean, it's like you always say. We both play our part in this partnership, ya know?'

Drake couldn't recall saying that but imagined he might have used words to that effect to cheer Jimmy up in the past.

'And now you've done your part.'

'Correct!' Jimmy almost yelled with excitement. 'So, now it's over to you to run things, ya know?'

Finished with his meal, Drake pushed his empty white box aside.

'Sure, I'm nervous,' he climbed back in, ignoring the who's-in-charge nonsense. 'We're going to a territory neither of us has ever been, delivering goods that are illegal to transport. So yeah, there is a lot to fear.'

The color drained from Jimmy's face.

'But I'm not afraid, Jimmy. I know we can do this. Driving a truck is what I'm good at. And with the skills and training we've had in the last few months, especially from Dina, I think we're good if something goes a bit awry.'

Slowly the color reappeared in Jimmy's face, hearing Dina's name. Together with her partner, Ziggy, the two Slavor women taught Drake and Jimmy how to use their weapons more efficiently and to make better tactical choices. If it wasn't for them, they would still be stuck in Lan-noi.

'Once we cross the border, I suggest our first task is to get hold of some pulse rifles, what do you say?'

The last of the color exploded back into Jimmy's face.

'Ooh, can I get an Artie again? Like the one Dina had?'

'Sure, buddy. You can have any pulse gun you want.'

* * *

A sign appeared on the Hydrostar's windscreen, indicating the turnoff for sector fifty-five. A turn-off they had taken multiple times. Drake looked at the sign on the screen and realized he would never have to take that route again. He was free from working for someone else. Taking orders from a person who hated their job. Hated their life. Someone who wanted to make everyone as miserable as they were.

Tires screeching, Drake suddenly took the turn, almost missing it, going way too fast.

'What the hell, man!' Jimmy yelled as the momentum threw him against his door.

Drake corrected the truck to go straight again, and Jimmy fell back into his seat.

'Drake?'

Smiling, no, grinning, from ear to ear, Drake said: 'Almost forgot to say bye to Jack.'

Everything had happened so fast, Drake almost forgot he was still employed by NF55. Not that he planned on leaving there with his bridges intact. Quite the opposite. The warehouse was located close to the off-ramp and before Jimmy had a response ready, Drake pulled into the yard.

Jackie stood in the middle of everything, screaming at people and ordering everyone to do what they already knew how to do. Drake made a U-turn around her, making sure the Hydrostar was facing the exit, and opened his window.

'Hey, Jack.'

'Fuck off and get to work. Whose truck is that? You can't drive for anyone else. You are under contract. Why are you smiling?'

Drake waited until the vein was visible on her forehead.

'I quit. Good luck trying to impress your dad, Jack.'

Jackie exploded. She sprang up and down screaming and threw her DDU at Drake. It missed and Drake didn't hear a word, as he had his window up and had already started to follow the green line away from there.

| eleven |

Night had fallen and Drake was ready for a rest. Having to use the outdated exo-lifter had taken its toll on him and his muscles were aching. A reminder that time waited for no one. They had covered a good distance today; he was happy to call it a night. Jimmy was still awake too, but Drake knew that would change in the following days. Jimmy was a great co-pilot but staying awake was not his strong suit.

'Side of the road or truck stop?'

'Huh?'

'Should we push on and look for a truck stop, or just park it and sleep in the back?'

Talking about sleep triggered a yawn from Jimmy.

'We'll stop here,' Drake answered for him.

Next to the highway, running alongside the shoulder, was a wide strip of even ground. They were traveling through a sparsely populated area and the terrain was almost dead flat. It was the perfect place to stop for the night.

Drake slowed the Hydrostar down, making sure there was no traffic behind him, and slowly steered the truck and cargo to the side. The steering yoke shook in his hands as the wheels left the predictable grip of the tarmac for the slippiness of the dirt. Drake had washed off enough speed by now, and the truck stayed straight. Gently, Drake applied more brakes and soon the Hydrostar was stationary. Jimmy helped him shut down all the driving systems.

'You go ahead and sleep, Jimmy. I'll finish up.'

'Okay,' Jimmy replied, offering no resistance. Drake watched him move Seymour to the foot end of his bed and saw him folding himself up to accommodate the ASR.

A cool breeze touched Drake's face as he climbed out of the Hydrostar. Twenty meters behind him a Hydrocomet blasted past on the highway. Then silence. Drake looked up at the night sky, the stars brighter than anywhere in New Franco. He missed seeing the spectacle of the stars, out on the road, away from the light pollution. Flicking on his Human Interface Console, he searched Mars' location and transferred it to his Augmented Retinal Projector. Displayed in the night sky, only visible to him, was the word MARS in big bold red letters, and next to it, on the left-hand side an arrow, also in red. Drake turned his head left until the arrow turned green. MARS was still red, so he kept searching until it also turned green, and a thin white line connected it to a bright star in the sky. Only this star was not a star. It was a planet. A planet that was at the heart of a war on Earth. He stopped himself before he started dwelling on everything that had happened and his part in it. What was the point?

Another Hydrocomet whizzed past, distracting Drake, but soon he had Mars back in his vision. From here it looked like just another star in the sky. Almost insignificant. Nothing differentiated it from the thousands of other stars around it. Unless you were clever enough to spot it not twinkling which most people didn't. Yet it had such a massive impact on what was happening here, almost eighty-four million kilometers away. Because of him.

Drake shook his head.

'And now you're following another stupid idea,' he said to the cool breeze around him.

Was there a word for the force that takes over once things are set in motion? Once a plan is hatched and the groundwork laid, it takes on a life of its own. Like right now. Everything was done. Nothing was stopping them from not going through with it, and yet there was. A force made him wake up, get in his truck, and drive to their destination, without thinking about it. Something drove him forward, towards the inevitable conclusion. Leaving him a passenger.

He had heard the word fate a lot but never liked the concept. But maybe that was it? Maybe it was fate that made him do these things?

Drake didn't like the thought of that. It made him sound helpless.

Get back to work. You're driving yourself nuts.

Shutting off the voice in his head, Drake walked around the truck and did a quick inspection. Using his ARP, he scanned for any mechanical, electrical, or hydraulic issues. The ARP wouldn't be able to pick up everything, but any damage that could lead to a breakdown should be visible. Nothing critical showed up, so he inspected the cargo. Sliding the door of the cargo trailer open, revealed everything was still in place. Drake climbed up into the cargo bay.

The crates were stacked on top of each other, in two rows running alongside the cargo trailer's walls. It left a walkway between them, that Drake used to load them. Each crate had a small Data Display Unit on it, which was used for tracking and also for locking and unlocking them. Looking up and down the aisle, Drake saw that the DDU's displays were red. Which was a good thing. Green meant, open and ready to be used. Yellow meant an error had occurred and the crates could be open or closed or damaged. Red meant they were securely closed. Everything was in order.

Drake jumped out, closed the door, and did one last walk around the Hydrostar before climbing back in. Once inside, he switched on the security protocol, making sure all the cameras were running and the sensors too. Everything looked in order, so he climbed up into the top bunk ready to join Jimmy in slumberland.

This is the life you want. Don't fuck this up.

Sleep came quickly.

| twelve |

Having been on the road for months together, living in cramped units, Drake and Jimmy knew each other's habits and routines. Within minutes of waking up, they were both fed, clean, and ready to hit the road. A well-oiled machine.

Jimmy completed all the waypoints on the map while Drake went through the pre-startup check list. When Drake finished, he looked up to see the green arrow, already superimposed on the windscreen, appearing on the road, curving back to the highway.

No traffic showed on the radar, so Drake slowly drove the Hydrostar to the highway and only accelerated once its wheels were in contact with the bitumen.

'So,' he broke the silence. 'Where's lunch today?'

Although they carried enough white box meals in the truck, Drake always liked to stop at a local diner. Some of them had local items on the menu, alongside the staple of white box meals. It also gave him the chance to catch up with fellow haulers and get a feel for what was on the roads. Bandits, other sketchy haulers, and the sorts. You had to stay in the loop and know what was happening on the road ahead.

Half the windscreen turned into a map. The windshield, which was also a DDU, showed a map of their progress on Jimmy's side, and a clear screen with all the telemetry and navigation on Drake's side. Jimmy traced their route, via his HIC, and as he did, a second arrow appeared showing an estimated time of arrival at the positions he passed with his finger.

'What time do ya want to stop?'

Looking at the telemetry, Drake said: 'We're good till tomorrow for fuel. So, noonish?'

Jimmy continued to trace the route, increasing the distance between their current marker and their future one, until it showed an ETA of 12 PM.

'Nothing around at that time, ya know, but let's see,' Jimmy continued tracing the path ahead. 'Aha! 12:37 PM. Truck stop at Epsir. You been there before?'

The name didn't ring a bell which Drake took as a good sign.

'Nah, but who knows? If it has food, it's good enough for me.'

The telemetry on Drake's screen changed as Jimmy typed in their new destination.

On the road, the green arrow stretched out into the distance and Drake settled in for the drive.

* * *

Epsir turned out to be a small, but charming-looking town. The truck stop was on the other side of town and Drake received a good overview of the town driving past it on the highway. It had no big factories or business sectors, and Drake assumed its residents used the Hyperloop to commute to a nearby industry, leaving the town untouched. Placing the truck stop a few kilometers out of town helped keep it quiet and serene. Drake didn't blame them.

As he pulled into the truck stop, he noticed two hydrocars and only one other truck. He turned the Hydrostar around and switched it into reverse. It was one process Drake was happy to hand over to the Autodrive system, and he was free to monitor the cameras. Once the truck parked itself, Drake and Jimmy ran the shutdown sequence and disembarked.

Inside the diner, Drake saw what had to be the driver of the truck, and two other occupied tables where he assumed the hydrocar drivers were sitting.

'I'll grab a table, and you order,' Drake said.

'I'll see if they have anything special, ya know?'

'Cool, but don't go overboard with the credits.'

'Do I ever?'

Assuming he was accidentally being rhetorical, Drake sat down at a small table which was two tables away from the other hauler. Being such small tables meant he was still in talking distance.

'Your 'Comet out there?'

The man nodded.

'It's quieter than I would have expected,' Drake said and looked around the almost deserted diner.

'I guess.'

One of the other table's occupants stood up, exchanged pleasantries with the other table's people, and left the diner. As Drake expected, they climbed into one of the hydrocars parked out front and left.

'This a usual route for you?' Drake asked.

'Sort of.'

At the counter, Jimmy was still standing overthinking the lunch order.

'I know the feeling,' Drake returned to the fellow hauler. 'I've been to so many places, that I can't say for sure if I've been here before.'

The man grunted. 'It's not too bad. Used to be much busier.'

Finally, a reply longer than two words.

'What happened?'

'What do you mean?' The man shook his head. 'The stupid war. Everyone is hauling for Penta now.'

Hauling for NFT55 left Drake out of the loop. To be more precise, working for NFT55 Drake decided to detach from the hauler network and had lost touch with what was going on. He just needed a reset, before diving back in. Seems he might have been detached for too long.

'Oh yeah, I mean, of course, I just thought there was another factor at play.'

A look of indifference answered Drake.

'So, why didn't you join them? Going to work for Penta, I mean.'

'Because everyone simply joined out of fear. Scared shitless Penta was going to draft the heavy vehicle operators and send them to the front line. So, they seized the first opportunity to haul crap for Penta. Now they haul all over the territory, except where the danger is.'

For a moment Drake thought the hauler was going to spit on the ground.

He didn't.

'And to think,' the hauler continued, 'it's one of our own who caused all this shit.'

Wiping his hands on his legs, the man stood up, nodded at Drake, and exited the diner.

Drake had lost his appetite.

* * *

'Sorry I took so long, but everything I wanted to order was out of stock, ya know.' Jimmy said as he placed two white box meals in front of Drake on the table.

'Doesn't matter. Let's eat and get back on the road. I wouldn't mind getting to Bulanalke as fast as possible.'

'You okay?' Jimmy asked.

'Always. Now let's eat.'

And to think, it was one of our own who caused all this shit.

Drake swallowed, and the food slowly made its way down. It was a struggle, as he tried another bite. The food resisted going into the body of a man who failed his people.

'What is going on with your face?'

'Huh?'

'You look like you're about to cry, ya know. Or are you constipated again? I can get you some meds.'

'I'm fine, Jimmy. Just keen to get out of here. Thanks for getting the food, by the way.'

'Anything for you, ya know.'

Jimmy sat eating his food, staring at Drake, his usual nervous energy higher than normal.

'I'm fine,' Drake said again.

Jimmy slowly nodded his head, his eyes never straying off Drake.

Ignoring him, Drake finished the last of his meal. He couldn't believe he made it through the whole box. Seeing Drake's empty box, Jimmy quickly shoved the last of his food into his mouth.

'Mmky, m good to gow,' Jimmy mumbled through a mouth full of unchewed food.

Leading the way, Drake stood up and left the small diner. Outside, Seymour was sitting next to the Hydrostar, keeping a watch on things.

'Let's go, Seymour,' Jimmy yelled next to Drake, and the orange ASR sprang up and followed him to the door of the Hydrostar. Drake was sure Seymour could manage to get in by himself, but Jimmy insisted on helping the ASR climb aboard.

'Yolanda, ETA to Jaxon,' Drake said as Jimmy made himself comfortable.

'Five hours and twenty-two minutes.'

Turning to Jimmy, Drake said, 'We'll be there at sunset and on the boat before the midnight departure.'

Jimmy replied with a nervous look.

'You'll be fine, buddy. You'll see. Bigger ships are much better than smaller boats.'

Drake's words did little to change Jimmy's expression.

* * *

The drive from the diner to Jaxon was relaxing and Drake enjoyed watching the landscape slowly change from open grasslands to greener dense vegetation. Trees lined the road on both sides creating a tunnel effect. Drake preferred the open spaces, but he also liked how the countryside changed as he drove along. He knew they had to be close to Jaxon.

'Jimmy, what's the ETA?' Drake asked loudly, waking Jimmy up.

'Um, yeah, not sleeping, ya know. Uh, what was that?'

Drake laughed.

'ETA?'

Jimmy rubbed his eyes and looked at the screen, that Drake could've read himself.

'Forty-one minutes,' Jimmy read out the number Drake had already seen.

'Thanks, buddy. Almost there.'

Trees made way for scattered buildings which became less scattered as they drove. The road widened and extra lanes appeared. Soon the buildings outnumbered the trees and the highway started to fill up with vehicles from the side roads. Jaxon turned out to be a fair sized city.

Following the green line, Drake took a turn off and followed it through some buildings. As they reached the crest of a hill, the ocean appeared.

'The ocean!' Jimmy yelled.

'Yup, saw it too, buddy.'

Driving down the road, they could see Jaxon harbor in front of them. At the same time, a multitude of advertisements and waivers came on the screen. Jimmy went to work, dismissing the ads and signing the waivers. The sun was setting behind their backs and the lights of the harbor welcomed them.

'Right, here goes nothing,' Drake said as they neared a gate. A man walked out of a small building and stood in front of it, hand in the air. A signal for them to stop.

The success of this venture depended on the next few minutes.

'Jimmy, deploy Seymour to check for guards or weapons. This could go bad, quickly. We need to be prepared.'

'Don't worry, we'll be fine, ya know.'

Confused, Drake turned to Jimmy. 'What the fuck? If we get caught here, we're screwed. We need to use Seymour.'

Jimmy didn't move.

Three white dots danced in front of Drake's face, obscuring the man in front of the truck, as he brought the Hydrostar to a standstill. Drake swiped his HIC and the dots merged.

'Benjamin Drake. Contracting for John Simons, cargo listed as hydrogen propulsion units, destination Rakad?'

This was a bit unusual. Usually whoever had the authority to stop them, whether it was a border crossing, private territory, or a harbor, would scan the truck, then have them sign off on the contents and they'd be on their way. Most of these gatekeepers processed hundreds of vehicles a day and tried to move them along as quickly as possible. Granted, there weren't any other vehicles around at the time, but it felt odd to Drake that the harbor officer would have a list of their names and itineraries. Almost like he had been waiting for them.

'That's us,' Drake finally replied.

'Please pull the truck into the inspection bay.'

Drake kept his face impassive. He had to stop any sign of the panic gripping his guts in a vice. He swallowed, a sour taste in his mouth. The meal he forced down hours earlier was threatening to come up.

| thirteen |

'I've got this, ya know? Let me handle it, okay?'

Drake shook his head at Jimmy.

'Absolutely not! What are you talking about? I've been through countless borders and checkpoints in my time. I'll handle it.'

A tap on the window grabbed their attention. Through the window, they saw the harbor official waiting for them to disembark so the interrogation could begin. Drake reached for the door handle.

'Drake! You have to listen to me, ya know. Let me do this.'

Hand still on the handle, Drake stared Jimmy down. Without success.

'What's going on?'

'I'll explain it to you when I'm done,' Jimmy said and leapt out of the truck.

Drake looked on as he saw Jimmy cross in front of the headlights and walk over to the waiting official. Together they walked to the back of the truck. Drake quickly asked Yolanda to show him the rear camera view. Only an image appeared – no audio. Maybe it was busted or never installed in this model, either way, Drake had a visual but no context. The man was doing most of the talking and making notes or ticking off items on his portable DDU. He motioned towards the door of the cargo hold, and Jimmy swiped his HIC, presumably to open it.

'Yolanda, cargo hold view.'

Jimmy climbed in first and waited for the official to join him. Lifting his DDU, the man started making notes or whatever he was doing, again. He pointed to one of the crates. Jimmy looked up at the camera, straight at Drake, and proceeded to open the crate.

Drake had the perfect angle to see the inside of the crate. So did the official. They both saw the same thing at the same time. A hydrogen propulsion unit.

Only Drake knew it wasn't one.

When Mr. Simons showed them the fake tops of the cargo boxes Drake was amazed. He had seen multiple smuggling boxes in his day, but these were exquisite. Although they were fake tops, they were made from actual propulsion units that had been sliced. It would have cost Mr. Simons thousands of credits per box, but it was worth every penny. Only a detailed scan would reveal the true contents, and only the biggest and busiest places had the equipment to do that. Places much bigger and busier than Jaxon. A location handpicked by Mr. Simons.

The official nodded and Jimmy closed the box. A conversation took place and Jimmy swiped something on his HIC towards the official. Instead of checking his DDU, he checked his HIC. Strange. Any documents Jimmy shared with the official would appear on his work DDU, not his HIC. Both exited the cargo bay and the door slid shut. Drake had Yolanda track them now, and the cameras automatically switched to the side of the truck, and then the front as they stopped in the glare of the headlights. Some more words were exchanged before Jimmy made his way back into the cabin.

'Okay, done. Just follow the new line, ya know, and we'll be on the ship.'

Jimmy typed the location of the ship into the truck's DDU, and a new green line appeared on the road, right next to the official. Seemingly satisfied their business was concluded, he stepped out of the way, allowing Drake to drive by.

'What just happened?'

'I told you, I'd handle it, ya know?'

Slowly Drake eased the truck forward, following the green line past a row of warehouses.

'Okay, you handled it. I'm impressed. Care to tell me the details?'

Drake followed the green line around a corner, revealing the docks. Four ships lay in waiting and following the line, ship number three was theirs.

'Not much to tell, ya know? I took him to the back, he confirmed we worked with Mr. Simons, I transferred the bribe, ya know, and he let us go.'

Drake slammed on the brakes. Not only because they reached their destination, but also because Jimmy bribed a Penta official.

'Why did you bribe him? Was he on to us? Did he have a scanner on him?'

'Uh-huh. Mr. Simons gave me some credits to use as a bribe, ya know, and the name of the person to give it to. So, I did.'

'Why didn't you tell me?'

'Because I had it under control, ya know?'

'Jimmy, I get it, you want to be an equal partner, but that doesn't mean you do whatever you want without telling me. That could've been a setup or the wrong official back there.'

'But it wasn't, ya know? Besides, you always do as you please.'

That one stung.

'Maybe, but I have experience, Jimmy.'

'So do I, ya know?'

Drake had been getting his way for too long. Jimmy was a well-known character in New Franco's underworld and he did have experience in areas Drake lacked. But sitting in a truck, what is more a Hydrostar, made it difficult for him to relinquish control.

'Is there anything else that I need to know? Any more details you might have left out?'

A shake of the head.

'Okay, let's get on this boat.'

* * *

Vehicles and cargo went into the bottom of the ship. The next level had crew and maintenance, and finally five levels of passengers. It wasn't the biggest ship in the harbor, but it was the biggest Drake had ever been on. After finding their cabin, they went exploring, as the ship wasn't leaving for another three hours. It didn't take them long to find the bar.

Judging by the people already filling the tables, this was not a luxury vessel. Most of the people looked like Drake and Jimmy. Workers. Dull clothes and scuffed boots. None of the vibrant colors the inner sectors liked to wear. Here, like in the outer sectors, everyone blended in with each other and the environment. Like an unnatural evolved camouflage.

Drake reached for his HIC to send an update to Lily but stopped himself. *No communication till this is over.* He took a deep breath and saw Jimmy approaching the table with two beers.

'Almost feel like home, ya know?' he said as he passed one to Drake.

'You're not wrong. I keep looking around thinking I might recognize someone.'

Simultaneously they took a sip of the beer, and staying in sync, they pulled the same faces.

'Oh boy,' Drake said and placed his drink on the table.

Jimmy took another tentative taste.

'It's better after the second try, ya know?'

If it wasn't for the expression on his face, Drake would've believed him.

Risking it, Drake took another sip and burst out laughing.

'What in the hell is this stuff?'

Jimmy laughed along.

'I mean,' Drake took a sniff of the beer. 'We have been to some dodgy places, Jimmy, but we never drank anything as bad as this slop!'

Jimmy took another sip to confirm Drake's statement.

'I think you're right, ya know. I can usually drink anything, but this,' Jimmy paused and took another sip, 'is truly disgusting!'

'At least wherever we go from now, we'll know that it can't be as bad as this.'

Despite their bad reviews of the beer, Drake went for refills the moment the glasses were empty. It didn't get any better, and neither did it when it was Jimmy's turn again. By the time Drake went back for the fourth time, it became almost palatable.

The atmosphere in the bar was electric. People came and joined their table for a few drinks, swapping stories, and then disappeared again. The music slowly became louder and louder, and the frequency of their refills became faster and faster. Soon everyone in the bar had become drinking buddies.

No one even heard the announcement that the ship had sailed out of the harbor.

* * *

'Have you found a pulse gun yet, Jimmy? I really need you to find one and shoot me. Please.'

Sitting across from Drake, his face buried in his hands, Jimmy shook his head.

'Urgh,' came the reply.

Going to the ship's mess hall, they grabbed a table with the full intention of having a meal, but once they sat down and smelled the food, things took a turn for the worse.

'I don't think I can eat, Jimmy.'

'I don't think I can stand up, ya know.'

Unlike the bar the previous night, the mess hall was deserted and the atmosphere depressing.

'Maybe we should just go back and sleep some more.'

Without saying a word, they both stood up and stumbled back to their cabin. When they woke, it was nighttime again.

'How you are feeling, buddy?'

'Not great, but definitely better, ya know.'

'Wanna try some food again?'

'I guess, but could we go for a walk first?'

'Wow, now I've seen everything. Jimmy Something proposing to go for some exercise?'

Jimmy lifted his hand in protest.

'No. No. No. Nothing extreme, just get some fresh air, ya know.'

'Almost had my hopes up there, buddy. Let's see if we can find you some fresh air.'

Jimmy ordered Seymour to guard the room, better to be safe than sorry.

Finding some fresh air meant an open deck and the only open deck, according to the schematics Jimmy downloaded, was on the top floor. The hallways between the rooms were narrow and the ceilings very low. Every time another person approached from the front, everybody had to do a little sideways shuffle to squeeze past. Soon they found some stairs and made their way to the upper deck.

All the fresh air they could ever need greeted them as they opened the door onto the deck. They sucked it into their lungs and were both refreshed. Drake walked over to the railing on the side of the ship and Jimmy followed him. They were surrounded by darkness, but the moon provided enough light to make out the surface of the ocean. A never-ending stretch of water disappeared into the distance.

'How are you feeling, buddy?'

Jimmy smiled.

'Better than ever, ya know.'

They stood there for a while, enjoying the breeze, the fresh air that it brought, and the feeling of being free.

Eventually, hunger pangs brought them back to the here and now.

'Time to eat?'

'I think so.'

Making their way down the stairs to the mess hall level, they managed the maze of hallways until they found the mess hall they sat in earlier. This time it was much busier, and although it still didn't match the energy of the bar from the previous night, it was much livelier than before. Only a few tables remained open, and Drake steered Jimmy towards one.

'My turn to grab the meals,' Drake said and left Jimmy at the table.

A line up of people showed where to find the food, and Drake joined the back of it. It moved along rapidly, a sign that there weren't too many options ahead. In fact, when Drake reached the front, he saw that there was only one option. Standard White Box Meals, with no variations. It didn't surprise or disappoint him. What he wanted right now was to fill the emptiness in his stomach. After grabbing two boxes and scanning his HIC, he returned to the table.

Jimmy wasn't alone.

On the table, two long muscular arms lay folded over each other. Strong shoulders connected the arms to a relaxed body, full of confidence. Long hair, braided into multiple skinny braids, fell down the back. And the biggest smile Drake had ever seen made his heart skip a beat and then race to catch up.

'Um, uh, who is your friend?' Drake placed the meals down and sat next to Jimmy.

'Isn't she gorgeous, ya know?'

'Jimmy, I don't think that's appropriate,' Drake snapped but agreed wholeheartedly.

'That's okay, really,' she said in an accent Drake had never heard before. It was easy to understand; he didn't even need his ARP to translate it.

'Her skin is so beautiful and dark, ya know,' Jimmy continued.

'Jimmy! Stop talking!'

A laugh to match her smile escaped from her.

'It's fine. I have never seen anyone with hair so red!'

'See? It's fine, ya know.'

Giving Jimmy his best-disappointed look, he turned to their table guest.

'I'm sorry about my friend. He's not used to people from other territories.'

Drake played it cool, but this was his first time talking to anyone from Bulanalke. New Franco consisted of every variety of humans on the planet, Drake always thought, but the more he traveled, the more he saw the small differences and nuances in the people from different territories. People in New Franco might have different colored hair, eyes, or skin, but they were all the same. No one in New Franco identified as anything other than a New Franconian.

When he had driven in the more remote sections of Penta, close to some of Shangcorp's borders, he had seen some people from Bulanalke a few times. But he never had the opportunity or a reason to interact with them. For some reason, it made him feel guilty.

'Everyone has to have our first experiences sometime.'

Drake realized he had been staring at her the whole time and turned his gaze toward his white box.

'I'm Drake, by the way, and this creature here is Jimmy.' He kept eye contact to a minimum. But when he did look at her his heart sped up again.

'Hi Drake and Jimmy, I'm Lerako.'

'Hey,' Jimmy mumbled as he had already started on his meal.

'Good to meet you, Lerako.'

A beautiful, charming lady on a vessel full of haulers and miners, making pleasant conversation.

Drake couldn't believe he had been so slow to catch on.

'It was really lovely to meet you, Lerako, but we are only here for two nights, and then were off completing a contract. I'm sure you'll find some other people in need of your services.'

Jimmy frowned at Drake. 'What services?'

Lerako lifted her arms off the table and folded them across her chest. Every movement made her muscles ripple under her skin. 'Yes Drake, what services do I offer?'

Her energy and confidence never waned.

'Um, you know, *services*.'

Jimmy shook his head.

'No, that's what I asked. What services?'

A tiny nod from Lerako said, *come on then, please tell.*

'C'mon Jimmy, you know. I mean, look at her.'

Jimmy's eyes darted between Drake and Lerako, whilst he unconsciously took another bite of food. Finally, he shrugged.

'Jimmy. She's a - you know, an escort.' Drake's voice was barely a whisper.

'Oh, okay,' Jimmy replied and ate some more.

Lerako sat, content to wait for Drake to speak.

'So, like I said, we just want to eat and relax for a day before we deliver our cargo. I'm sure you are very good at your job, but,' Drake hesitated for a second, 'it's not something we're after right now.'

Next to Drake Jimmy was eating away, taking no further interest in the conversation. Across from him sat one of the most striking people he had ever seen, quietly observing him. He had never been so uncomfortable in his life.

Finally, Lerako leaned forward and put him out of his misery.

'I am exactly what you are looking for.'

Drake couldn't swallow.

'You were right, I am an escort.'

Relieved that he was right, Drake relaxed a bit but didn't move.

'But I'm not the type of escort you had in mind, Drake.'

Confusion set in, and then clarity came. It was a con. Some sort of scam.

'Lerako, just tell me what it is you came over here to sell so I can eat my meal.'

'Fine,' she replied. 'I work for a man who specializes in protection. Bulanalke is a very, very dangerous place, Drake, and most people do not know how to survive in it. Especially people from Penta. My job is to escort foreigners to their destination, to make sure they come and go safely.'

'Jimmy, did grandpa mention this to you?'

'Who? Oh, yea, no, nothing. Only the bribe at the border, ya know.'

'Listen, Lerako, I've traveled to most territories, and we were even trapped behind Shangcorp's borders for a while, so I think we'll be safe traveling by ourselves. I appreciate the offer, but you are wasting your time.'

'I can guarantee you, right now, that you are making a mistake, but I can see you are a strong and proud man, Drake, so here are my details.' Lerako pulled out an old Human Interface Device, similar to the ones Drake and Jimmy used in Lan-Noi and swiped her details over to Drake's HIC.

'I'll be seeing you again soon, Drake.'

She stood up and walked away.

| fourteen |

Jimmy's sea legs were firmly underneath him now, and shortly after Drake and he woke up, they went to the upper deck again. The breeze felt amazing, and in the bright light of day, they could take in the vast emptiness around them.

'It's so big, ya know.'

Waves splashed against the side of the boat and the breeze played on Drake's face. A few clouds had gathered, cooling everything down a bit. He didn't want to be anywhere else in the world.

'Do you think that lady last night had a point?' Jimmy asked.

'What do you mean? That we need protection?'

'Maybe?'

'Do I need to tell you the same things I told her, huh? How we outsmarted the mighty Penta and stayed one step ahead of them the whole time? What about how we evaded the clutches of Shangcorp and although we have nothing to show for it, we are still alive?'

'This feels different, ya know?'

The breeze had turned into a wind, and bigger waves splashed against the hull. More clouds rolled in, darker and more menacing than before.

'We'll be fine. She's just a con artist trying to take advantage of a pair of foreigners. See, there she is talking to another poor sap.'

Jimmy turned to where Drake pointed.

Lerako stood talking to a group of men, who were gazing at her in rapt silence. They had obviously fallen under her spell.

'See? She's just out to make some credits. Doubt she's going to offer any real help to them once they are on shore.'

Big fat raindrops fell on their faces and a loud crack, closely followed by a bright light, rumbled in the distance.

'Let's go inside before we get caught in this storm,' Drake said and caught Lerako's eye as they left.

She seemed unfazed by the weather and mouthed something at Drake.

Something that looked like, *call me.*

* * *

The storm lasted the whole day, and everyone had to spend it indoors. Which meant the bar. Drake and Jimmy made an oath to keep each other in check. They entered the already packed space and looked for a table to join. They had a mission today. Find some haulers and do some reconnaissance work on Bulanalke. Everyone here could pass for a hauler, so Drake switched on his Augmented Retinal Projector and used his HIC to scan the faces around him. To haul, one needed a license, so any hauler in here would be on the Hauler Network Database. Drake wouldn't have permission to look at their information, but he would be able to make a positive ID. As he scanned the room, a few names popped up, with a corresponding image taken of the person when they applied for their license. As he was using his ARP, all the information floated above their heads. Some of the names sounded familiar, but no one Drake would call an acquaintance. A table of four haulers took his fancy, for the simple reason they had two empty chairs.

'Mind if we join you?'

Four indifferent faces looked back at him.

Taking a page out of Jimmy's book, he ignored the slightly hostile vibe and grabbed a seat. Jimmy had already done the same.

'Benjamin Drake. This is Jimmy Something.'

Three indifferent faces and one amused face stared back at him.

'Bullshit!'

Drake turned towards the amused face. He looked a lot younger than the other guys and way more energetic.

'I assure you it's not. Do I know you?'

Amused Face slapped the table a few times.

'No way! Do you guys know who this is?' He slapped the table again.

Drake assumed this to be a rhetorical question to the group since he had just introduced themselves. The number of indifferent faces stayed at three.

'Benjamin Drake guys! The guy who took over Mars!'

'Hang on, I didn't take over Mars, just so we're clear.' Drake regretted his choice of table.

'No, but we definitely helped, ya know?'

Drake was happy that the number of indifferent faces stayed consistent, even without Jimmy's help.

'So, it is you! Wow! I've never met anyone famous before.'

Drake was about to excuse himself and find another table, when one of the other haulers said, 'Leave him alone, kid. I'm sure he's had enough of people harassing him for being an idiot.'

He had found his people.

'Can we buy you guys a round? We're looking to swap some tales and shoot the shit.'

Four interested faces looked back at him.

Knowing his way into any hauler's heart, albeit temporarily, Drake motioned Jimmy to go with him, and soon they returned with six beers.

'To the road,' they called out, one after another raising a glass.

'So, Benjamin Drake, what sort of information were you after?' the man who spoke earlier asked.

'Seems like I picked the right table. You get straight to the point.'

'No, but I'm also not one to turn away a fellow hauler. Especially one who is willing to buy my friendship.'

Drake liked this guy.

'My mother named me Joe D. Rutledge. But everyone calls me Rut.'

'Well, Rut, my partner and I are hauling our first contract to Bulanalke, and we thought, why not speak to the people who've already done this route? Assuming you have, of course.'

Rut didn't look at the others for permission to keep talking.

'So, you've never been to Bulanalke?'

Drake shook his head. 'No.'

Everyone at the table had their eyes on Rut.

'What do you know about the place?'

Drake recited back the information Lyle Miller gave them, about corporations, especially Shangcorp, stripping the continent of its valuable resources and then leaving the people behind to fend for themselves with no corporation or any authority to help govern.

Rut huffed.

'That's the version they tell kids. The reality is far worse.'

The other three solemnly nodded their heads in agreement.

'But it's also far better. It's the last free place on earth. For better or for worse, in Bulanalke, you can do whatever you want.'

Drake saw the look of pure excitement on Jimmy's face.

'Sounds great, but what about the warlords?'

Rut took a long swallow of his beer.

'The warlords. That can be a problem. The easiest way to get around is to remember that every town, every village, no matter how small, has a leader. They go by different titles and names, but each of them has one. Some are subservient to another leader, but as long as you are in their area, you abide by their will. Do not ever, and I mean fucking ever, undermine the leader of an area. Ever.'

Rut looked Drake in the eye to emphasize his point and Drake waited for him to speak again, sensing he wasn't done yet.

'Most places have benign leaders, only concerned with feeding their people and keeping them safe. Some, the warlords as you called them, are only interested in one thing. Power. And they'll do anything to increase it.'

They had passed the halfway point some time ago. Drake considered staying on the ship and going straight back home.

'It sounds crazy. Why do you guys risk it?'

Rut smirked, but the other three laughed.

'The credits, man! So many credits!' the younger hauler yelled.

Drake kept his gaze on Rut.

'The kid is right. There are credits to be made here. But it's so dangerous that most haulers refuse to do it. My advice is make as many credits as you can while you are here, and never come back.'

Lerako made her way past a table close by, and Drake found himself staring at her again.

'You ever came across her?'

Rut turned his head away from Drake and when he turned back said, 'Not personally, but I know of her. Her dad's some bigshot up north. She runs a protection team. It's like insurance-you only need it when you need it. And even then, they'll try to get out of helping you or increase the price. If you know how to use a pulse weapon and don't act like an idiot, you won't need them. You'll be fine.'

Everyone's beers had run out and it was decision time. Buy more beer and information or walk away.

'So, what are you hauling?'

A simple question, but also one that could get you killed. A question usually reserved for haulers you have a history with. Telling Rut what they had in the back of the Hydrostar would make them very vulnerable. Not telling Rut would raise suspicion.

'First, I think another round, yes?' Drake motioned for Jimmy to follow him.

'Sit down,' Rut said.

Drake stood motionless.

'It's our turn. Robbie, go get some beers.' Apparently, the skinny kid and a name.

'So,' Rut started as Drake sat down again, 'what are you boys hauling?'

At the last second Rut turned to Jimmy, phrasing the question at him. Drake knew if he cut in and answered, it would raise suspicion. They were outnumbered, in the middle of the ocean. Drake had no idea what Rut was playing at, but he'd have to let it play out and hope that Jimmy was paying attention.

As cool as you could get, Jimmy said, 'That's a bit rude to ask, ya know, but it's hydrogen propulsion units.'

Drake prayed that Rut didn't have his ARP on to measure Jimmy's biometrics, as he would see the spike in Drake's heartbeat. He would not see any evidence of lying from Jimmy, as Jimmy sat there scratching his head.

'That's true. State-of-the-art never used propulsion units. No idea what the client's proposed use for them is, and we don't care. Right, Jimmy?'

Jimmy nodded.

Robbie returned with the beers and placed one in front of Drake.

'They must be worth a lot of credits.'

Drake took it as a statement and didn't offer a response.

'What are you guys doing in Bulanalke?'

Now it was time for Rut and his friends to tell half-truths and not reveal any details. .

'When Shangcorp left, they did so in a hurry. They took all the big machinery but left most of the infrastructure in place. So, the people of Bulanalke started to mine what was left. They only have limited tools, but they still get some valuable minerals out. Not enough for the likes of Shangcorp, but enough to keep themselves fed. We take whatever they mine and sell it on their behalf on the black market.'

Rut made it very clear-cut and businesslike, but Drake had a feeling that there was a lot more going on. More under-the-table deals and backstabbing than Rut was admitting to. The way the kid went on about all the credits they were making gave Drake the impression that the people in Bulanalke were still being exploited.

'Sounds like a good gig.'

'It is, but we don't need no more haulers.' Robbie arced up.

'Settle down,' Drake snapped back. 'I have no interest in taking any of these abundant credits you are making.'

A strange quietness fell over the table and Drake noticed a few glances between the older haulers. Something was up.

'Did I just say something wrong? Won't be the first time, right Jimmy?'

Jimmy rolled his eyes.

'Things have been slowing down lately, that's all.'

'Oh. The mines drying up?'

'Yes,' Rut said. 'Like I said. This is a place to make your fortune or lose your life. It depends on what you are willing to do. We'll be fine.'

If Drake had learned anything in the last few months, it was not to stick your nose where it didn't belong. Let well enough alone. Stick to your lane. Other people's problems were theirs and theirs only to fix.

'Maybe Mr. Simons can help, ya know?'

What a fool. Jimmy had blundered into dangerous waters.

'Jimmy,' Drake hissed at him.

Drake's reaction made it even worse. Four interested faces stared at him.

'Who is this, Mr. Simons?' Rut asked, alternating his gaze between the two.

Anything but the truth, and Rut would know.

'The person we're under contract for.'

'Huh. And why could he help?'

Jimmy's face reflected the realization of what he might have done.

'He runs a transport company and does a lot of work in Bulanalke. I guess Jimmy thought he might have some work for you. Is that it, Jimmy?'

Jimmy's face was one of regret and confusion.

'Uh, ya know, yea, something like that.'

Five unconvinced faces looked at Jimmy.

'Anyway,' Drake said loudly announced as he stood up. 'We're gonna hit the sack and rest up for our first taste of Bulanalke tomorrow.'

Jimmy jumped up, almost knocking his chair over.

'Hopefully we'll bump into each other again soon,' Drake said as he left, dragging Jimmy with him.

'I'm sure we will,' Rut replied.

| fifteen |

Orange and pink hues filled the morning sky as the sun started to peek out over the horizon. According to Data Display Units around the ship, their arrival at the harbor in Bulanalke was less than an hour away. After catching a quick glimpse of the sunrise, Drake and Jimmy set off to the cargo bay to inspect the Hydrostar before disembarking.

Most of the haulers had the same idea, as the cargo bay was a hive of activity. Everyone was making sure they could get off the ship and back on the road. After checking the Hydrostar's functions and operating systems and being satisfied everything was in order, it was time to check on the payload.

Drake opened the latch and climbed in. A grunt and a thud announced Jimmy's arrival behind him. Rows of red lights greeted them, which meant all the boxes were locked and secure. Out of habit, Drake did a visual check as one could never be too sure. Satisfied everything was in order, Drake motioned for Jimmy to jump out.

'Hope you boys have a safe journey.'

Rut was standing next to Jimmy and looking up at Drake, craning his neck to see the cargo.

'Thanks,' Drake said and jumped down, closing the door behind him.

'Well, good luck then,' Rut slapped his shoulder and disappeared into the crowd.

'That was kind of him, ya know?'

'Sure. Unnecessary, but sure.'

* * *

Light spilled into the cargo bay as the dock door lowered onto the harbor loading area. The moment the door doubled as the loading ramp. The moment it hit the concrete, people spilled into the cargo bay. At first, Drake assumed they were the officials, checking manifests and permits, but soon realized that was not the case. The first person to reach the Hydrostar had bags of some sort of fruit in their arms, yelling and pointing at them. Not an official, but a street vendor. A knock on Jimmy's window turned their attention to another seller, with the same merchandise. Drake's ARP caught up and started to translate the sales pitch.

'Very nice, very nice, very fresh, super sweet. Please mister. Very sweet.'

The other pitch was along the same lines.

Loud bursts of pulse rounds echoed through the cargo bay and sent most of the informal merchants running. Standing at the exit ramp, uniformed personnel shouted instructions to the civilians to get out and leave or be shot. A few more rounds echoed in the cargo bay, and more people ran.

'Please, mister. Very sweet.'

Drake looked into the pleading eyes. He despised salespeople, but this was not one.

Opening his window, he shouted, 'Quick! How much?'

The local man gave him a price and held up a Human Interface Device that was hanging around his neck. Drake swiped his HIC to transfer the credits and the man ran off as soon as Drake took hold of the bag. Keeping his eyes on the merchant, Drake watched until he saw him safely exit the ship.

'What are those?' Jimmy asked.

Drake had no idea and shrugged.

'Well, give me one, ya know.'

A person at Drake's window interrupted them.

'Please follow the instructions on screen and disembark.'

Looking up Drake saw a purple line on the road ahead of him, indicating an official path to follow. The person moved onto the next vehicle and Drake set off, following the line. Even brighter light filled the cabin as they left the dark hull of the ship and finally set foot on Bulanalke ground. Drake followed the line, and procession of other vehicles, whilst Jimmy signed all the waivers popping up on screen. The vehicles bunched up and came to a standstill. After a few seconds, they moved forward a few meters, before stopping again.

'Must be an inspection or customs point up ahead,' Drake guessed.

They moved forward again, allowing Drake to see a boom gate operating ahead.

Soon it was their turn at the gate. The waivers Jimmy had already signed flashed up on the screen again, with green signs indicating everything was in order. A singular Shangcorp security guard staffed the gate. No sign of any other Shangcorp activity, except for the waivers, was apparent. The solitary man pressed a button and the gate opened.

'Welcome to Bulanalke,' Drake said as they drove underneath the gate.

* * *

Abandoned buildings, dead trees, and burned-out vehicles lined the road. Not that it was much of a road either. Potholes the size of the Hydrostars wheels made it impossible to go full speed, and Drake pitied the haulers who relied too heavily on automation to get around. Steering the Hydrostar manually, Drake tried his best to avoid the worst of the holes.

The purple line ended at the boom-gate, and Jimmy programmed the new route into the Hydrostar's DDU. Between the holes in the road, a semitransparent green line was now visible and led Drake to their destination.

Although the buildings looked run down and abandoned, people still lived there, going in and out of them and filling the sidewalks. Some buildings even had people sitting outside on crates and old vehicle seats. On the surface, the town looked dead, but Drake soon realized it was just in disrepair. Slowing down at an intersection, people swarmed over the Hydrostar. Some held up more food, some signs and some just tried to get a glimpse into the truck.

Drake pulled away slowly, making sure he didn't run anyone over.

'Good lord,' Drake mumbled as he had to concentrate on avoiding potholes and people alike.

'Drake, you have to try this.' Jimmy held out one of the fruits. 'The skin is shit, ya know, but the inside is so good!'

Drake took the yellow and orange fruit from Jimmy and took a bite. Sweet sticky juice ran down his face and filled his mouth.

'Oh my,' Drake mumbled as he took another bite.

'Right?'

After devouring a fruit each, they quickly grabbed another. Occasionally truck stops and some food stores had fruit in them, but they were so expensive that Drake never bothered buying any. Once or twice, at the beginning of his hauling career, he bought some fruit, but it always left him disappointed. But not these. These tasted as good as they looked.

An acrid smell drifted into the cabin overpowering the sweet aroma of the fruit. Something Drake had smelled before. It grew stronger, and Drake slowed down.

'Do you smell that?'

Jimmy flared his nostrils.

'Yup. Burned plastic, or synthetic or rubber, ya know?'

All materials found in a vehicle.

'Is it us? Can you see any alarms?'

Both scanned the telemetry and even checked the sub-menus, but no alarms sounded and no warnings flashed on screen.

'There!' Jimmy yelled out.

Drake looked up at Jimmy who was pointing to something outside of the vehicle. Something up the road.

Drake saw it too. A still burning Hydrocomet. The cargo bay was open and it was empty. A figure lay on the ground next to it.

'Get our pistols, Jimmy,' Drake said and parked a few meters behind the truck.

Handing Drake one of the pulse pistols, they slowly made their way towards the wreck. Drake switched on his ARP to look for any heat signatures. The signal was very weak, and the ARP struggled to make a connection, but once it did it showed no heat signatures, except for the heat from the burned-out vehicle. It didn't mean there wasn't anyone around, as ARP sensors were severely limited, but their immediate surroundings should be clear. Switching back to normal mode, he crept closer to the wreck, with Jimmy closely behind.

'Crap,' Drake said under his breath. 'Jimmy, go back and put Seymour on surveillance. This might be a trap and they could be circling back on us.'

Jimmy nodded and disappeared. When he returned, he gave Drake the thumbs up.

With three meters to go, Drake could tell the driver of the truck was dead. A huge pool of blood surrounded his head. He also recognized his face from the ship. They never interacted, but he saw the guy a few times. This meant he must have left the ship only minutes, if not seconds, before them. Flipping on his ARP, Drake did a scan for biometrics as well as one for electronics. As suspected, his vitals showed him to be dead and the electronic scan did not reveal any functioning devices or weapons on him. There was nothing they could do. It was time to go.

A siren blasted. Drake had to cover his ears. A siren he had heard before. Seymour's siren.

Someone had entered the truck's proximity. Drake signaled for Jimmy to cut the alarm, and staying low, huddled up next to him.

'Do you have eyes?' Drake asked. Jimmy nodded. He must have already switched on his ARP for Seymour's point of view when he heard the alarm go off.

'Looks like a group of ten, all locals, all armed, ya know, currently hiding but advancing.'

'What weapons?'

It took Jimmy a few seconds before he answered.

'It keeps cutting out, ya know,' Jimmy sounded frustrated. 'Pulse rifles, not current models. Looks like old SA74s.'

One of Shangcorp Armory's original and most popular rifles. Even when it was released, it wasn't a very powerful rifle and it wasn't accurate. It did have one attribute that small forces and militias loved. It was almost unbreakable.

'Will Seymour's EMP take them out?'

'Nah. It'll deactivate the pulse rounds, but they will still penetrate flesh, ya know.'

Old tech with almost no electronics.

'Okay, seems we'll do this the hard way. Let's save Seymour's charge for a last resort.'

'I think they are getting ready to take out Seymour, Drake.' Jimmy popped his head out from behind the cover to see better.

'Get down,' Drake pulled him back to the ground.

'But they might shoot him, ya know?'

'Let me think.'

The sound of a pulse round crackled through the air.

'Seymour!' Jimmy yelled.

Multiple rounds went off.

There was no time to think.

Drake popped up and saw ten people running towards them, all shooting.

* * *

The advantage of being shot at by an angry mob carrying SA74s is that they hardly ever hit their target. Running and shooting from the hip didn't help their accuracy either. They were clearly on some stimulant too, as most of them had crazy big eyes and had their lips drawn tightly against their gums, exposing discolored teeth. Drake steadied himself and lined up a shot. Squeezing the trigger, he hit center mass. He quickly acquired his second target and squeezed the trigger again. Two people fell before Jimmy even joined the fight. Seven more to go. Seeing their comrades go down, the rest panicked and ran for cover. As they scattered, Drake and Jimmy both took out one more each. Five left.

Falling back behind cover, Drake and Jimmy gave each other the thumbs up, confirming they had not been hit. Having secured more stable shooting positions, the angry mob started pelting them with pulse fire, and hitting much closer to their targets than before. Jimmy and Drake crouched further down, as pieces of debris flew around them.

The firing stopped as both sides reevaluated their positions.

'What do we do?'

'I don't know, Jimmy. Do you have enough ammo?'

Jimmy nodded.

'What if reinforcements show up, ya know?'

Drake hadn't considered that possibility. If that was about to happen, they had to act quickly while the numbers were still sort of in their favor.

'Let's see if we can draw them out. I'm gonna shoot a few rounds and the moment I duck down, you pop up and shoot, okay?'

It wasn't the best plan, but Drake relied on the inaccuracy of their weapons to make it work. Jimmy scooted over as much as he could, staying behind cover but moving as far away as possible from Drake.

Drake popped up and shot a few rounds where he imagined the assailants had taken cover. He waited a second until he saw some movement and made sure that the return fire would be in his direction, before ducking down. As he did, Jimmy popped, and not having any of the pulse rounds flying his way, took his time and downed two more. Three to go. Drake couldn't help but be impressed by how much their marksmanship had improved.

The same tactic wouldn't work again, and Drake had to come up with a new plan. The other guys were just waiting for them to do something, realizing they were outgunned.

'Jimmy, sound Seymour's alarm. When it goes, we split up and flank them. Hopefully, they would be concentrating on Seymour and not see us move. What do you think?'

'As long as they don't shoot him, ya know.'

Drake bit his tongue. 'Hopefully that doesn't happen, but let's worry about getting us out for now, okay?'

Jimmy nodded and went to work on his Human Interface Console. Seymour's loud alarm filled the air again. Moving fast in opposite directions, they made a run for it, keeping an eye on the enemy. No one fired at them. Drake found cover and a good vantage point. The alarm was driving him crazy, but it was doing the same to the enemy. He needed to grin and bear it. Raising his pistol, he lined up the holographic sight and acquired his target. The target was a man, dressed in tattered clothes, gun leaning against him, his hands covering his ears. He did not look like a threat. Drake hesitated. A crackle, barely audible over the siren, meant Jimmy had taken down another target. Two more. The man still sat, crouched, hands on his ears.

A movement caught Drake's eye. Behind him, another man, almost an identical copy, broke his cover and started shooting at Drake. Sporting the same bulging eyes and menacing grin as some of the others, his shooting was wild, from the hip and not even getting close to hitting him. Drake took his time placing his sights on the man's chest and with one shot took him down. Jimmy's face popped up right behind the crouching man, and both looked surprised as they scrambled to grab their weapons. Before either of them could, the man in the tattered clothes hit the ground. Drake lowered his pistol.

'Wow, thanks for that. I thought he had me.' Jimmy swiped his arm, and the alarm went quiet.

'I feel really bad,' Drake started.

'It's because you're bleeding, ya know.'

Drake looked down at himself and inspected his torso. It was fine, but crimson red was spreading across his left arm.

'Oh,' he said.

'Let's get some protein in you and some synth skin on that arm.'

Jimmy helped him up and took him to the Hydrostar. As he dressed the wound, Drake drank some proteins to replenish the lost blood.

'Feeling better now?' Jimmy asked, admiring his handy work.

'Yeah,' Drake said.

He closed his eyes and saw the man, tattered clothes, and with his hands clamped over his ears.

'I feel fine, thanks, buddy.'

He didn't.

| sixteen |

Rakad was a three-day drive from the harbor but after being on the road for only one hour, they had been ambushed. Three days was an eternity.

Shortly after leaving the burned-out Hydrocomet and the dead mob behind them, they hit the open road. Funny enough, the highway was in better shape than the local roads at the harbor. A legacy from the Shangcorp era.

It took a while for the adrenaline to wear off, but eventually, their heart rates returned to normal and the paranoia disappeared. The bandits preferred to stay close to the harbor and attack new visitors as soon as they landed, catching them off guard. Jimmy stopped checking the cameras and monitors for people chasing them and Drake became acutely aware of the wound on his arm.

'I didn't even feel it,' Drake said clutching his arm.

'It's because those SA74s are shit. The pulse round most likely never had a charge in it, ya know.'

Jimmy reached behind the seat and grabbed something.

A SA74 pulse rifle.

'I didn't even think of taking one,' Drake said, impressed by Jimmy's initiative.

'Grabbed one for you, too,' Jimmy reached behind the seats once more and produced another pulse rifle.

'They are as ugly as they are useless, but they're better than nothing, I guess.'

Stroking the gun as if it was a prized possession, Jimmy said, 'Things don't have to be beautiful to be useful, ya know.'

Drake laughed.

'No, definitely not Jimmy. I'm glad you grabbed those, buddy.'

Pride washed over Jimmy's face.

'That was not quite the welcome I expected. I mean, Rut and Lyle Miller both warned us, I guess, but to get ambushed minutes after arriving? That's a bit crazy.'

'Do you think it'll happen again?'

'Yeah, it means it might happen all the time. We'll have to be as alert as we can be, buddy.'

Jimmy squinted his eyes, looking serious.

The green line stretched out in front of them, straight and true, disappearing over the horizon. All the telemetry in the Hydrostar looked fine, and they settled in for a long drive. They had a few hours before their next big test.

Their first village.

* * *

'Jimmy, wake up!'

Waivers and warnings filled the screen, waiting to be dealt with. This was something Drake could easily do by himself, but he knew Jimmy saw it as his responsibility. A village was fast approaching, and it was time to get themselves organized.

'I don't think these waivers are valid, ya know?' Jimmy said as he dismissed one waiver after another.

'What do you mean?'

'It's Shangcorp stuff. Mining and security, ya know. Nothing specific about this village.'

'Maybe it's another leftover piece from when they ran the show?'

'See,' Jimmy pointed to the screen. 'I just declined a few, and nothing happened.'

Under normal circumstances, not agreeing to a town or territory's terms of entry would trigger a warning of an impending shutdown, unless the vehicle turned around or accepted the terms. None of that happened, and they were able to continue without any harassment. No one was monitoring the entries into the territory, not even an AI system.

'I guess Shangcorp really is done with this place.'

Up ahead, Drake could see buildings and structures flanking the road. If he had to guess, this village popped up after Shangcorp built the highway, and they placed themselves around it, making it impossible to miss. A lot of traffic must have passed through here in the past, allowing them to trade or offer services.

'Put Seymour on standby and make sure the pulse weapons are ready to go. If anything happens, the first plan of attack is to outrun them, but if we get bogged down, we'll have to shoot our way out. Shit, I can't believe it's this crazy already.'

Jimmy made all the preparations and Drake instructed Yolanda, the truck's AI, to start scanning for any people or vehicles.

As they approached the first buildings, Drake's prediction was confirmed. It had been a prolific little village but no longer. Empty buildings lined the streets, shattered windows, and their insides stripped bare. Large DDUs hung on the exteriors. Once used to display the vendors' goods, they hung limp and broken, swaying in the wind.

'There's no one here, ya know,' Jimmy said aloud.

'I guess I expected something more, with the waivers and stuff.'

'Nah, this place is dead.'

Keeping their speed low, Drake rolled through the town. Chairs and tables littered the sidewalks as if the people had fled from a surprise attack. Drake imagined what a vibrant place this must have been. Now everything was broken and covered in sand. The whole place was making him feel depressed. He increased the speed of the Hydrostar and placed his focus back on the green line.

* * *

They passed two more abandoned towns, before finally seeing signs of life. First, some light traffic on the highway. Not much, but a few beaten-up hydrocars went past them, and a few joined the highway from connected dirt roads. Waivers appeared again, but being the standard Shangcorp ones, Jimmy dismissed them. They saw more buildings and around them, the first people.

Unlike the other towns, the buildings had intact windows, and the chairs and tables sat firmly on the ground, most of them had people sitting, drinking, eating, and talking. Like the previous towns, the highway separated the town in two, and Drake slowed down as they entered; one hand on the yoke, the other resting in his lap, holding his pulse pistol. People on the street pointed and shouted at the truck and little kids ran alongside it, laughing. Nervously Drake scanned his surroundings waiting for someone to jump up and start shooting. Soon they reached the end of the town and Drake picked up speed again as the road opened before them.

'That was much better, ya know.'

Drake relaxed his hand clutching the pistol.

'Maybe our little run-in at the harbor was an abnormality. Those people seemed happy. But we need to always stay alert, Jimmy.'

Feeling slightly more relieved, Drake pushed on to the next village.

* * *

Long brown grass covered the landscape, and enormous trees stood clumped together. It was a sparse environment, but Drake loved it increasingly as he drove through it. Inside the cabin, the air was cool, but outside the temperature was soaring. The sun was beating down harder here than any place he had been before. It was a long drive to the next village, and the shadows of the trees started to grow longer, stretching further away from their roots. Jimmy had been asleep for hours, and Drake nudged him to wake up.

'I was thinking about our sleeping arrangements tonight,' Drake said once Jimmy had focus in his eyes.

'You wanna swap bunks? Because I've been thinking the same, ya know?'

'No, Jimmy, I meant do we stop next to the road and risk another attack or go on to the next village hoping they are friendly.'

'Oh, yeah.'

For the last few hours, Drake debated with himself what to do and decided to push through to the next village. If they were friendly, it would offer them some security through the night. If they weren't, they'd have to deal with them, sooner or later. They had to drive through the village and it was fifty-fifty if they were going to be met by gunfire or laughter.

Waivers filled the screen, and Drake placed his pulse pistol on his lap.

Lights were already on in some buildings, but people still lined the streets. Nobody was in a hurry to get anywhere soon.

Two men, carrying SA74s, stepped off the sidewalk and onto the street, putting their hands up for Drake to stop.

'Here we go,' Drake said as Jimmy grabbed his pistol too.

Once the truck stopped, Drake waited for the communication to come through on his ARP, telling him what to do. Instead, one of the men walked to the driver's window and knocked on it.

Drake pressed a button to open the window and shifted his pistol out of sight.

'Who are you and what do you want?'

The language was the same as the one spoken at the harbor, and Drake's ARP translated it instantaneously.

'Hey, buddy, name's Drake. What's yours?'

A small voice echoed from the man's chest, and Drake saw a HID hanging from a string. No HICs or ARPs here. Not that it mattered. Both their HIDs had been struggling to find a signal since arriving, and the deeper they drove into Bulanalke, the worse it became.

'What do you want?'

Seems hospitality was also missing.

'What's your name?'

A hardened face looked back at Drake. A face that was not interested in small talk.

'Um, just passing through, on our way to Rakad.'

The other man spoke into his HID and waited for instructions.

An answer came through promptly. He whispered it to the man at the truck window's ear.

'The General would like to meet you.'

Drake knew this was not a request.

'Lead the way.'

The two men exchanged a look and the man at the window landed on the sidestep of the Hydrostar. Clinging onto the outside of the truck, he said, 'This way,' and pointed to where Drake had to go. Ignoring the warnings flashing on the screen of an unsecured object hanging off the truck, he went ahead in that direction.

Although it was a short and uneventful drive, Drake was relieved when the man hopped down safely at their destination.

Like most of the towns and buildings they had passed through, the large building in front of them needed some repairs, but it looked better than most of the other buildings in town. Large gates prevented anyone from entering and two guards stood at the entry. Drake and Jimmy's guide walked over to them and a conversation took place that Drake could not make out. The man came back to the truck and pointed to the gate, before running back in the direction they came from.

'Guess we're going in,' Drake said and moved the truck forward.

As he neared the gate, one of the men ran up to his window, and now familiar with the procedure, Drake opened it in anticipation.

'Give me your weapons.'

'Is everyone here this friendly?'

The man gave him a puzzled look, as the little voice spoke from his HID.

'Give me your weapons,' he repeated himself.

'Looks like we need to give this man our weapons, Jimmy.'

Jimmy reached for his pistol but Drake shook his head slightly and pointed to the back of the seats with his eyes.

'Hurry up, Jimmy, the man is waiting for those *rifles*.'

As Jimmy reached behind the seats, Drake smiled at the man at the window and tried to gauge if he suspected anything. Drake wagered that this man would not have an ARP and would not be able to scan the cabin for weapons. Jimmy passed Drake the two SA74s and he gave them to the man.

'Right. Go in.'

The gates opened, and Drake moved forward.

The two men took up position at the Hydrostar's doors and waited for Drake and Jimmy to disembark.

'Just switching everything down,' Drake yelled through the open window.

'Jimmy, quick. Grab the pistols and attach them to Seymour. Put him on standby and leave a window open for him to get out if needed.'

Staying low, Jimmy did as Drake asked.

'C'mon Jimmy, I'm done, let's go!' Drake yelled and rolled his eyes at the guard at his window. He turned in his seat and saw Jimmy finishing strapping the pistols to Seymour.

'All good,' Jimmy whispered as he made his way back to his seat and opened his door.

'Okay then, take me to your leader.'

The men walked behind Drake and Jimmy, nudging them along towards a door. A dead DDU screen sat next to the door, and the man pulled the door open. They entered the building and stepped into a brightly lit room. A few doors and a hallway led out of the room. One of the men knocked on a door, and after hearing a voice from within the room, opened it. Drake half expected to see a person sitting on a throne as he entered, but instead, he saw a man behind a desk. The man nodded and the two guards left.

'Good evening gentlemen. My name is General Saba. Please, take a seat.'

Once they sat down, the General continued. 'What brings you to my village?'

Drake had a few questions regarding the General's rank, and who bestowed it upon him, but decided to keep it to himself.

Since arriving, Drake had spotted about twenty men, all carrying SA74s walking around the premises. He had no doubt they would fill this room in an instant if the General ordered it.

'Just passing through, General. We did consider staying the night, but we do not want to impose, so—'

'Impose? Never! Tell me, who are you? I know most of the foreigners trading in my country, but I've never seen your faces.'

The General wasn't dressed in any uniform, but he carried himself like a man who was in charge. His demeanor was relaxed as if he had nothing to fear from these foreigners.

'Um, well, I'm Benjamin Drake and this is Jimmy Something.'

'Something,' the General laughed. 'Did you forget your friend's last name?'

Drake looked at Jimmy to see if he wanted to explain himself, but he just sat staring at the General, who was still laughing.

'No, General, no one can pronounce his last name, so it became Something through the years, and now it's stuck.'

The General shook his head.

'Now *that* is something.' The laughter continued.

'Anyway, like I said, we are only passing through, and if there wasn't anything else?'

The laughter stopped.

'As I said before, I know the faces who travel through here. Do you know why I know them?'

The General's voice still had a friendly tone, but Drake feared it was about to change. He shook his head.

'Because I make connections. You see, we do not have a mine nearby, and we don't have any food to sell, so the most valuable thing we can offer is information. We are the first town most foreigners travel through if they come from the harbor, which gives us an advantage. People pay a lot of money for information. So, when I see someone I haven't seen before, it means new information.'

Seymour was ready to run into the building and supply Drake and Jimmy with a pistol each but considering the twenty-armed guys Drake had already seen, plus the unseen ones, they would be outgunned. They were trapped until the General decided they could go.

'So, what information would you have for me, Mr. Benjamin Drake? What could you offer me, that would be worth my time?'

'I'm afraid not very much. This is our first time here, as you said, and I don't think we have anything valuable to tell you.'

'I see. But everyone has something. Tell me, what's in the back of your truck?'

The fake propulsion units would fool anyone, and Drake felt certain the General wouldn't be able to find the pulse weapons.

'Boring stuff, unfortunately. Some hydrogen propulsion units. I think they are designed for trucks or big machinery, but I wouldn't really know.'

The General would make a horrible gambler. His eyes lit up like the headlights on a hydro when Drake mentioned the propulsion units.

'Thank you for your honesty. I agree, that is very boring,' the General laughed, trying to mask his interest.

The General placed both his hands on the desk and studied the two men in front of him.

Jimmy squirmed under the scrutiny, but Drake remained calm. The General liked what he heard about their cargo, and

Drake knew he was making up his mind what to do with the information. And with them.

'Guards!' he yelled, startling Jimmy and Drake. Four men entered the room, each carrying a SA74 pulse rifle.

Drake looked at Jimmy, ready to give him the signal to activate Seymour. If the General locked them up, there was no guarantee they could figure out a way to escape. That's if they were lucky. Getting rid of them would be a much faster solution for the General. Even with the odds against them, Drake knew he would rather fight than roll over. Jimmy looked back at him, expecting the signal.

'Take these men to the guest room so they can freshen up for the feast.'

| seventeen |

'What the hell is that?' Jimmy asked, grabbing Drake's arm, and sliding behind him, using Drake as a human shield.

Tied to a tree, next to the fire, a four-legged animal with horns was making a terrible noise.

'I think, I'm not sure, but I think it's a goat, Jimmy.'

Like most kids, Drake had seen pictures of animals at school, and a few times he saw some when he was on the road. Always just a blur, as the Hydrostar barreled down the highway. Drake had never asked Jimmy before, but he always assumed that school was not something Jimmy bothered with. Although Drake had seen pictures of goats as a kid, this was the first time seeing one up close. It looked terrifying.

'Why is it here, ya know?'

Drake was about to guess when a man stepped up to the goat and answered for him, by lifting a huge knife and chopping it's head off. The people standing around cheered, and some went over to the dead animal. Drake and Jimmy watched on in horror as they hoisted the animal in the air, and systematically pulled it apart. First, they removed the skin, then the insides (which made Jimmy throw up), and then they stretched it out on a frame and placed it over the fire. In less than an hour, the goat went from screaming its head off to having no head and slowly turning over a fire. An aroma like nothing else wafted over to them.

Only a few times in Drake's life could he recall smelling something so good. It made his mouth water and tummy rumble and erased his memories of seeing the goat butchered.

People filled the courtyard and everywhere there was laughter and singing. Kids ran around chasing each other and the grown-ups were talking and laughing, obviously enjoying each other's company. Even the guards looked a bit more relaxed, although they were still on duty and walking around the crowd.

General Saba, sitting at the main table, waved for Drake and Jimmy to come over.

'You enjoying yourselves?'

'Not really, ya know.'

'My friend here didn't quite take to the butchering of the goat,' Drake said, hoping to be correct on what type of animal it was.

'Bulanalke is not a place for weakness, my friend. Here, only the smartest and strongest survive.'

'So, is this some special occasion?'

'Yes. Today has been a very special day. First, I met my new friends Drake and Mr. Something,' the general paused for a little chuckle. 'And then some of my men found this goat. What a fortuitous day indeed!'

Still smiling, and clearly in a great mood, the General gestured for them to sit at his table. Someone brought over huge cups of something that looked like beer and before they could even taste it, plates of food arrived. The smell was almost overwhelming.

'I don't know if I can eat this, ya know?'

'Are we smelling the same thing?'

'It smells good, but—'

Drake couldn't wait any longer. Considering the General was already eating, he assumed he would not breach any etiquette by getting into it himself. Taking one last sniff of the aroma, he took a bite.

A memory of a dusty little man and his happy family came rushing out of nowhere. A happy memory, of loving caring people, sharing the little they had with a stranger. Drake took another bite, savoring the taste and more importantly the memory.

A loud moan pulled Drake back to reality. It was Jimmy, juices dripping down his chin, eyes closed, chewing and moaning.

'Told you!' Drake chuckled.

'I'm so glad we came here, ya know?'

Looking at the happy people, eating, drinking, and laughing, Drake had to agree.

** * **

Stretching out as far as one could see, the road disappeared over the horizon. A long black strip, with a long green line, pulled them forward.

Leaving the small village was hard. Not because of any resistance but knowing they had to leave all that food and hospitality behind. General Saba had urgent business to attend to, so Drake and Jimmy left him a thank-you message and hit the road.

The next village was almost five hours away and Drake settled in for the long drive. Jimmy did too, and soon his rhythmic breathing turned into a snore.

A warning of an approaching vehicle sounded, and Drake switched the telemetry on screen over to radar. This was not something he'd usually do, except when hauling in remote areas. It was a precaution against faster-moving Hydrocomets blasting past him, but also possible raiders. The vehicle on screen was catching them, but not at great speed. If only it was traveling faster. A faster-moving dot would imply a Hydrocomet, another hauler getting to their destination as quickly as possible. Something traveling only slightly faster than them could mean anything. Anything included raiders.

Ten minutes later, the dot on the radar closed the gap enough so that Drake could use the rear-facing cameras on the Hydrocomet to zoom in for a visual. Hoping it was nothing more than a local vehicle, Drake left Jimmy sleeping and did it himself. Although close enough, he couldn't make out what it was. Drake gave it another three minutes and tried again. This time the picture was much clearer. Drake relaxed. It was another Hydrostar, similar to his, but traveling much faster. Not having had this truck for long, Drake had not made many modifications, but obviously the owner of the approaching Hydrostar had. Watching the distance decrease on the radar, Drake gave the other truck more than enough room to speed by and not lose any momentum. A professional courtesy.

The truck came up behind them, swerved out of the slipstream, and sped on by. A non-event.

Except the situation changed when it slammed on its brakes, setting off multiple alarms and automatic collision protocols in Drake's truck. Sliding and shuddering, barely avoiding crashing into the other truck, Drake's Hydrostar came to a standstill. Alarms died down, and new ones replaced them. Drake hit the mute button; he'd check out the problems once he had a chat with the idiot who decided to stop in the middle of the road.

'What — why did you brake so hard?'

'Stay here, but grab a rifle, and keep your eyes on me. Hand me my pistol.'

Jimmy grabbed the pistol and handed it to Drake. 'We never got the SA74s back, ya know.'

'Dammit. Never mind. Use your pistol. It's probably nothing but stay alert.'

Jimmy nodded.

* * *

Once outside, Drake switched on his Augmented Retinal Projector and scanned the truck and the surrounds for any heat signatures, but there was no signal. He tried connecting to Jimmy, but that too didn't work. With his back against the other truck's cargo door, Drake looked back at his Hydrostar and saw Jimmy. He was glad to see him looking alert. Drake craned his neck around the corner and waited. Nothing moved. He started to make his way down the side of the truck to the front cabin. Still no movement. Reaching the door, he hesitated a second, listening for any sounds. When nothing happened, he reached for the handle and pulled the door open. Cold air escaped from inside and spilled over him. Slowly, he raised himself and peered inside. Nothing. Then a sound came from behind the seats. A door closing. Drake lifted his pistol and aimed it into the cabin. He saw a man who stopped in his tracks. .

'Cheese and crackers, what are you doing?'

'Shut up. Why did you stop?'

Looking puzzled, the man said, 'Do you want me to shush, or tell you why I stopped?'

Drake waved the gun at him.

'Talk.'

'Fine, no need for any of that.' The man looked around. He was clearly hiding something from Drake.

Drake waved the pulse pistol around again. 'Seems there is. Do I need to do a stupid countdown, or are you going to tell me why you tried to take us out, eh?'

'It's quite embarrassing, you see. I had the most ill-timed bowel movement in the history of defecations fall upon me. I had no choice, but to adhere to the loud and unexpected call from nature.'

'So, we almost collided, because you were about to shit your pants?'

'Well now, I never said that. I can assure you that I made it to the facilities in time, thank you very much.'

Drake lowered his pistol.

'Fine, but I still don't get why you couldn't have just pulled over, man. That could've ended up real bad.'

The man smiled awkwardly and opened his mouth to speak as a large hole appeared above his left eye, followed by a delayed electric crackle in the distance. A sniper. Both men fell, Drake taking cover, the man taking his last breath. Everything went quiet. Drake looked up and saw Jimmy peeking over the yoke of the Hydrostar, looking at him. Glass showered onto Drake, as he heard another crackle. Judging the direction the shots originated, Drake crawled to the other side, putting the truck between him and the shooter. It didn't help much.

Storming across the open landscape, kicking up a dust cloud, three vehicles came charging towards them. Two had flat beds on the back of which were mounted gunmen. High-pitched whistling and whirring filled the sky as Drake's position was pelted with successive pulse rounds. Crawling underneath the truck, Drake found himself caught between a sniper and assault rifles. He had to act fast. Sliding forward on his belly, he moved towards the back of the truck and closer to Jimmy. All he had to do was sprint two meters and he'd be at his truck's driver's door. Hoping that Jimmy would have it open and the truck ready to go, they would be able to make a getaway.

Bracing himself to run, a volley of pulse rounds smashed into the road in front of his face, sending debris flying around and cutting into his skin. He had no choice but to crawl backwards. Screeching tires announced the arrival of the vehicles carrying the men with the assault rifles. Yelling became the new gun-shots and it sounded like fifty people screaming instructions and threats. Every time Drake moved, the sniper placed a round as close as possible to him. What saved him was the angle of the shooter, as he couldn't reach Drake from his position.

The yelling gave over to excited chatter, and Drake heard doors closing, muting most of the voices. He heard the sounds of gravel and ground being crushed, as the vehicles left. Drake waited until there was complete silence before he moved, slowly, toward the back of the truck. No shots rang out or pelted the ground. Drake reached the end of the truck and crawled out from underneath it.

No one was there. All the vehicles were gone too.

Including Drake's Hydrostar.

Jimmy was gone too.

| eighteen |

A dark cloud enveloped Drake. He shook his head as if to wake himself up from this disaster. If fear and hopelessness took hold, he would not survive. Things were bad but he had to use his head and not give in to negative thoughts. He had to focus. Be proactive. He started by inspecting the truck and found multiple flat tires, hydraulic leaks everywhere, and holes in almost every outside panel. This truck was not going anywhere.

Drake tried his HIC and ARP again. Both connected. The only thing on his mind was to call Jimmy.

The three dots danced for a second before merging into a bigger circle with a message on it.

The user you are trying to contact is offline. Please try again later.

Although he had a signal, Jimmy did not. There was also a chance that his devices had been compromised or blocked by some other device. Drake shrugged it off for now, vowing to try again later.

The busted-up truck was the only thing he had to work with. Climbing into the cabin, he tried to run the start-up procedure, but even without having the proper codes, he didn't get far. All the DDUs remained blank. Maybe there was something valuable elsewhere in the cabin. To access the small living quarters in the back of the cabin, Drake had to step over the dead man. He tried lifting him, but he weighed a ton. Doing his best not to step on him, he managed to get past. Unlike Jimmy and Drake's Hydrostar, this model only had one sleeping bunk. Drake rummaged through the cabinets but found nothing of use.

Time to look in the cargo bay.

The DDU next to the cargo door was as blank as the ones in the truck and shattered to boot. Pulling on the door did nothing. It was locked.

'Fuck!' Drake yelled punching the truck.

Turning around, Drake slid down the side of the truck, until he sat on the ground. Heat waves rose from the road as the sun sat at its peak, burning brighter than ever. At least he had some shade to sit in.

The longer he waited to do something, the smaller the chances were of getting Jimmy back. With his Hydrostar missing, the other truck shot to pieces and armed only with his pulse pistol, he had no choice but to do the one thing he hated most.

Ask for help.

Activating his HIC, Drake scrolled through the names on his contacts list.

Lt. Wells was out of the question. Calling her, and involving her, would be the end of their friendship. Only if Jimmy's life was threatened would he call her. Hopefully, that was not the case, yet.

What about Dina? She would know what to do. If Dina could get here, she would find Jimmy in hours. But the last he heard from her, she and Ziggy went off the grid to work on their relationship and some serious trust issues.

Rut's name popped up. He hardly knew anything about him, but he had experience in Bulanalke and might have some connections. But something about Rut unsettled Drake.

Then there was Lerako, gun for hire. No strings attached. If he paid her enough, she would come running. If he paid her enough. Something he couldn't do. He only had a few hundred credits in his account. Jimmy had access to the Numbers money they borrowed.

With nothing to lose, Drake made the call.

* * *

'I hoped I would get a call, but not this soon. What happened to your face?'

Wiping his hand over his face, it came away bloodied.

'We were ambushed. Twice, actually. They stole the truck.'

'Oh, I'm sorry to hear that. Are you guys okay?'

'No. They took Jimmy too.'

'That's not good. Gives them leverage on top of the cargo they took. What was the cargo?'

Drake hesitated.

'Hydrogen propulsion units.'

'Could be valuable, I guess. Why did you call me, Drake?'

She was going to make him say it.

'I need your help, Lerako. I should have taken your offer. I'm sorry. But they took Jimmy. I need to get him back. In one piece.'

There was no urgency from Lerako, just confidence and patience.

'I'm sorry. Please can you help?'

She had all the power.

'Please.'

'Of course, I'll help, but you need to understand that you'll be hiring me to do a job. A job that I need to be paid upfront. There are no guarantees in this business, you understand, but if anyone can help you, it's me.'

Drake believed her.

'I accept your terms, Lerako. I'll send you my coordinates now.'

'Hold on. First, payment, then we get to work.'

Payment he didn't have.

'I'll pay you, I swear, but we need to get moving before something happens to Jimmy.'

'That's true, so the quicker you get me the credits, the faster we get him back.'

Lerako's face disappeared.

* * *

The next call hurt even more to make.

'Mr. Drake. I didn't expect a call from you. Especially one so early in our partnership.'

Drake hated Numbers. The way he talked. The way he dressed. The way he preyed on desperate people. Even more, he hated how he was the only person he could call right now.

'We have a problem.'

'Huh,' Numbers replied. 'Not the sort of thing one likes to hear, but admittedly not a big surprise.'

Drake clenched his teeth hard enough for pain to shoot up his temples.

'Jimmy and the truck are gone. So is the cargo.'

'Gone? Did you misplace them?'

'No,' Drake took a breath and stopped himself before he screwed up his only chance of getting the credits he needed to pay Lerako. 'We were ambushed, and they took the truck with Jimmy still in it.'

'I see. That is unfortunate, but as you know, Mr. Drake, we entered into a partnership, a mutually beneficial agreement. I upheld my part of it by investing a large sum of credits into this enterprise. So, I'm wondering why we're having this call?'

He was about to make the biggest mistake of his life. He knew it. Numbers was not going to hand him the credits without making sure he indebted Drake to him forever. That was something for him to try and fix and work out in the future. Right now, the clock was ticking, and Jimmy's life was in peril.

'I need to borrow credits so I can hire a local fixer.'

Numbers studied Drake for a second, before saying, 'You know I don't lend credits, Mr. Drake.'

He wished he could punch that smug face until his knuckles bled.

Number's face started to move around and deconstruct as the signal weakened. Drake waited for it to go back to normal before he continued.

'Numbers, please, Jimmy's life is at stake. So is this whole contract if we don't get the truck back. The only way we get paid, and you get paid, is if we find the truck and finish the job.'

'Drake, you are not paying attention. I've done my part, and if you get your truck back or Jimmy lives has nothing to do with your obligation to pay me back my investment.'

Drake clenched his fists so hard that his arms shook. He had no one else to turn to. This had to work.

'Tell me what I need to do to get more credits, Numbers. What do you want? Just tell me. No crap about making my dreams come true. My dream is to find Jimmy. Whatever deal we need to make, I'll make.'

Hearing the words come out of his mouth made him feel sick.

'I'm not going to bore you with the details of the contract I have with Jimmy, as you know it well. So, we can skip right ahead to the new contract. The one between you and me.'

Drake felt that invisible force pulling him down into a hole. That force that takes over once things are in motion. Fate, as some people call it.

'Same deal, but I receive five percent of your future earnings for the next ten years, on top of the deal I made with Jimmy. There is no negotiating on this deal.'

There was no time to do the math, to work out what the contract would cost him. He knew what it would cost him if he didn't take the deal.

'Okay,' Drake said as *fate* took over.

* * *

Two men jumped out of the beaten-up hydro vehicle, holding SA74s, and scanned the area. Happy with what they saw, they nodded at the hydro. The driver's door swung open, and Lerako climbed out.

'Drake. So nice to see you again.'

'I assume the credits cleared,' Drake stated the obvious.

'It's why I'm here.'

'Great. So, what now?'

Lerako inspected the truck behind him, taking a walk around it.

'What's in it?'

'I don't know. The door is busted. But can we focus on Jimmy?'

Looking over at the men standing at the car, she yelled, 'Get someone over here right now. There might be something valuable in here.'

'Now,' she returned to Drake, 'before we set off, there are a few things we need to cover.'

'Okay.'

'This is not Penta or Shangcorp. This is Bulanalke. If you want to survive and find your little friend, I suggest you stick close to me and do as I say. Even if you don't agree with me or my actions.'

Not a statement one should blindly agree to, but Drake was now completely in the hands of fate. Things were in motion that he had no control over.

'Sure. Yes. What else?'

'There are no guarantees or refunds, but I'll do my best to help you.'

More unsettling terms.

'Lastly, do you have any requests for a burial if things go to shit?'

Drake shook his head.

'Good, let's go then.'

Lerako made for the hydrocar. Drake followed and sprang into the passenger seat next to her. If he was paying, he wanted to be as close to the action and any decisions being made. That meant the front seat. The two armed men jumped in the back, and Lerako took off in a cloud of dust.

* * *

'Think harder, Drake. There must have been something that made them stand out. Something that could tell us who it might be.'

Lerako had been grilling him for the last forty-five minutes, trying to get some useful information out of him, but the whole ambush was a blur. He tried to recall the details, but for the most part, he was lying underneath the truck. He only saw boots and dust. Even if his memory came back better, he wouldn't have much to say.

'I really didn't see much.'

Before heading out, they did a sweep of the area. All the tracks left the same way they came, except for one, which went to where the sniper must have been, then circled back again. Not finding anything at the sniper's post, they headed in the direction of the other tracks.

'Using a sniper is unique. That gives us something,' Lerako thought out loud.

'Why?'

'What do you know about the history of Bulanalke, Drake?'

Drake was in no mood for another history lesson.

'It was a paradise, then Shangcorp came in and ruined every-thing, and now there's violence and disorder. No disrespect.'

Lerako mumbled something, barely audible, but Drake's ARP caught it.

Arrogant foreigners.

'Keep scanning the area and make some calls to the nearby villages. Find out if someone has seen anything. Don't offer too many credits for information, but if you think it'll help, use some,' Lerako instructed the men sitting behind them in the hydrocar.

'Drake, we have some time, so I'll enlighten you. Bulanalke has never been a paradise. Since there have been people here, there has been war. Fighting between villages, tribes you name it. It is who we are as people. Warriors. So please, do not ever pity us. We are a strong and proud people.'

The car bounced along the corrugated dirt road at a speed much higher than Drake would have tried it.

'When Shangcorp came, they tried to unite the people of Bulanalke with empty promises of riches and power. They suc-ceeded, and almost everyone replaced their weapons with tools. Tools they used to strip our land of its bounty and give it over to our new master. A master that had no intention of fulfilling its promises.'

A turn in the road made Lerako pause, as she navigated her way around it.

'Once Shangcorp left, the people went back to their towns and villages. Boundaries were reestablished, and the fighting resumed.'

'Great,' Drake replied once he was sure she was done. 'Doesn't explain your curiosity in the sniper.'

'Even before Shangcorp came here, they had already flooded the market with their SA74 pulse rifles. Years before they came, they armed the people in the hopes of eliminating some and manipulating the rest. So, when they arrived, they already controlled the leaders of the bigger towns and villages, and they had their willing puppets to control the rest of the populace.'

'So everyone has a SA74. So, what makes the sniper so special?'

'The town you left yesterday? It had a general, right? Did you see anyone in uniform?'

He knew she knew the answer, but he said it anyway. 'No.'

'Because no one in Bulanalke has an army. There are militias and armed groups, but only a handful are organized, trained, and this well-equipped.'

Drake was starting to catch on.

'So, whoever used a sniper is not just another local group.'

Lerako touched the tip of her nose.

| nineteen |

Dusty people walked the streets, feet dragging, clearly tired, yet they had huge smiles on their faces and laughed as they chatted. A common sight in Bulanalke, Drake noticed. The village looked like all the ones he'd seen so far – run down but functional.

'Are we stopping here?' Drake asked.

'Yes. We've been on the road since before you called us, and I am starving. We'll go over the information my men gathered and see if there are any leads.'

Everyone climbed out of the hydrocar and stretched themselves out as they followed Lerako into the nearest building.

'Four meals, please,' she announced as she walked in and grabbed a table.

'So, what information did you guys get?' Drake asked the moment his butt hit the chair.

Ignoring Drake, they looked at Lerako.

'Go on.'

For the first time, Drake noticed that the three of them had Human Interface Consoles embedded in their arms. It wasn't the newest models, in fact, they were older than Drake's outdated model, but it was still a rare sight to see around here. He recalled

Lerako using a HID on the ship but didn't bother asking her why she had two devices. There were more important things to concentrate on. Both men started scrolling through their devices, collecting the data from their inquiries.

'We launched some drones early on, but due to their limited range they didn't provide too much useful info, except for the tracks and the general direction, which we are following.'

'Also,' the next guy cut in, 'we contacted people in the towns they might have passed through. If they sounded like they had some information we told them we'd set up a meeting when we arrived in their villages.'

The two men shared a look as if congratulating themselves on a good day's work.

'And?' Lerako yanked them back to reality.

'Um, yes, there's more, of course. We have set up a meeting with a local informant, who should be here any moment.'

Instead of looking pleased with themselves this time, they eagerly waited for Lerako's approval.

'Good. Let's hope it's someone useful.'

The meals arrived and everyone dug into their white boxes. It was hard not to compare it to the previous night's feast, but hunger helped the meal go down quickly. As Drake finished his last mouthful, a scrawny, nervous-looking man approached the table. He reminded Drake of Jimmy.

'Sit down,' Lerako ordered him, without asking any questions as to who he was or demanding any form of identification.

'My men tell me you might have some information for me?'

Shaking, he turned and studied each face at the table.

'I was told I'd be paid.'

'That depends on what you have to tell me.'

Weighing up his options, the man took a second before he replied.

'A group of hydros and a truck came through town earlier.'

'How many?' Drake asked.

'Three. Plus the truck.'

Drake leaned in to ask another question, but Lerako stopped him.

'Why do you think that these are the people we are looking for?'

'Because most trucks travel alone. Also, you guys said there were two flatbed hydros in the group you were looking for, right? Well, there were two flatbed hydros in the group I saw.'

'What's your name?' Lerako asked the man.

'Um, it's Seepo.'

'Okay, Seepo. Did these vehicles stop anywhere, or go anywhere that you saw?'

'Yes,' Seepo said excitedly, remembering something that might earn him some credits. 'They turned off to the mines.'

'The mines?'

'Uh-huh. They went down the road but came back only a few minutes later. I almost forgot about it.'

Lerako looked quizzically at her men, but they both shrugged.

'Are these mines still working?' Lerako asked. Drake could tell she was working towards something and knew the answer already.

'They sure are. Most people in town work them. Not that Shangcorp left us much. Some days we come back empty-handed.'

'Did Shangcorp leave any machinery behind?'

'Yes, but most of it has broken down, and no one here knows how to fix or maintain them.'

'But if they used them for a while, they would have the means to refuel them. Right?'

'Oh yes,' Seepo said. 'The hydrogen refueling station is still in operation.'

Standing up from the table, Lerako faced her men.

'Pay him and get the coordinates for that refueling station.'

* * *

A constant line of people walked through the gate of the mine, and another line walked out, everyone dusty and done for the day. One flatbed hydro, with a mounted heavy pulse rifle on the back, sat at the gate. Two armed guards stood next to it, guarding the entrance. No one paid much attention to the exit gate. As they approached, the guard operating the heavy pulse gun, swung it around, aiming straight at them.

'Do you think that thing works?' Drake asked.

'Unfortunately, I do. Along with the SA74s, Shangcorp also gifted us with hundreds of them.'

Lerako slowed the hydro down and stopped a few meters short of the gate. No one approached the vehicle or issued instructions on what to do next.

'Stay here,' Lerako said and made her way to the guards at the gate.

A lengthy and animated discussion followed between her and the two guards, but they were out of range of Drake's ARP.

He was able to zoom in for a better visual, but audio-wise he was stuck.

'What do you think they're talking about?' Drake asked the two men in the back.

Stoic faces looked back at him with no reply or opinions.

'Yeah, that's what I thought,' Drake said as he turned back in his seat.

Lerako was making her way back to the hydro.

'Get out,' she said to Drake. 'You two, stay here and make sure no one else comes after us or our shit.'

'Where are we going?' Drake asked as he tried to keep up with Lerako's long strides.

A small building sat close to the gate, and Lerako made her way towards it. It had no door, or the door was busted, but nothing stopped them or anyone else from going in. A row of three large Data Display Units sat above a desk that had two chairs. No one was using the room as the chairs were empty. Drake followed Lerako's lead and sat down in a chair.

As expected, the DDUs were used for security and multiple camera feeds were displayed in a grid pattern. Lerako located the one with the best view of the hydrogen pumps and enlarged it to fill one of the DDU screens. On-screen, a few people walked past the pumps, but there were no vehicles.

'Okay,' Lerako said, 'let's roll it back in time.'

The image became unstable as Lerako scrolled back through the timeline.

'There! Stop it! I saw something,' Drake yelled.

'I got.'

After a few seconds of going back and forth, Lerako paused the image.

'Let's see what we can find.'

On-screen, an old hydrocar, two flatbed hydros, and the Hydrostar rolled into frame. The flatbeds parked to the side, each facing in an opposite direction, both gunmen on the backs scanning the area. A door on the hydrocar opened and a man emerged who then proceeded to connect the hydro to the hydrogen pump. Crossing his arms, he leaned against the hydro and waited for the pump to finish. It only took a minute or two before he uncoupled the pipes and opened his door again. Nothing moved, the screen was frozen. The door of the hydro opened again, and the man reemerged. He walked to the rear door and opened it up. He stuck his head in to do something, then closed the door and climbed back into the hydro. This time it sped off immediately, with the two flatbeds and the Hydrostar in tow. Soon they were out of frame. Lerako switched to another camera and followed them until they drove up to the gate. She switched cameras again and watched them drive off until they were out of range. The screen went motionless.

'Did you notice anything familiar? Anything at all?' Lerako asked.

'I noticed they had logos on the side that had been spray painted. Did you notice that?'

'Yes, but that's common. All my vehicles have insignias on them. It's a tribal thing. The best bet would be that they are stolen vehicles, which isn't surprising. Anything else?'

'No. I mean, I'm sure it was the Hydrostar. The plates were removed, but I'm sure it was. It has to be them, right?'

'Maybe,' Lerako said and scrolled back to the time stamp that showed the man leaning on the hydro. She pressed play.

Together they watched as he finished refueling the hydro and climbed back in. Then they waited for him to climb back out again and go to the rear. As he opened the door, Lerako paused the video. Zooming in on the open door, the picture became bigger but blurrier. The more she zoomed, the more pixelated the image became.

Even with everything pixelated, and hard to recognize, Drake knew exactly what he was seeing. Next to the man's shoulder was the shape of a face. A very pixelated face, but a face for sure. And on top of that face was a bunch of uniform-colored pixels.

It was orange.

* * *

'That must be him! I'm telling you, no one else has crazy hair like that. It's Jimmy!'

Keeping her eyes on the road, Lerako said, 'Maybe.'

'Trust me, it's him.' Drake smiled, his heart beating with excitement.

'Drake, you need to keep your expectations in check. We saw something orange in that image. It could be Jimmy, but it could also be a hundred other things.'

'Like what?'

Lerako shot him a look.

'Sorry. I just know it's him, though.'

'Run the registration numbers on those vehicles, not that I expect much, but it's worth a try, and also contact the surrounding villages. Send out a copy of the screen shot from the mine footage and see if anyone bites.'

Drake heard mumbled responses from the back as Lerako's men immediately set to work. He might have made a deal with the devil to be able to afford her, but Lerako filled him with confidence that they would find Jimmy.

They drove in silence for a long time; Lerako was following her gut about the direction, and her men doing everything they could to confirm it.

'You and Jimmy been working together for long?'

The honest and personal question took him by surprise.

'Uh, yes, few years now. A few crazy years.'

'Why crazy?' Lerako sounded genuinely interested.

'Well,' Drake started but had no idea where to begin. 'We met when he hired me for a contract that turned out to be dangerous, career-ending, and illegal. Luckily, we met some people who helped us to come out alive. Since then, it's been one crazy adventure after another.'

'Sounds like you'd be better off without him.'

'It may sound like it, but to be honest, he saved me.'

'He saved you?'

'I mean, my life wasn't so great before I met him, so I guess after everything we've been through, I owe him.'

'I don't get it.' Lerako shook her head.

'Me neither.'

| twenty |

Drake flinched as he heard the crackle followed by the impact on metal inches from his head. They had been pinned down for a few minutes, with nowhere to go.

'I need a rifle, Lerako. This pistol isn't doing shit!'

Drake felt like throwing it at her.

'Let us do our job, Drake, and stay down.' Lerako wasn't having any of it.

The village looked like any other he had seen so far, and there were no signs that an ambush was awaiting them.

'I know how to shoot a gun, just give me one.'

The last piece of glass in the hydro exploded.

'Stay down,' she shouted and popped up, taking aim and shooting at a target not visible to Drake.

'You got him,' yelled one of her men.

'Do we have a head count?' Lerako asked no one in particular.

Their silence said no one had.

Judging by the age and state of their HICs, Drake had to assume their ARPs would be equally as outdated. For once, his archaic equipment outshone everyone else's.

'Cover me, I can do a body scan.'

Lerako frowned at him.

'I can scan for body heat signatures. It's not very accurate, but it will give us an idea of what's going on in our immediate surroundings.'

'If they shoot you, we are out of here. I will leave you to bleed out, you understand?'

'Sure,' Drake replied.

'Suppressive fire on my count.'

Lerako counted them down, and Drake popped his head over the side of the hydro the moment they commenced firing. He didn't have very long before their weapons overheated, and they had to duck behind cover. Another thing he didn't have was a signal.

'And?' Lerako asked.

'No good. The signal here is very bad. I'm afraid—' As he spoke his HIC came online from the faintest of signals. 'Wait! Cover me! Be quick! I have a signal!'

Lerako and her team opened fire again, and Drake popped his head out.

'Four. Spread out. Two on the sides at the opposite corners of the first street crossing. Two more, hiding in the building on the left.'

Lerako's face turned serious.

'You,' Lerako pointed to one of her men, 'come with me. You two cover us.'

The men nodded, and Drake kept his objection to himself.

Lerako gave them a nod and ran at full speed towards the building on the left, slamming into it as she reached it. Pulse rounds blasted into the ground around her as she ran, but none made contact, as Drake and the other team members shot at their assailant's positions preventing them from aiming properly. She took cover and waved for her team member to follow suit. He did and made it safely too.

Lerako raised her rifle and poked it into the window of the building housing two of the gunmen. Blindly she swung it around, letting it rip, till it overheated. With her index and middle fingers, she pointed to her eyes, and then at Drake. *What can you see?*

'Cover me,' Drake told his nameless partner and popped up for a scan, as he fired his pulse rifle.

Drake dropped back down into cover and peered around the side to get a view of Lerako. Once they made eye contact, he held up three fingers. Confirming that there was only one left in the building, she held up one finger and nodded. Drake nodded back. Out of earshot, Lerako spoke to her team member and then turned back to Drake and the other team member. Holding up her hand, she counted to three with her fingers and nodded. The message was clear. On three they would lay down suppressive fire and she was going to do something.

Lerako raised her hand. She extended her thumb, then her pointer finger, and after a slight delay her middle finger. Immediately Drake poked his head and upper body out and blasted his pulse pistol in the direction of the enemy fire. As he did, he saw her leaping through the window and her team member taking up a spot at the window, firing into the building. The enemy's pulse rounds were getting too close for comfort and Drake ducked down again.

'I hope they made it,' he turned to his nameless team member. Who was now a faceless partner.

Multiple rounds must have peppered the poor guy in the face and Drake could not distinguish any recognizable features. Switching on his ARP, he checked for any vitals, but as he suspected there were none.

Drake caught a movement out of the corner of his eye and saw Lerako's partner giving him a thumbs up. Drake didn't know how to communicate the loss of the other team member and simply gave the man a thumbs up back. More pulse rounds hit the ground around Drake, but the enemy was now diminished, as the rate of fire had declined.

Being cut off from the rest of the team, Drake had no idea what to do next. On the ground next to his leg was his ex-partner's SA74. Drake grabbed it, made sure it looked functional and started firing blindly in the direction of the street corner, hoping to be of some help. When it overheated and he crouched down again, he heard some returning fire. It was even less intense now. Maybe Lerako had taken down another gunman.

'Drake!'

Hearing his name yelled out so loudly startled him. It was Lerako.

'You okay?' he yelled back.

'Yes! There is only one left. We have him cornered but can't get to him. Run to the building on your right and see if you can spot him.'

Drake picked up on her intention: to lure the man out, and he did as she asked.

Reaching the building, he could see Lerako and her team member, but not the enemy. Lerako did the two fingers to the eye thing again, pointing them in a direction for Drake to follow. He craned his neck around the corner of the building and saw the man huddled behind some rubble, his back towards Drake.

Unsure what Lerako wanted him to do, he raised his gun and shook it at the man. *Should I shoot him?* She nodded and raised her gun to show she had him covered.

Drake stood up and aimed. The man had no idea he was there and fired blindly in Lerako's direction. It felt wrong to shoot him in the back. Why, Drake didn't know. He had no problem shooting someone who was trying to kill him, but this would be too cold-blooded. He couldn't do it. Instead, he walked forward until he knew he was within earshot of the man.

'Raise your hands and drop your weapon. Do it now or we will shoot you!'

Startled, the man turned around, aiming his gun at Drake.

'You know we outnumber you. Just drop it.'

The man stood up, gun still aiming at Drake, and said, 'Why are you shooting at us?'

The question didn't make sense to Drake.

'Drop your gun and we can talk.'

Instead, the man took another step towards Drake, putting himself in Lerako's line of fire. Which she utilized. Before Drake could react, the body had already hit the ground.

'You okay?' Lerako asked as she walked up to Drake.

Lerako's man ran towards the fallen enemy and searched him.

'Yeah, I guess. Um, the other guy, he, uh, didn't make it.'

'That's fine,' Lerako replied.

Lerako's man came back and gave her an update and an all-clear for the area.

As the adrenaline started to fade, dizziness took over. Drake sat down on the ground before gravity compelled him to. Lerako looked unfazed by the events.

'What just happened?' Drake asked.

The sun was right behind her, and Drake could only see her silhouette.

'We were ambushed. Considering we sent out messages to all the villages, it's not surprising someone would be waiting to jump us.'

'I guess,' Drake said.

Drake remembered rolling into the small town, not seeing a lot of activity. So far, the towns in Bulanalke have either been bustling, or dead, but this one was in between the two extremes. He recalled them driving and Lerako ordering the men to be vigilant. The next thing she slammed on the brakes and leapt out, yelling it was an ambush, and started shooting. Did she shoot first? He couldn't remember.

'The man, the one who walked towards me, asked me why we were shooting them. Isn't that an odd thing to ask?'

Lerako's silhouette towered over Drake.

'I suppose, but what did he expect? We were defending ourselves.'

He remembered Lerako jumping out of the hydro and firing her gun. He knew the human brain and especially its memory function, was super unreliable and only ARP recordings were considered evidence in court but he could not recall hearing gunfire before she jumped out.

'What's bothering you?' Lerako asked.

'Nothing. It's just, I don't know. Not a big fan of killing people, I guess.'

Crouching down and becoming more than a silhouette, Lerako came face-to-face with Drake. Her eyes were as dark as any he had ever seen, and it felt like they were looking straight into his mind.

'Drake, you need to stop judging us by your standards. This is not Penta. We did not grow up like you. You have never suffered as much as we have. To live here in Bulanalke is about survival. Everything else is a luxury. You might not agree or like how we do things here, but trust me, I'm one of the good guys. Believe me, you'd much rather be on my side than anyone else's.'

Standing up, she once more became a silhouette and walked away.

* * *

'Okay. Let's pack up and get out of here before reinforcements show up.'

Drake only heard the end of their conversation, and they wrapped it up the moment they saw him walk over.

'Did we learn anything?' he asked.

'Yes. But it's not good. Except for us, no one else has passed through here in the last few hours. We'll have to backtrack and head in another direction.'

'I thought we followed the tracks?'

Lerako shrugged.

'So why did they shoot at us? Could they be lying?'

'It's a small village, Drake. My best guess would be they saw an opportunity and tried to grab it.'

Heads were sticking out of door frames now, and a few braver souls even wandered out into the street. They seemed curious rather than malicious. Drake doubted anyone else was going to attack them.

'Drake, why do you keep frowning? What answer will satisfy you, huh?'

Pointing it out, he became aware of the scowl on his face and tried to relax his facial muscles.

'Nothing. It's just a bit off, don't you think? The whole ambush.'

'We are wasting time, Drake. If you want your friend alive, we better get moving.'

Lerako didn't wait for his answer and instead made her way to the hydro.

Which sat flat on the ground, its tires shot out, and smoke coming from somewhere underneath the hood.

'Damnit!' Lerako kicked the hydro for good measure.

'What now?'

'I can have another hydro delivered here, but it will take hours,' Lerako trailed off in thought. 'Here's what we're going to do. This seems like a small town, right? And no one has shown up to inspect what the shooting was about. So, my guess is there aren't many fighters left, and whoever is left will be guarding the leader. And it doesn't matter how poor a village is, the leader will have a hydro.'

The surviving member of Lerako's crew nodded along as if he knew exactly what the plan was.

'Can't we steal another one? Does it have to be the leader's?'

Lerako made a sweeping gesture with her arm.

'Sure Drake, take your pick.'

Except for the shot-up hydro they arrived in, there were no other vehicles to be seen. On closer inspection, Drake realized that this town was smaller and more run-down than any of the other towns he had seen so far.

'Nothing grabs your fancy?' Lerako taunted him.

Drake didn't answer.

'Let's go before it gets dark.'

| twenty-one |

By the time they reached the leader's house, the sun hovered close to the horizon. Drake found it interesting that the leader of the village would live outside of it, but Lerako assured him it was the norm. Creeping up to the house, using the long grass and some trees for cover, it was clear they were expected. Four men stood guard in front of the house, facing the entrance. Drake had to assume there would be more in the back and possibly inside too.

'What's the plan?'

Lerako stayed quiet and kept her focus on the house.

On closer inspection, the men guarding the house looked relaxed, chatting to each other and laughing. Occasionally one would scan the area, as if to look busy, and then continue the banter again. Drake started to doubt there were more people in the back, or inside. It was something about the way they were on duty yet relaxed that told him it was the whole gang. He tried a scan with his ARP, but with the low signal, it barely picked up the four men in the front, let alone anyone behind a wall.

'I'll be right back. Stay here and don't let them see you.' Lerako gave Drake one of her serious looks and disappeared into the bushes.

'One tough lady, huh?'

The man's expression never changed, and Drake wondered if his HIC was maybe malfunctioning and not translating for him.

A commotion behind him startled Drake and he spun around, rifle drawn.

'Put that away,' Lerako ordered him.

'That was quick,' Drake said as he obeyed her instructions and lowered his rifle.

'It's not a big house. I couldn't see anyone behind the building, but I did spot a hydro.'

Lerako squeezed herself in between the two men.

'Our best option is to get as close as possible and try to take them out before they even know we are here.'

The man next to Lerako nodded and she turned to Drake to receive his acknowledgement.

'That's one option. Another is to sneak around the back and steal the hydro. That way we only have to shoot these guys if they see us and start shooting at us.'

Lerako did nothing to hide her frustration.

'You paid me to do a job, and it wasn't to take you sightseeing. We don't have the time to fidget around with the hydro's DDU and figure out the codes.'

'But what if I could hack the hydro's DDU, quickly? Could we at least try?'

'Sure, why not? Let's do it your way. Please show us poor Bulanalkese how to do things in our own country.'

'Lerako, I didn't mean it like that, it's just I have these hack codes that Jimmy gave me, and I'm sure I can get that hydro up and running in no time. I'm just offering an option with less bloodshed.'

'People die every day, Drake.'

He waited for her to finish, but she was done.

'Please.'

'You have five minutes. If the hydro is not working by then, I'm shooting everyone that's in my way.' Lerako turned to the other man. 'Cover us from the front. If they move to the back, start shooting. If we are successful, we'll circle back and pick you up at the big tree down the road. Got it?'

The man nodded and disappeared.

'Let's go,' Lerako said to Drake, her face still displaying every bit of frustration she had for him.

* * *

ERROR – CODE NOT RECOGNIZED

Drake moved his body to cover the hydro's DDU and to make sure that Lerako couldn't see the message. Luckily for him, she was watching the house and not him. The countdown timer on his HIC dipped below three minutes.

Trying the next code, Drake couldn't help but think that Jimmy would have had this thing up and running by now. Pushing any thoughts of Jimmy away, before they took over and distracted him, Drake pressed on with the next code on the list.

ERROR – CODE NOT RECOGNIZED

Less than two minutes remained.

'Looks like we're doing things my way,' Lerako added some more pressure.

A sweat bead ran down Drake's forehead, bypassing his eyebrows, and landed in his eye. Stinging like hell, he tried to ignore it, as he knew time was about to run out. He still had a few codes left but Lerako was about to do it her way.

CODE CONFIRMED

Drake almost missed the message, as he was already getting the next code ready.

There was less than a minute left.

'Lerako. Lerako!'

Scowling at Drake for making a racket, she made her way over to him.

'Get in. It's working.'

A look of surprise and disappointment came over her face, but she ran around the front of the hydro and jumped in next to Drake. Once she was on board, Drake ran the start-up procedure. He waited as long as he could before starting it up, for fear the hydrogen-powered vehicle's engine sound might attract attention. Making sure the path was clear, with no obstructions, he turned it on.

The hydrogen power unit came to life, making the uniquely muffled bubbly sound of being underwater. Being an aging model, it took a while for everything to get up to working tolerances. The propulsion unit grew louder and louder, and the bubbling sound made way for a whining buzz.

'Time to get out of here,' Drake said as he floored the accelerator and drove the hydro past the stunned guards.

Big round eyes stared at them in disbelief, unsure what was happening or what their reaction should be. In the rear-view monitor, Drake saw the door to the building open, and a man with a pot belly appear, yelling and waving his arms. the guards snapped out of their daze, but it was too late as Drake disappeared around a corner.

'There!' Lerako pointed out, soon after.

Drake turned his head to see Lerako's man, running parallel to the road they were on, heading towards the tree they agreed upon as the rendezvous point.

'Looks like a race, Drake said and sped up a bit, ensuring he reached the tree before the man.

This prompted a rare chuckle from Lerako.

A minute later the man arrived, sweaty and out of breath.

'Hey, you should have flagged us down. I didn't even see you,' Drake said.

The man gave him a deadly look as he climbed into the hydro.

'Where to, boss?' Drake asked, feeling confident having a steering wheel between his hands.

'Follow this dirt road until it crosses the highway. It's a long way away, but I'll warn you when we are close.'

With no green line to guide him and pull him forward, Drake pressed down on the accelerator and followed the brown strip of brown dirt instead.

* * *

Night had fallen by the time they reached the highway. It was unlike any highway Drake had ever been on. It was a simple two-lane sealed road, barely bigger than a normal road in New

Franco. It was littered with potholes, but traffic was light, and avoiding them was easy.

Lerako directed Drake to take a left on the highway when they reached it, and he duly followed orders. There were no lights on the highway, and the only illumination was from the hydro's underpowered headlights. It made driving harder, but the view spectacular. Stars filled the night sky, shining so bright, that Drake knew they were nowhere near a large city.

'I guess we should have zigged when we zagged,' Drake broke the silence.

'Huh?'

'Nothing. I mean, we took a left when we should have taken a right someplace.'

It was hard to read Lerako's expression in the daylight, and almost impossible now in the darkness of the hydro's cabin.

'You are correct, Drake. I made a mistake. But I promise we'll catch up to Jimmy.'

Instead of reassuring her he didn't mean she was incompetent, and that he was merely making small talk, Drake left it there. It gave him some power, having her apologize. He had no idea what to do with it, or if it was worth anything, but he decided to hold on to it.

They drove on in silence. A sudden vibration in Drake's arm startled him.

A message on his HIC.

'Maybe it's Jimmy,' he said out loud.

Not wanting to lose the signal or misread anything, he brought the hydro to a standstill on the side of the highway.

He put the hydro on standby, and with a shaky hand accessed his HIC.

One unread message.

Tapping on the notification, he opened the messaging app, displaying the unread message.

Mr. Drake

What's going on? I've been trying to contact Jimmy all day but haven't heard back yet. The customer is expecting delivery tomorrow afternoon and wants assurances. Please confirm that everything is in order. This is not the kind of customer one wants to make wait. Trust me!

John Simons

'Well? Was it Jimmy?'

'No,' Drake replied. 'Just a friend checking in on me. Let's keep going.'

Driving off into the night, Drake replayed the message over and over in his head.

This is not the kind of customer one wants to make wait. Trust me!

* * *

'I hate to be that guy, but I can barely keep my eyes open. Do we have an ETA on the next town? Or maybe a truck stop if you guys even have those.'

From the back seat came a loud snore, and then more rhythmic breathing.

'We don't have many of those left. I think the best would be to stop and rest for the night. We aren't close to any villages or towns that I know of, and I don't think anyone will bother us.'

Lerako tried to stifle a yawn.

'Cool. Where should I stop?'

Lerako accessed the hydro's DDU and used the system's rudimentary navigation program to find a spot for them.

'In about two kilometers there will be a turnoff on your right. Take it and follow the road for about five minutes. That should give us enough distance away from the main road.'

Following Lerako's instructions, instead of a green line, Drake saw the turnoff and took it. After what he guessed was five minutes, he pulled to the side of the small dirt road.

Lerako disembarked and looked around, while Drake shut down the hydro. After he finished, he joined her outside.

'I'm worried about Jimmy.'

The stars were closer than he had ever seen them.

'I told you, no guarantees. But I believe we are on the right track now.'

'Why? All we've been doing is driving with no more information coming our way.'

'Because,' Lerako said, her voice tight with tension, 'we are on our way to Jotown. It's one of the biggest in the area. The biggest, I guess. Anyway, I know a lot of people there, and someone like Jimmy would have been noticed by now.'

'So why haven't we heard anything?'

'Not everyone here is connected, like the people from Shang-corp or Penta. Most Bulanalkese are poor, and things like HICs, HIDs, or ARPs are not on their minds. Food, shelter, water. That's what people worry about, Drake.'

'And you think someone there will have seen him?'

'If not seen him, they would have heard something. He's unique-looking, at least here he is. You don't see anyone that light or with orange hair like him.'

He had to agree. Jimmy's appearance was the opposite of most Bulanalkese.

'I really hope we do. I fear the longer we take—'

Silence settled over them. The night air was cool but pleasant. In the distance something made a noise, that Drake assumed to be that of an animal.

'I wouldn't recommend sleeping on the ground,' Lerako said. 'There are things here that might bite you.'

Drake gasped loudly and looked around his feet.

'In the hydro then?' he asked.

'Won't be comfortable, but it will be safe.'

* * *

Being half awake already, it didn't take too much for Drake to be fully alert. The vibration in his arm did the trick.

Let me know when the delivery is made.

John Simons

Leaving the vehicle behind, Drake walked a few meters, stretching out his body. It felt like he was right back in Lan-noi, sleeping in a wreck under a bridge. The place Jimmy told him he was happiest.

The sun was on the rise painting the sky in beautiful pink and orange hues. The landscape was flat and open with only a scattering of trees. This was not the first or most breathtaking sunset he had ever seen, but somehow it was the most peaceful. Maybe it was because of all the violence in such a short time since arriving in Bulanalke that made this isolated place feel serene. It felt untouched by humans.

'I forget sometimes how lucky we are.'

Drake turned to see Lerako's face, smiling, displaying the same serenity he felt.

'Lucky? People have been shooting at me since I arrived. Pretty, sure, but lucky?'

'Yes, lucky Drake. And can I tell you why?'

'Sure.'

'Because we are free. We are not chasing around, trying to make more credits. Running off to places we shouldn't be. We are content to live here and have what we have. Every time I have to protect a foreigner it is for the same reason. They are here, chasing credits, risking their lives.'

The hues in the sky faded, as the big yellow ball made its appearance.

'What about the warlords and generals?'

'They are free too.'

'They are, but what about the people they oppress and exploit.'

Lerako looked at him, confused.

'Who says these people are exploited? Why do foreigners always make us into victims?'

'Are you saying the warlords and generals who run these towns are the good guys?'

'I'm saying that the people of Bulanalke are free to follow whoever they want. And if they want to follow a strong leader, that is up to them.'

On cue, Lerako's man walked over. 'We have a lead in Jotown.'

Dismissing him, Lerako faced Drake. 'People need a strong leader.'

| twenty-two |

Jotown was not what Drake had expected.

Waivers and warnings filled the screen, alluding to a bigger town ahead. Drake accepted them blindly and drove on. A steep hill tested the hydrocar's resolve, but eventually, they reached the peak. Sitting on the crest gave them a 360-degree view of the surrounding area. They had already seen what lay behind them, so Drake only looked ahead. To the left-hand side of the road, it looked like a typical Bulanalkese landscape-arid and vast. On the right-hand side of the road ahead was a huge hole. Drake couldn't see the bottom of it, or judge the diameter from this distance, but it was the biggest crater he had ever seen. He kept driving, and as they neared it, he started to identify buildings around the crater. The closer they came, the more he could differentiate between the buildings and realize how many there were. Which also meant the crater was bigger than he expected. They reached the bottom of the hill, and the crater disappeared from view. Jotown came into view on the horizon, looking like a normal town.

'That's a massive crater in the middle of it.'

Lerako laughed. It was an uninhibited sound, perfectly matching the confidence she always displayed.

'That, Drake, is not a crater. It is the biggest man-made hole in the world.'

Drake had a few questions, but summed it up with, 'Huh?'

'Jotown started as a small mining town, close to an open-cut mine. Normally mines are deep underground here, but this one was different and the planners for the town made a mistake in building it too close to the mine. As the mine grew, it encroached on the town. It also needed more people to mine it, which meant the town grew. Instead of building it somewhere new, the people who arrived simply claimed spots around the massive hole. Soon the town encircled the mine.'

The old hydro didn't have much in the way of a display on screen, but Drake could see the town approaching fast.

'As far as holes go, it is pretty impressive, but I expected Jotown to be bigger somehow.'

'You'll be surprised,' Lerako replied.

Buildings started to line the road. Only a few, at first, but as they drove, they became more frequent and more closely spaced. Soon there was hardly any space between buildings and even the roads had traffic on them. It still felt smaller than Drake expected.

'You ready? Turn right over there.'

Intrigued, Drake followed Lerako's instructions and turned onto the street she pointed to. Buildings flanked the street on both sides, and he followed it until the road disappeared. They've reached the edge of the big hole. The street curved to the left and Drake followed it. Gravity pulled him forward in his seat as the nose of the hydro dipped, and they started to descend into the pit. Drake glanced out his side window, looking into the hole.

Lerako was right. He was surprised.

Like a big corkscrew, the road circled the big hole, gradually reaching the bottom, where more buildings and roads made up Jotown.

'Wow,' Drake admitted his surprise.

'That's not all. Turn there,' Lerako instructed him again.

They were only a quarter of the way down the corkscrew, but Drake saw the road Lerako pointed to. He took it, and at once went into a tunnel.

It was a whole new world.

Tiny buildings sat on top of each other and lined the road. Lights were on everywhere, some strung across the road. People were going about their days as if they lived in a normal town, not one underground. Drake kept on driving and the buildings kept on coming. Occasionally roads veered off the main street, and as Lerako remained silent, Drake started to explore more. These streets contained even more buildings, most appearing to be housing units. People were everywhere.

'This is insane. I've never seen an underground city before.'

'I said you'd be surprised. Once Shangcorp left. People kept coming to Jotown for work, but there wasn't any, so they stayed, as they had nowhere else to go, and occupied the empty tunnels.'

Drake kept on driving, taking detours, and after a few min-utes, he saw sunlight again, as they came back to the tunnel entrance.

'This place is truly amazing, Lerako, but I'm not here to sightsee.'

'Give me the details,' Lerako turned to the back of the vehicle, sounding a bit annoyed.

She made it clear that there were no guarantees, and a feeling that had been lingering in Drake's mind became stronger. Had he been played? Back on the ship, Rut told him not to trust her, but he decided to hire her anyway. Now, he couldn't stop the feeling that they weren't getting anywhere, driving in circles, and she was in no rush to rectify it.

'Turn around. It seems our informant is back in the tunnels.'

The feeling stayed with Drake as he turned the hydro around and followed Lerako's instructions to an unassuming gray living unit.

'You stay here and look out for the hydro. It seems like a safe area, but who knows.'

It took Drake a second to realize she was asking him to stay behind, not the other guy.

'Absolutely not! If they know anything about Jimmy, I need to hear it.'

To prove how serious he was, Drake exited the hydro and walked to the living unit's door, waiting for Lerako. She did not look happy when she caught up.

'Stay quiet and let me do the talking. Remember, you paid me so let me do my job.'

Lerako knocked on the door since there was no sign of a DDU.

Nothing happened, so she knocked again, this time a bit louder.

A shuffling noise came from the inside before the door slid open.

'Yes?' The voice belonged to a typical Bulanalkese man, short hair, dark skin, and skinny, with muscular arms.

'You answered a post we placed about this man?' Lerako held up her arm so the man could see the image on her HIC.

Squinting, the man took his time studying the image. Drake didn't blame him, as it was barely visible on Lerako's out-dated HIC.

'That's him.'

'Could you be more specific, please?'

The man looked nervously at Drake, before addressing Lerako. 'The credits?'

'The credits are for helpful information. I'll need to know what you know before we can decide if it's valuable.'

'It is.'

'So, tell me then,' Lerako said and took a step closer to the man. Standing next to him, the smart bet would be on Lerako to win in a physical altercation. The man must have felt the same and cowered in front of her.

'I work on a farm, outside of town. Sometimes, if we get a bonus, I go to the canteen close to work and drink. Not often, but sometimes. Last night, I went. But like I said, I don't go there a lot. There was a group of people at a table, and I could tell they weren't from Jotown. That happens a lot at the canteen since it's outside of town and people from smaller villages go there. I overheard them saying something about the red-haired ghost in their village. Is that good enough?'

Red-haired ghost. Not the most flattering description of Jimmy, but it fitted, nonetheless.

'It's him,' Drake said.

Lerako shot him a look to shut him up.

'Can I have my credits?'

'Do you know what village they were from?'

The man went silent as he tried to remember.

'No, but I did see hydros parked outside before I went in.'

'So—'

'They had tribal logos on them.'

Drake recalled the hydros with the painted-over logos they saw on the hydrogen station footage. The shape of the logo was still visible, but he couldn't place it. It was an image he had seen at school, many years ago. It was on the tip of his tongue.

'And what was the logo?' Lerako asked.

Drake mouthed the words as the skinny man answered Lerako.

'An elephant.'

* * *

'This is not good,' Lerako said as they closed the hydro's doors.

'That's the same ones I saw at the hydro station!'

'What?'

'At the old mine. The hydrogen station. Remember how I saw a logo on the hydros, but it had been painted over? And you said that it was normal?'

'Yes.'

'It was the shape that was painted over. An elephant's head. I'm sure of it.'

Lerako backed up the hydro, spun it around, and took off for the tunnel entrance. When they left, Drake went for the driver's door, but Lerako brushed him aside and took his place. She was businesslike, so Drake kept his mouth shut and jumped in next to her.

'Get me the coordinates to that canteen,' Lerako ordered her man in the back.

Within minutes he had it and Drake entered it into the hydros DDU. No telemetry, or a green line appeared, instead a tiny voice issued directions. Drake had to turn the volume to its maximum setting to ensure they didn't miss anything. Soon the directions had them on the outskirts of Jotown. It didn't take them long to arrive at the canteen.

Nothing but a big shack, the canteen's main building material was corrugated tin sheets. Rocks on the roof supplied insurance that the roof was secure. Dirt surrounded the canteen and served as the parking lot. A painted sign, not a DDU, hung above the door. Shebeen. It didn't translate to anything meaningful on Drake's ARP, but he understood the gist of it. He stood outside buildings like this many times and knew they were at the right place.

Strings of lights hung from the tin roof, giving the interior a warm feeling. The worn-out wooden floorboards pointed to a well-visited establishment. Being early in the day, only a handful of people sat inside drinking. There were no vehicles outside, so Drake had to assume none of them belonged to the Elephant tribe. Patiently, he waited for Lerako to take the lead.

She exchanged pleasantries with the woman behind the bar before getting down to business.

'Do you know who uses an elephant head for their emblem? I think they might have a camp nearby.'

The woman behind the bar was friendly, but Lerako's question made her cross her arms and take a step back.

'What do you want with them?'

'A friend of my friend over there has gone missing. We heard that the tribe we are looking for might know where he is. Please, we do not want to cause any trouble for anyone. We just want to find his friend.'

'They spend a lot of credits here and offered me free protection if someone were to bother me. Like this right now.'

The time had come for them to leave.

'Like I said, we mean no—' Drake grabbed Lerako's arm and smiled at the woman, as he pulled her towards the door.

'What are you doing, Drake?'

'Outside,' Drake replied.

Lerako shook her arm free and walked out towards the hydro.

'Why did you stop me? I had it under control.'

Drake held up his hands.

'I know. I believe you. But everyone was watching you. By now the word has reached the tribe that someone was asking about them. I bet very soon we'll see a hydro or two with elephant heads on them rock up.'

Lerako's face did not hide her frustration, but she did her best to sound neutral.

'Maybe. We'll hide the hydro and find an advantageous spot for us and see if you're right.'

Twenty minutes passed before a cloud of dust signaled an approaching vehicle. Everyone gave the thumbs-up signal, letting the others know they were ready for what was coming. The dust cloud grew bigger, and the noise of the hydro became audible. It only took a few seconds before they had a visual. A flatbed hydro raced up to the canteen, slamming on its brakes, and allowing the dust cloud to overtake it. Two men left the cabin in a hurry while a third man stayed, positioning himself on the flatbed, ready to use the mounted pulse rifle. After a quick inspection of the empty parking lot and surrounds, the two men entered the building.

Lerako held up her hand to show everyone to wait.

Sweat dripped down Drake's back, as the sun reached its peak. He hoped Lerako would make a decision soon so that they could get out of this heat.

The door to the canteen swung open and the two men re-appeared. They looked around for a while, before jumping back into the hydro. Leaving the way they came, they disappeared into another cloud of dust.

'Go! Get in the hydro!' Lerako shouted.

Before they took cover, they parked the hydro down a narrow path in the trees and covered it with some branches. Once they removed the branches, they quickly took up their places in the hydro and Lerako set off, following the dust cloud hanging in the sky.

From what he'd observed, no one here used or had functional radar systems as Lerako chased the dust cloud, well within range of a radar beam. The road was heavily corrugated, and Drake had to hold on as the hydro shook and slid on the loose dirt surface. Visibility was almost zero, and Drake hated not having control of the vehicle. If only he was driving.

An alert on his HIC drew his attention away from their imminent crash.

It was from Mr. Simons.

Drake swiped it away. Whatever it was, he would deal with it later. Right now, he had to focus on Jimmy.

| twenty-three |

There was some method to Lerako's driving madness. Once the dust cloud ahead stopped, she pulled into the scrub and bashed through it as far as she could. Having stayed so close to the other vehicle, the two dust clouds merged into one and there was no sign of an approaching vehicle. They had the perfect cover.

'Let's move closer and see what we have, okay?'

They agreed and followed her through the scrub. It was slow going, as the shrubs had massive thorns which grabbed onto their clothing. A few penetrated and nicked their skin. It didn't faze Lerako or her minion so Drake kept his complaints to himself.

'Hold up.'

Drake stopped, but not seeing anything, inched forward.

A small village, small enough to be fenced in, sat in the middle of a clearing. Guards stood at the gate and walked the perimeter. Some guards were busy carrying boxes.

'Is this some military compound?' Drake asked. Everyone he saw was armed. There was hardly any women, but he saw a few kids. They too carried pulse rifles.

'Sort of. It's one of the local warlords. That's the term they use, but they are nothing more than what you'd call a gang. They raid and steal from other villages, trying to increase their territory. The kids are usually stolen and forced to fight for them.'

Something changed in Lerako's voice when she spoke of the children. If not for Jimmy, he would have asked her about it, but now was not the time.

'We are completely outnumbered,' Drake stated the obvious. 'Do you have any more people working for you? Can we get some backup?'

'Even if I called in more people, it would take them a day to get here. The way everyone is moving around, they are busy. With purpose. They are planning something.'

'Then what do we do?' Drake asked.

'For now, we can only watch. See if we can learn anything from here.'

Jimmy could be here, a few meters away, and sitting there doing nothing made Drake feel hopeless and angry.

But he couldn't think of a better plan than Lerako's.

A message alert made his arm vibrate. Making sure no one was watching him, he accessed his HIC. Two unread messages from Mr. Simons. Reluctantly, Drake read the first one.

Mr. Drake. The delivery should have been made by now. Please confirm. I have lost all contact with Jimmy and the cargo, and I'm extremely concerned. John Simons.

Drake closed the message and read the next one.

Mr. Drake. The client is not happy. Please contact me ASAP. We can still fix this. John Simons.

Maybe he had been wrong in keeping Mr. Simons in the dark. Perhaps he could help, somehow? Considering he had been dealing in Bulanalke for years, he might have resources Drake didn't consider.

A loud noise pulled Drake's attention away. Lerako craned her neck, trying to find the source of the noise.

'There!' she said as she found it.

Drake looked in the same direction and saw the source too.

Their Hydrostar.

The noise came from two big sliding doors that were clearly in need of some lubricant and maintenance, but behind them sat what mattered. His truck.

'That's it! That's my truck!'

After shushing him, Lerako said, 'Calm down. It's easy to get carried away so close to the end. This is the time mistakes happen. You must listen to me from now on, okay?'

Drake nodded, only half listening to what she was saying.

Slowly the Hydrostar made its way out of the big shed. Multiple hydros, some with mounted guns, some civilian vehicles with the elephant emblem sprayed on them, lined up in front and behind the Hydrostar. They were forming a convoy. If they were able to drive the Hydrostar it meant they had the codes. The question was, did they take it from Jimmy, or did they use him to input the codes?

'We need to find out if Jimmy is in the truck.'

'I don't see how we can, Drake.'

Drake tried to imagine Jimmy sitting in the back on his cot, most likely tied up. At least he'd have Seymour for company.

'Seymour!' Drake blurted out which earned him another scowl from Lerako.

'Who's Seymour?'

'It's an ASR that Jimmy found, and he is never without it.'

'So?'

'I had completely forgotten about him. Jimmy's HIC and ARP are somehow blocked or broken, but maybe I can contact Seymour.'

'It's worth a shot, but you need to hurry. That convoy is going to leave soon.'

Drake had only used Seymour on a few occasions as Jimmy had set him up as the only other authorized user. No doubt with limited access, but access, nonetheless. Finding the app Jimmy installed on his HIC, Drake tried to link up with Seymour. He watched on as three dots ran across his screen, making the linking process visual. Every time they reached the end, they reappeared at the start and made their way across the screen again.

'C'mon,' Drake said, urging the pixels on.

A message appeared telling him the connection failed. Looking at his HIC's telemetry he saw he was without a signal again.

Trying to calm himself, he cursed the poor technological infrastructure as graphically as he could and tried again. Clearly, the swearing worked, as the three pixels reappeared and started their journey across the screen again. It didn't take long before a menu with multiple options replaced them. None of the options were helpful, except one. LOCATE. Drake immediately clicked on it. The three dots started running across his HIC again.

'They're moving,' Lerako whispered.

The three dots reemerged and started their journey across the screen again.

'Drake, talk to me.'

Another lap completed. Another lap started.

'It's not connecting to his location. I don't know!'

The guards at the gate opened it, and the convoy slowly rolled through it.

'We need to make a decision.'

The dots disappeared and a map of the area appeared. Having such an outdated Human Interface Console, Drake struggled to make out much. He zoomed in and waited for the image to refocus.

'They're out of the gate, Drake.'

A little dot on the map showed Seymour's position. It was still vague, so Drake zoomed in again and waited again for it to refocus.

'They're getting away, Drake.'

The dot remained motionless. Drakes' heart rate increased as he zoomed in one more time.

At the gates, the last vehicle exited, and the guards started to roll them shut.

'It's now or never, Drake. I suggest we follow the convoy.'

Slowly the image on his HIC became clear, finally showing details to identify the village. He now had a clear location of where Seymour's signal came from.

The last vehicle disappeared around a bend.

Seymour's signal stayed static.

Drake's heart was racing.

'Follow the trucks. I'll go to Seymour's location.'

'We need to stay together.'

'No, this is our best shot. Follow the trucks. Even if Jimmy is with Seymour, we still need to follow the truck and try to recover our cargo.'

Lerako shook her head.

'You're the client, but I think this is a mistake.'

She didn't wait for an answer. Tilting her head towards the convoy's dust, she ran towards the hydro, her man closely behind her. Drake watched them disappear into the thick scrub before he moved towards the village.

* * *

After the convoy disappeared, calmness settled over the village. The dust dissipated and the remaining guards were no longer alert but stood around, kicking at the dirt with their boots. About half the people departed in the convoy, and of the remaining ones, most went indoors. A few sat around in the shade, but no one looked vigilant. A handful of men patrolled for a while, then took up a spot in the shade and joined the others for a chat. Only the gate was guarded.

According to the map on Drake's arm, Seymour was in a building right behind the big shed where the Hydrostar came out. After he orientated himself to the map, Drake made his way around the perimeter, staying deep in the scrub, and moved as close as possible to Seymour's location. The only obstacle between him and Seymour was a rusty chain-link fence. A small building, no more than a shed, was five meters behind the fence. It was where Seymour's beacon was signaling.

Accessing the app that controlled Seymour, Drake went through the menu again. He found the one he was looking for and selected it. After waiting on another slow connection, he finally connected to Seymour's camera. Drake's ARP kicked in and Seymour's POV displayed in Drake's view.

Total darkness.

Drake checked all the settings and reconnected again, but still, his ARP remained dark. Maybe Seymour took damage, and its camera was broken. There was no way for Drake to tell. What mattered was that he was in the building in front of him, and possibly so was Jimmy.

Chain-linked fences weren't used that often in New Franco or the Penta territories as most people and businesses relied on scanners, cameras, and drones to keep themselves and their valuables safe. Still, he had seen enough of them on his travels to know that they were very noisy when rattled. Climbing it was out of the question. He also didn't have his little plasma cutter with him. That was still in the Hydrostar. He only had his pulse pistol and an SA74. Both super noisy tools.

Scaling it seemed impossible. Except for the noise it would make, the fence was also twice as high as Drake. Sitting down on a rock, Drake's shoulders slumped as the negative voices in his head grew louder. He had to get over that fence, but how? There we no trees close to the fence, and the shrubs were dry, with thin, brittle branches. The only other things around were rocks.

Out of desperation, and with no better plan, Drake started to pile the rocks on top of each other. An exolifter would have made light work of the rocks, but instead, Drake had to struggle to lift and carry each one by himself. Unless someone came around the corner, looking for something behind the shed, no one would be able to see him. Still, Drake worked as quietly as possible to make sure he didn't alert anyone. After almost an hour, he had a pile, right next to the fence, and almost as high as he was. Since Lerako left, she hadn't been in contact, and Drake had not been able to connect with her either. He checked his HIC one more time before he would attempt to jump the fence. Still nothing. Time to go.

Climbing the rocks was harder than he expected since they weren't very stable and some rolled down the pile. Luckily, they didn't make a lot of noise. Finally, he reached the top, and fearing he might fall off if he lingered, he jumped. Back in Lan-noi, Dina taught Drake plenty of tactical skills, one being how to fall from heights. So, the moment he hit the ground, he tumbled over and rolled. It wasn't pretty, but when he stood up, nothing hurt. He tried to be as quiet as possible but took cover against the building Seymour was in and waited. Once he was certain no one was coming, Drake stepped back from the building and inspected it.

About two meters high and three wide, it wasn't very big. No windows were visible on this side. He would have to move around it to find a way in. Carefully Drake poked his head around the corner. From here he could see the side of the building, but also some people. Fortunately, they had their backs to him. A scan of the building revealed no entry points, so he quickly retracted his head. He repeated the process at the other corner with the same result: no entry points and people sitting around. The only way in was from the front.

Slowly, Drake began to inch his way to the front of the shed, keeping an eye on the guards sitting twenty meters away. As he reached the front corner, he paused to make sure no one looked his way and poked his head around, hoping no one was there. No one was, and there was even better news. The front of the shed was wide open. Without hesitation, Drake flung himself around the corner and into the small shed.

Once inside, he scrambled to the side, and pushed himself against a wall, making himself as small a target as possible. Keeping his eyes outward, he waited for a beat to make sure no one heard him or made their way over, before turning his attention to the inside of the shed.

Tarpaulins, empty crates, and rusty parts sat on broken shelves. This place was nothing more than an oversized storage closet.

In the corner on the ground, too big for the shelves, sat a dark gray box. It had an elephant head logo on it. Drake bent down and opened it up, knowing what he'd see.

He was right.

| twenty-four |

Sitting on the ground, legs splayed out in front of him, Drake took Seymour out of the box. It was even more banged up than normal but was still working. It took Drake a few minutes to figure out how to take it out of standby mode. The orange ASR rose on its four legs and walked in a small circle, checking all its systems. Once done, it came over to Drake and stood next to him, ready for its instructions.

Finding Seymour was bittersweet. It all but confirmed that Jimmy was still alive, but it also meant he had left with the Hydrostar. It made no sense for the local militia to take the Hydrostar for a joyride so Drake had to assume they were on their way to a new destination. Probably a rendezvous with a buyer for the truck or the cargo. Both, most likely. At least Lerako was in hot pursuit of them.

The network in Bulanalke was the worst Drake had ever experienced. Half the time he had no connection, and when he did have a connection, it was laggy and patchy. Lerako didn't have an ARP, so he had to resort to messaging via his HIC. Not as instantaneous as he would have liked, but still better than radio silence.

Jimmy's not here, just the ASR. He must be in the truck. Please let me know once you have a visual.

Seymour stood motionless, still awaiting a command.

Waiting for Lerako to reply made Drake feel like Seymour. They were both standing around waiting to be told what to do next.

Drake refreshed his message app, but no new messages appeared. He had no idea how far away Lerako and Jimmy were, or even what direction to go in. The scrub was a maze of trails and small roads. He'd be sure to get lost the moment he ventured out there by himself.

But not doing anything was not an option.

It was time to come up with a plan.

Sitting still, thinking, Drake became aware of the noises around him. Not weird animal noises like at night but familiar noises. Sounds of people talking and laughing, things banging together, doors being shut. Normal human noises. He was not sitting in a military compound, but a village. Everyone in the village was armed and working for the militia but it was still a village.

What he needed to do was grab someone and interrogate them. He could hear kids playing, but immediately pushed that thought aside. Although some of the armed guards he saw looked no older than ten, he was not going to participate in any violence towards kids. Which was the only way he had ever seen interrogation handled. Penta was a law unto themselves, and they didn't shy away from using whatever technique produced the fastest results.

Not that his morals were that high. Any grown-up, any gender, any age would do. As long as they were smaller than him. No point in picking a fight you can't win.

Placing Seymour on standby, Drake moved out of the shed. Straight ahead was the bigger building from where he saw the Hydrostar appear. It was as good a place as any to start, as there could be a clue hidden in there. Staying low, Drake ran to the rear of the building. Everyone was going on with their lives with no signs of being alert. This made it easier for Drake to move around. He had to stay low and not attract any attention.

A door on the back of the building was an obvious place to gain entry to the building and Drake crawled over to it. No DDU was visible, so he tried to push, then pull on it. It budged slightly but made a loud screeching sound. Drake paused and listened. A light crunching sound came from around the corner of the building. The sound kept repeating itself and grew louder. Foot-steps. Drake's only option was to make a run for the small shed that had Seymour in it, but running could expose him. Instead, he decided to wait, leaning as hard as he could against the build-ing, but still clearly visible. Tucking his head down, he tried to make himself as small as possible. The footsteps continued, and Drake could swear they were headed straight for him. His only choice was to jump up and defend himself. Yet, he stayed down, listening to the increasing sound of the footsteps, keeping their rhythm steady. The crunching was now right next to him and started to move away. Cautiously, Drake lifted his head to take a peek.

And saw a goat.

In two days, he went from never seeing one, except for a picture when he was a child, to seeing two.

Knowing he might not be so lucky next time, Drake picked up a rock. Aiming at the goat, he placed his right foot on the edge of the door. Pulling back his arm, he braced his leg and threw. The rock hit the goat on its hind leg, and the animal let out a loud cry as it scampered away. At the same time, he threw the rock, Drake kicked the door. If he missed the goat, or the goat didn't make a sound, he would've been in real trouble. It made a loud creaking sound, but Drake timed it perfectly with the goat's cry. To be safe, he waited briefly before moving inside.

Darkness engulfed him, and it took his eyes a second to adjust to the low light inside the large building. It was easily the biggest building in the village. Tiny windows, close to the roof provided the only light source. As Drake's eyes became used to the light, he made out some familiar shapes. Not only did they store the Hydrostar here, but also their other vehicles. Drake identified the shapes of two hydrocars in the dim light and made his way over, careful not to bump into anything and make a noise.

The first hydrocar Drake approached looked like nothing more than a spare parts donor. Missing all its doors and its hood, Drake noticed that most of the propulsion unit was missing too. Closer inspection showed the inside also to have been stripped of most of its parts. Moving on to the next vehicle, Drake felt some hope, as its doors and hood were intact. Pulling on the door handle, the door swung open. More good news. The interior was in good condition.

Drake climbed into the driver's seat and switched on the Hydro's DDU. Hopefully one of Jimmy's codes would work.

The DDU screen remained blank. Drake flicked the switch again. Same result. Drake slumped back into the seat. Trouble-shooting this problem could take hours. And even if he found the problem, he'd have to work in the dark to fix it. He tried one more time, closing his eyes and crossing his fingers, but no superstition in the world would make this hydro come to life.

Getting out of the hydro, he searched the rest of the building. It was a general storage building. Besides the vehicles, there were also crates, boxes, and various lockers and shelves. Tarpaulins covered some items, but most sat in the open, covered in dust. Drake's hopes of finding anything useful here started to fade.

A small window in the front of the building, next to a door, looked out on to the village. Dust and grime covered the window, and Drake dared only clean a tiny hole for him to peak through. From here he had a great view of most of the village. It matched what he had heard before. People walked around, kids played and even the goat was there. Only a handful of people were armed. If he had to guess, he would say most of the militia went with the Hydrostar to their destination, leaving only a few people to guard the base.

Moving to the side to get a better view around the corner, Drake bumped into something with his hip. It felt pretty solid, but also soft. A tarpaulin covered whatever it was, and out of curiosity, he pulled the cover back.

And smiled.

The hard but soft object was a rubber grip. A grip that was attached to a bar. Before he pulled back the canvas sheet, Drake already knew what he would find. A hydrocycle. A simpler, easier machine to work on. It wasn't new, and it didn't look big, but it would do. In fact, a hydrocycle might be better suited to a quick escape than a hydrocar.

Flicking on the power switch, Drake saw no sign of life in the cycle. Unlike the hydrocar, the battery sat on the side, easily accessible. Drake pulled it out and found the LED battery indicator. Five bars indicated a full charge. Three meant half. One meant charge now. What Drake saw was a faint glow, barely visible emitted from a single bar. The battery was drained, but not dead.

It took Drake almost half an hour, but finally, he found a charger. Fingers crossed, he plugged it into the cycle's battery and waited for the LED bars to come to life. For a second, he feared it was hopeless, as the dull light from the LED bar disappeared. Franticly, Drake tapped on the charger to try and magically fix the problem. It worked. In a beautiful sequence, which is normally overlooked, the LED bars lit up, one after the other, before dimming down again. Then it started over again, one bar, then the next, and so forth. The battery was charging.

Dark thoughts of him wasting too much time and showing up too late kept lingering, but Drake pushed them aside. He had to wait a few minutes before trying to start the cycle, so he decided to go fetch Seymour. Jimmy would never forgive him if he left Seymour behind.

As expected, Seymour stood in the same spot he left him. Opening the app that allowed him to control Seymour, Drake selected the command he thought deemed the most appropriate. Follow. To make sure it was working, Drake walked a few meters away from Seymour. The ASR turned its head and walked towards Drake. Drake gave another few steps to the side, and Seymour copied him again. Everything was working just fine.

Back in the bigger shed, Drake found some rubber straps, and after a bit of a struggle, he was able to secure Seymour to the back of the hydrocycle. The battery LED indicator showed five full bars. Show time. Holding his breath, Drake flicked on the power switch. And waited. Then, slowly, the DDU mounted on the handlebar came to life. No issues, just an old system, taking it's time to power up. Relieved, Drake went through the codes on his HIC again, and after a few failed attempts found one that gave him access to the hydrocycle's operating system. First priority was to run a systems check to see if everything was operable. It only took a few minutes. Most systems were operational. Only one major red flag. There was no hydrogen.

Having already searched the shed before, Drake knew there were no hydrogen pumps or refills in there. His only hope was that the two hydrocars had some left in their tanks. It was impossible to tell, due to their lack of power, so Drake pushed the hydrocycle over towards the hydros. Once there, he uncoupled a pipe leading from one hydro's tank towards its propulsion unit. Doing the same on the hydrocycle, he then coupled the two pipes together. Accessing the hydrocycle's DDU, he put it in emergency refueling mode and waited to see if the fuel gauge went up or stayed still. The hydrocycle's fuel pump made a loud whirring sound as it tried to suck the gas out of the hydro's fuel tank. Drake doubted the sound would carry beyond the shed, but he ran over to the window to check for signs of someone being alerted, nonetheless. An alarm went off on the hydrocycle, and Drake sprinted back to mute it. The alarm was an error message. There was no more fuel in the hydro. The hydrocycle's fuel gauge was less than a quarter. Not worth the risk. Drake uncoupled the hydro and repeated the whole process with the other hydrocar.

This time it took the alarm much longer before it went off. And to make things even sweeter, the tank registered as full.

'Time to go,' Drake said to Seymour, who silently stared back at him.

| twenty-five |

One of Drake's most recognizable character traits, as agreed on by everyone who knew him, was his ability to act before he thought it through. Above anything, Drake always trusted his gut, and if something felt right, he would do it. Immediately and without further thought. This was such an occasion.

The sun had long been past its peak and daylight was running out. Finding the hydrocycle, charging the battery, and then refilling the hydrogen tank had taken hours. Without knowing the destination, he would need to follow the tracks left by the convoy and do so before nightfall. Drake doubted the area had a lot of traffic, and hoped the tracks would remain visible for a while. His plan was to break out of the village and chase down the convoy.

Ensuring Seymour was secure, Drake powered up the hydrocycle. It only took four tries, and considering how long it could have been sitting there, he counted himself lucky. No major errors came up, and no alarms went off. It was time to go. Opening the door, Drake pushed the hydrocycle out leaning it from side to side to maneuver the handlebars through the narrow door. Once outside the building, he jumped on and twisted the throttle.

Everyone he passed had the same surprised look on their faces but none tried to chase him down. The entry gate was fifty meters away now, and Drake kept the throttle open. Out of the corner of his eyes, he could see some kids running alongside him laughing and hollering. It only lasted a few meters as they ran out of puff. Twenty meters to the gate.

The guards turned and looked on, with the same surprised expressions. They did not attempt to move out of the way or raise their rifles. Drake ducked down as much as he could and braced himself for the impact of crashing through the gate.

It was much harder than he anticipated.

The gate gave away, but it took a lot of energy and momentum out of the hydrocycle. Combined with the soft sand on the road, the front wheel slowed down much more than Drake expected. He was about thirty meters away from the entrance when he finally lost his balance and toppled over.

'Hey! You! What are you doing?' Someone, most likely one of the guards, yelled.

The hydrocycle was heavy. To buy himself some time, Drake drew his pulse pistol and shot at the man yelling at him. Grabbing his arm, the man fell, dragged himself up again and scurried back to the busted gate. Another man ran towards Drake and opened fire. None of the shots hit him, and taking his time Drake aimed and downed the second man with a single shot.

The whole village came to life. Voices yelling and people screaming, but no pulse rounds came his way. Drake grabbed the handlebars and with his back to the bike, walked it backwards. Without too much effort he had it back upright.

A pulse round whizzed past his head.

The hydrocycle was still on, and Drake felt a sense of relief as it lurched forward with the twist of his hand. Following the narrow dirt road, he crouched down as low as he could and left the village behind.

* * *

Everything was going smoothly, but much slower than Drake had hoped. The roads were nothing more than dirt tracks, which were very narrow and heavily rutted. He toppled over a few times, but luckily, he never hurt himself or the hydrocycle. Whenever he found a better piece of road, he twisted the throttle wide open and hung on for dear life. The hydrocycle would squirm underneath him, its tires slipping on the dirt, but the momentum always carried them forward.

It was easy to follow the tracks left behind by the convoy at the beginning but became harder to spot them the further they traveled. The sun was also sitting right behind him, casting long shadows on the path ahead. Soon it would be dark, and Drake feared he might lose the trail. Drake rode even harder and faster, trying his best to outrun the sun.

Eventually, he lost. Darkness surrounded him and although the headlight on the hydrocycle cast a bright light, it created even more shadows and Drake struggled to stay out of the ruts. His progress slowed down to a crawl. Distinguishing between the convoy's tracks and older ones became almost impossible.

Getting off the hydrocycle, Drake switched off the machine, and failing to find a kick stand, leaned it against a tree. Seymour still sat securely on the back. The riding was exhausting, but Drake vowed to continue after a small break. Walking in circles, hands on his back, he tried to relax his body. Doubt and a feeling of hopelessness kept pushing their way into his head. Every fall and slip on the bike gave them another inch. He needed to regroup and banish them, even if it was only for a while.

He was down, but giving up was not an option.

It was time to get back in the saddle and keep grinding it out. An animal or a group of them made some noise in the distance. Drake hoped they were friendly. The noise continued, and a familiar sound joined the cries. A unique human sound. It was the sound of a pulse rifle being fired. The noises continued and a few more pulse rounds joined them. Drake did his best to pinpoint the origin of the sound. The pulse rifle seized, but the noises continued. Jumping on the hydrocycle, Drake took off in the direction of the noise, keeping his headlight off.

After a few minutes, he stopped and listened, to make sure he was still heading in the right direction. Satisfied he was, he took off again and repeated the process a few more times. When he stopped again to listen, he also received a bonus. In the distance, through the trees, a bright light shone. Carefully, as he was now riding in the dark, he rode closer until he had a visual of the light source.

What he found was a village, at least three times the size of the one where he found the hydrocycle. It was a hive of activity, most of it centered around the vehicles parked in an open space in the middle. Vehicles that included a Hydrostar.

The people gathered around it were talking and laughing, and Drake sensed a familiarity between them. Everyone acted very relaxed. Clearly, the elephant head tribe and whoever this was had an alliance.

The question on Drake's mind though was where was Lerako? The convoy made it to their destination, but what happened to her? Was she also observing them from somewhere in the surrounding scrub? Drake checked his HIC but there was still no reply from her.

A crackle of pulse rounds rang out in the night sky. The arrival of the Hydrostar had caused everyone to celebrate, as another man shot his rifle into the sky. Drake took a second look. It was Lerako's right-hand man. And as always, he wasn't too far away from Lerako. Drake had completely missed her earlier, but there she was, standing and chatting with the new tribe. What was her plan? She made it in and infiltrated them, but now what?

A man approached her, and by everyone's reaction, he had to be important, maybe even the leader. As he passed people, they parted to make way for him and Lerako shook his hand, and even her body language looked different to Drake. Her normal confidence had vanished, and she was subdued. The man turned around and walked back the way he came and Lerako followed him. Was she a prisoner?

As he watched the scene unfold, Drake realized there was no fence between him and the village. Unlike the smaller one, this village was only surrounded by thick scrub. An idea came to him.

Turning back to the hydrocycle, he untied Seymour and placed him on the ground. Accessing his HIC, he activated the ASR and made him stand up. Next, he found the menu that allowed him to see through Seymour's sensors and activated it. A small view from Seymour's perspective floated in Drake's view via his Augmented Retinal Projector.

Drake was nowhere as competent as Jimmy when it came to operating Seymour. After stumbling down the road and avoiding crashing into anything, Drake turned Seymour towards the village. Being nighttime, and having only a few lights burning, Drake found enough shadows and dark passages for Seymour to walk in. At times it became confusing as he tried to keep one eye on where Lerako was going and steer Seymour in that same direction. Luckily, everyone's attention was on the Hydrostar and the convoy that arrived with it.

Lerako followed the suspected leader into a building, and Drake moved Seymour into a dark spot, right underneath a window. So far so good. Drake kept expecting someone, maybe a child, to grab Seymour and take him away. But no one had noticed him. Drake turned up all Seymour's sensors to get anything audible, and even then, the quality was poor. Poor, but good enough to follow.

'...long day. But I'm sure my offer will please you.' Drake recognized Lerako's voice.

'I am interested, but to be honest, finding something like this doesn't happen every day. And then someone shows up at the same time with an offer for the items? It sounds too good to be true.'

Was Lerako trying to buy back the Hydrostar? Drake knew he didn't pay her enough to do that, and wondered whether he would have to make another call to Numbers.

'I'm sure it seems strange, Chief Neldella, but I assure you this is strictly business for me.'

'I've heard of you, Lerako. And I'll be honest, it's not been all good.'

'Well, then we know it's been true, at least.'

The chief laughed.

'So,' he continued, 'why do you want to buy these propulsion units so desperately?'

Great. No one had any idea that there were weapons in the back of the Hydrostar.

'A client of mine needs to repair some mining equipment. He's trying to reopen a few mines. And before you ask, no, he is not in your territory or even close.'

'Something tells me if I hold out a bit longer, I'll get even more for them.'

'Maybe. Or maybe you'll be stuck with them. And then you'll have to sell them one at a time or even parts of them. Could take you weeks or even months to make any credits out of them. Sure, they are valuable but they only hold value if someone else wants them. So right now, the only value they hold is my offer.'

Nothing but silence. Drake made some adjustments to ensure his equipment wasn't malfunctioning. As he played with the settings, the voices came back.

'I also know who your father is.'

Silence again, but this time Drake waited it out.

Finally, Lerako spoke. 'This has nothing to do with him.'

Drake wished he could see their body telemetry or even their body language. These silences said so much, yet he did not know what.

'I've never had any run-ins with your father, Lerako. But he is expanding his empire, and I would prefer if he stayed clear of us.'

He couldn't see them, but he knew the sub text.

If I sell you the cargo, your dad promises to stay away from here.

'Like I said, this has nothing to do with him. I don't work for him. But, if it will make this deal happen, I'll have a word with him, chief Neldella.'

Dreaded silence again.

'Okay. I'll sell you the truck and the cargo. Not because it makes financial sense, but more, let's say, political sense.'

'Thank you, chief Neldella. I'll make sure to tell my father of your generosity.'

No one said anything, and assuming the deal was done, Drake maneuvered Seymour back to him.

Lerako exited the building as Drake's HIC buzzed.

I have your truck, but it cost a lot of credits. We need to discuss new terms.

Drake didn't care. What he wanted to do was to get back in the Hydrostar and see Jimmy again.

Drake's HIC vibrated again.

This time, it was not a welcome message.

Mr. Drake. The client has lost faith in our arrangement and has started a search for the lost cargo. Unless you can deliver the goods within 24 hours, I'm afraid our deal will also be terminated, including your payment. John Simons.

It was time to hit the road.

| twenty-six |

Although not fenced in, Drake could not risk moving closer to Lerako or the truck. Guards and civilians were walking around, and everyone was carrying a pulse rifle. No one in the village shared Drake's pale complexion and he would shine like a beacon if he wandered into the crowd.

Where is the rendezvous point?

Drake stared at his HIC, waiting for an answer. He lost visual of Lerako as she walked into another building but he could see the Hydrostar still sitting there.

Minutes passed and still Lerako didn't reply.

He considered moving to a better vantage point but the sea of people and the amount of firepower deterred him. Having no better plan, and time to spare, he activated Seymour again.

This time he couldn't maneuver the ASR straight to the building Lerako had disappeared into. There were too many people along the way, and no other ASRs were patrolling the area, which would make Seymour stand out and raise suspicion. He'd have to take the long way around and walk Seymour along the boundary of the village and cut back towards the building where he last saw Lerako.

Operating Seymour was getting easier, and soon he had the ASR making its way around the edge of town toward the target building. Drake kept monitoring his HIC in the hope of Lerako replying, but nothing appeared. Soon he had Seymour in position again and started scanning for audio. After trying for a few minutes, with no result, he moved the ASR around the building and tried again. This time, he found a source almost immediately.

Jimmy's voice!

'...ya know. But I'm just happy to get out of here and see Drake again.'

'But let's not get carried away. I had to pay a large sum of credits for the truck and its cargo. I'm here on business, Jimmy, so I need to know I'm getting my fair share out of this.'

A small hydrocar stopped a few feet away from Drake, blocking his access to the building and the route he used to get Seymour there. Two men climbed out and made themselves comfortable on the hood of the hydro. Any movement or noise, and they would surely find him. Drake hunched down as much as he could and concentrated on the conversation again.

'...so, as long as we get the weapons to the client, I'm sure we can work out a deal, ya know.'

Drake wanted to jump up, run over there, and slap his hand over Jimmy's mouth. He was about to cost them a lot more credits. Until now, everyone operated under the assumption they had propulsion units in the back of the truck. Valuable items, but not crucial cargo. Now things would change rapidly. With the hydro in front of him, he had no option but to sit still and bear witness to his profits disappearing.

Franticly he typed a new message and sent it to Lerako. It stayed unread.

'Sure, yes, the weapons. Drake told me about the cargo, obviously.'

He had to give it to her. She was a smooth operator.

'I take it it's still secure?'

'Oh yes. I never said anything, ya know?'

It hurt Drake to hear Jimmy's pride. Earned, but so misplaced.

'Good. Good. I think the best thing would be for us to get out of here, and then catch up with Drake.'

'Can't wait to see him again, ya know.'

Lerako knew Drake was there, yet she didn't tell Jimmy. Instead, she made it sound like he was far away and unaware of their position.

She was lying to Jimmy, and she knew about the weapons.

She had no intention of meeting up with Drake later.

Jimmy was about to be kidnapped again.

* * *

Lerako and Jimmy emerged briefly, before turning a corner and making their way to the Hydrostar. Seymour sat stranded on the other side of the hydro, and Drake was pinned down on the opposite side.

Time to put the ASR to use. Maybe for the last time.

'What is that?' one of the men shouted, as they slid down the hood and approached whatever it was that caught their attention.

'It looks like a robotic goat,' said the other.

Drake ordered Seymour to run back to him and perform the dance routine that Jimmy programmed into it. It had worked before to get them out of a tight spot, and Drake was hedging his bets that it would do the same again.

'Look at it go, man!'

Judging by the laughter, Seymour was commanding their attention. It was time to make a break for it. Drake braced himself against the hydro and inched forward to get a better view of where Lerako and Jimmy went. It was easy to find it, and Drake looked around one last time to make sure no one could see him. Everything looked calm, and with Seymour distracting the two men, it was time to move. As he started to lean forward to make a run for it, something big came at him from the side. Drake stopped himself, and looked up, straight into the oncoming Hydrostar. Without hesitation or thinking, Drake threw caution to the wind and sprinted towards the Hydrostar, arms waving and screaming at the top of his lungs.

'Jimmy! Jimmy!'

It lasted two seconds.

Drake concentrated so hard on the truck, that he never looked down at his feet or saw the drainage ditch next to the path the Hydrostar was on. His foot slipped into the ditch and Drake fell forward, hitting the ground hard, almost knocking himself out. A wheel of the Hydrostar went past his head, barely missing it and almost crushing his skull. Drake rolled on to his side, his ankle throbbing with pain, and yelled again. But he could hardly hear himself over the drone of the truck. The Hydrostar picked up speed and disappeared in a cloud of dust.

'What are you doing? Who are you? Hey!'

The voice pulled Drake back to this current predicament.

The two guards who had been enthralled by Seymour's performance, were now equally intrigued by the pale-looking man, lying on the ground in front of them.

'Who are you?'

Everything was right there. Jimmy, the truck, and the cargo. Just meters away from him and he let it slip out of his grasp.

'I don't think he can hear us.'

The dust settled, and Drake saw Seymour still dancing away. He swiped his HIC to put him on standby.

Using the end of his pulse rifle, one of the guards poked Drake.

'Get up, man. Let's go.'

Annoyed, defeated, and extremely angry, Drake swatted the rifle away.

'Stop poking me!'

Both men pulled back, surprised not just at his actions, but also that he could talk.

'Who are you?'

'Benjamin Drake. Who are you?'

The men looked at each other in confusion.

'Clearly, I'm not from here, and it seems that you two are not in charge of making decisions, so how about you lower your weapons, and I can get out of here? '

Standing up, Drake dusted himself off and looked around trying to remember where he parked the hydrocycle.

'I think we need to take him to the chief?'

'Yes, that's what I was thinking.'

'Right then, tell him.'

'I will.'

Drake waited.

'We're taking you to the chief.'

'Why?'

Again, they shared a look of confusion between themselves.

'Because you shouldn't be here.'

'Says who?'

If their aim was as bad as their intellect, Drake figured he would stand a good chance if he made a run for it.

'Just let me go, guys. I'm just a little lost. I'm not a threat. Let me grab my ASR and hydrocycle, and I'll be on my way, yes?'

Drake started to move towards Seymour. He had almost reached him when they came up with another thought.

'You could be a spy.'

Drake let out a chuckle.

'For whom? Also, if you caught me so easily, I'm not a very good spy, am I?'

'Um—'

'He's trying to trick us. Be quiet and walk!'

'Take it easy,' Drake lifted his hands. 'I'll go wherever you want.'

'Good.' A rifle poked him in the back. 'Walk straight ahead, and no more talking.'

Drake nodded his head and finally did as he was told.

* * *

'Who is this?'

'Just open the door. We caught him. We think he's a spy.'

'For whom?'

'Open the door, before we take you in as well.'

'For what? Where did you find him?'

'Stop asking questions and do your job.'

'My job is to keep people out.'

'And if the chief finds out you kept a spy out, what would your job be then?'

The guard at the door sneered at Drake and reluctantly opened the door. The rifle prodded him in the back, and Drake stepped inside the building. Drake couldn't wait to meet the next incompetent yet power-hungry employee of the chief.

He didn't have to wait too long.

'Stop. Who is this?'

'We caught him. He's a spy. Let us in.'

The newest, and hopefully last member of Chief Nadella's security team stepped away from the door and came face to face with Drake.

'Who are you?'

Trying his best not to flinch at the repugnant breath entering his nostrils, Drake forced a smile.

'Benjamin Drake. Truck driver. Definitely not a spy.'

Stinky breath gave him an equally stink eye.

'Promise,' Drake smiled at him.

'Let us in. We caught him, and we need to take him to the chief.'

The goal was to gain favor with the chief.

'You've done your part. I'll take it from here.'

Shoving Drake aside, the three men grabbed each other and started a staring contest. Unfortunately, they were blocking the exit, so Drake took a step back and waited for the thrilling outcome. The staring and grabbing contest went nowhere fast, so it evolved into a verbal insult match. Which grew loud enough for a door to swing open behind them.

'What the hell is going on here?'

Everyone froze, then quickly stood down and started to inspect their feet.

'Who is this?'

All their bravado had deserted the men, and no one spoke.

'Hi, chief Neldella I presume?' Drake extended his hand. 'Benjamin Drake.'

One of the guards slapped Drake's hand away. 'Don't touch the chief.'

The untouchable chief smiled at Drake.

'This seems to be a day full of surprises. Tell me, Benjamin Drake, why did you show up minutes after I sold a truck that had another pale man in it? Surely it is not a coincidence, is it?'

'We caught him, Chief. We think he's a spy.'

'A spy?'

'Yes, chief.'

'What was he doing when you caught him.'

'Well, he was running and fell in front of us.'

'So, he stumbled into you. You didn't actually catch him?'

'But we brought him straight here, chief.'

A grunt let them know it was time to leave.

'Are you a spy?' Straight to the point.

'No, I'm not. I'm a truck driver. A hauler. And that truck you sold was mine.'

Accusing a local chief was not a smart move, and Drake knew it, but he also had no more time or patience. The chief nodded at the remaining guard before walking back into the room he came from. For a second Drake assumed the guard just received the nod to *take care* of him, but a gesture from the chief, now sitting on a large chair inside the room, told him he was safe. For now.

Inside the room, Drake noticed a lack of tech, like he did most places in Bulanalke. No Data Display Units were visible, and even the furniture looked dated. A soft glow from the chief's arm did show him to have a HIC at least.

The guard that stood outside the door must have followed Drake inside, as he was now guarding the door from this side. Another man joined them. He did not look like anyone else in Bulanalke but would have gone unnoticed in most Shangcorp territories.

'What is it that you want, Benjamin Drake?'

A very good question and one Drake needed a second to think about.

'I take it you are ex-Shangcorp security, and it was you who stole my truck. Am I right?'

The man who now stood next to the chief said nothing, but a smile was answer enough.

'I would advise you to answer me when I speak, Benjamin Drake.'

'I have to get my truck back. That's it. I have no issue with you having it and selling it. All I want is to get it back.'

The ex-security man whispered into the chief's ear.

'Who do you work for?' The chief asked.

'No one. I work for myself.'

'So, who is going to come and help you find your truck?'

'No one. If you let me go, I'll hunt them down myself.'

'But you'll call someone for help, won't you?'

'No, there is no one—' Drake caught on. He was not going anywhere. He was being held for ransom, and the chief was trying to find out who would pay for him.

'Chief, I have no one to call. I promise you. I've put everything I had into this venture, and right now I'll be lucky to just get out of here. I have no credits to offer you, and I promise you, no one is coming to look for me.'

Drake wondered if it was true. If the chief decided to throw him in a hole, would anyone come? Lt. Wells gave him clear instructions not to involve her in any way. Mr. Simons would most likely write them off as a loss and move on. If only Dina was here, she would be able to bust them out of any predicament.

It was true. No one was coming for him.

'I believe you, Benjamin Drake. I don't think anyone is going to rescue you or pay to have you released. And I do not want to waste resources to keep you around to test my theory. But, as it's quite late already, and I'm very hungry, I'll wait till the morning to make my decision on what to do with you. Lock him up and make sure he stays put.'

A nod from the ex-security guy instructed the guard to grab Drake and drag him out of the room.

'I hope for your sake the Chief wakes up in a good mood,' the guard said as he kicked Drake into a room and slammed the heavy metal door behind him.

| twenty-seven |

Sunrise was in less than nine hours. Assuming the chief would deal with him first thing in the morning, it left him with only a few hours to plan and execute an escape.

His plan was to distract the guard at the door, grab Seymour, and ride off on the hydrocycle. Simple, except he had no idea how to distract the guard, or how many there were. He couldn't rely on Seymour again, as he was already in the room when Drake arrived. The only weapon Seymour had was an EMP burst, but with the lack of technology around, it was useless.

Drake thought about the list of people he was sure wouldn't come to help. He tried to think of any circumstance under which one of them would step up, but he couldn't find any. Not anyone that he thought was worth the risk of potentially losing.

Out of sheer desperation, Drake began scrolling through his list of contacts. He had to move around the small room to find a strong enough signal, but finally, he did. Most of the names were other haulers and known associates. He thought about calling Numbers again, but he was already so heavily in debt to him, he didn't dare. Reaching the end of the list, the newest and last added contact showed up. Someone he had not considered asking for help, but now it was an obvious choice. Someone with local knowledge and a shared interest. A fellow hauler.

Joe D. Rutledge. AKA Rut.

Drake knew that credits would be involved, as the hauler brotherhood had its limitations. Rut was the perfect person to get him out, help him hunt down Lerako and find Jimmy and the truck. Rut had shown contempt for Lerako, which gave Drake hope that he could convince him to come on board.

The three white dots danced in front of him, and it took a while before they merged to form Rut's face.

'What is it, Drake?'

First hurdle cleared. He answered.

'Hey, buddy. Thanks for taking the call.'

Rut grunted.

'Okay, here it is. I need your help. I lost the truck, Jimmy, too, and I'm held in some village. I don't know the name, but the leader is called Neldella.'

Drake paused to gauge Rut's reaction. Unfortunately, he didn't have any.

'Please Rut. I have no one else to ask. No one nearby enough, anyway. I really need your help.'

Still no reaction, but finally he spoke up.

'Why don't you try Lerako? You were keen to get involved with her on the boat. She's a gun for hire and exactly what you're looking for.'

For a second, Drake considered lying to Rut.

'Funny story. She's the one who stole the truck and took Jimmy.'

This time Rut reacted. It was not the one Drake had hoped for. He simply shook his head and had a chuckle.

'Well, it sounds like you're done for then.'

'Huh? No, wait Rut, please. You have to help me. What's your price?'

'Credits will only get you so far in Bulanalke. Do you even know who Lerako really is?'

That didn't sound very promising.

'I guess I don't and you're about to drop a huge truth bomb on me.'

Rut sighed as if this conversation was taking years of his life.

'Lerako is the daughter of Chief Tjaka.'

Rut stopped as if that was all Drake needed to know.

It wasn't.

'That doesn't mean anything to me, Rut. How is that supposed to help me? I need actual help, man, not a family tree. I need to get out of here!'

'Chief Tjaka controls the biggest area in the region and let me tell you, Drake, he did not achieve it by playing nice. He is not someone you want to deal with, trust me.'

Drake had no more cards up his sleeve. Except for one last desperate card.

'The cargo is weapons.'

'I figured.'

The card was useless.

'Oh,' Drake mumbled, his brain racing to try and come up with a new strategy.

'Listen, the best I can do is to take you to Nandi. From there, you are on your own.'

Nandi. The client, who had been waiting for their weapons, and who, according to Mr. Simons, was not incredibly happy. It was also a name that Drake could not recall bringing up with Rut before.

'How did you know that is my client?'

As always, Rut's face remained expressionless.

'Does it matter?'

Drake wasn't sure.

'Maybe?'

Rut showed a little emotion. Maybe the only emotion he had. Irritation.

'I had the kid look into you when we met.'

'The kid?'

'Yes. Robbie.'

Drake recalled the enthusiastic skinny kid who sat with Rut's crew on the boat.

'Why?'

'I'm about to hang up, Drake. If you want my help, now is the time to say so.'

He didn't have anyone else to ask. His choice was already made for him.

'Yes, I do, Rut. I need to find Jimmy.'

'Okay. We'll be there in the morning.' Rut disconnected.

Now all he had to do was stay alive.

* * *

Long before the sun rose, Drake woke and sat staring at the door, willing it to stay shut. He had no idea what schedule the Chief kept, and what priority he placed on Drake's execution.

The door could swing open at any moment, guards piling in, grabbing him, and taking him away. Or, the Chief could enjoy his breakfast first, before he had a man killed. Maybe the chief preferred his blood spilling after lunch. Drake had no idea, but the longer it took, the better chance he had of Rut showing up on time.

Minutes passed, and eventually so did the hours. Although he was getting very hungry, Drake was happy to wait as long as he had to, if it meant staying alive. After another hour passed, voices started to grow louder outside the door. People were approaching. Drake stood up, ready to put up a fight.

'He's all yours.'

Drake balled his hands into fists as the door slid open.

Rut walked into the room.

'Thank you—'

'Save it. We need to get out of here. People tend to change their minds very quickly around here.'

With that instruction, Rut turned and left again. Drake scurried after him, clutching Seymour.

No one said a word until they sat in his hydrocar.

'Where is your truck?'

'On the road. Robbie is driving it.'

'Rut, I can't thank you enough for this.'

'Uh-huh.'

'I mean it. You were right. I'm way in over my head. I've just stumbled from one disaster to the next. I've lost my truck, the cargo, and most importantly, my partner. How do you work here? Everyone is just taking and stealing from each other the whole time. This place is insane.'

Turning the hydrocar around, Rut made his way out of the small town and took a dirt road that led into the scrub. Rut concentrated on his driving, not showing any interest in engaging in a conversation.

'So, where are we going? I mean, what's the plan?'

The small dirt road merged with another one, to form a wider dirt road. A highway of sorts.

'I'm taking you to Nandi, like I said.'

'The last message I received from Mr. Simons said that she was not very happy with me. Understandably, I guess. Have you ever dealt with her?'

'No.'

'How far away is she?'

'We'll be there soon.'

Drake gave up. Rut had driven through the night to come and rescue him. If he wasn't in the mood to talk, so be it. Drake wanted to ask him about payment, and how much he owed him for the rescue but decided to wait. Rut would bring it up when he was ready. Besides, he had no credits to offer.

He had another question too. One that was bugging him, but he decided to wait with that one too. He hoped it wasn't something he would regret not asking later. It felt important, but the vibe from Rut was clear: no questions now. Still, he was dying to know.

How did he get him out of the holding cell so easily?

* * *

A cloud of dust announced the arrival of a vehicle down the road. It took a few more seconds before the outline suggested it could be a truck.

'Must be him,' Drake said.

It was the first word said in the hydrocar since Rut pulled over to the side of the road and waited for Robbie to appear.

Nothing inside the hydrocar looked like it belonged to Rut, or any hauler for that matter, and shortly into the drive, Drake concluded it was a stolen vehicle. He must have told Robbie to steer clear, but stay close in case of trouble, and meet up with them a bit later. This way he wouldn't risk his truck being taken, but if needed, Robbie could crash into town, if they took Rut prisoner, too.

It didn't feel like Rut's first jail break.

Except it wasn't a jail break. It felt too civilized.

'Get out,' Rut grunted as he leapt out.

Drake followed and they waited for the truck to come to a halt.

'Hey, Drake!' Robbie greeted them as they climbed aboard.

'Thanks for the lift, man.'

'Anything for you, Drake!'

Rut grunted.

Once everyone found a seat, Robbie pulled back onto the road. Unlike Rut, he wanted to chat.

'So, how's things been going for you in Bulanalke?'

Having busted him out of a prison cell, Drake thought that would answer his question, but Robbie looked at him eagerly, waiting for more.

'Rough, to say the least.'

'Oh, I bet! I remember my first time here. Man, what a shock to the system it was.'

'I know you guys warned us, but I don't think anything can prepare you.'

'So, what happened? Tell me everything. I want to know the details of the newest Benjamin Drake adventure.'

Rut grunted, again, squeezed through the seats, and plopped down on one of the bunk beds. Moments later, he was snoring.

'And?'

The kid was so excited, and Drake had no idea how much time he had to kill, so he started at the beginning.

'Well, the moment we hit the ground, we knew trouble would be around the corner. It always is, with us.'

Robbie's eyes grew even bigger.

'And we were right. A group of bandits ambushed us, and we had to go into tactical mode, of course.'

'Of course,' Robbie whispered back.

'We were outnumbered, but, with our training, we knew we had the situation under control.'

'Training?'

'Oh yes, from the best Slavorian Special Security Unit operators. The bandits never stood a chance.'

'And did they?'

'I'm sitting here, aren't I?'

Robbie squealed.

'Oh man, I wish I could have seen that.' Lifting his hands, he aimed down the barrel of an imaginary pulse rifle. 'Zap. Zap. Zap-zap-zap.'

'Then,' Drake continued, 'a local leader, a General, invited us to a feast. We spent the night drinking and singing, whilst heavily guarded soldiers walked around us, making sure no one came near.'

Robbie was lapping it up.

'What happened next?'

Remembering the next part, Drake paused.

'Well, that would be the part where we were ambushed, again, but this time our enemy was prepared. These guys were not a street gang. They were organized. There was nothing we could do.'

Drake recalled the events, in vivid detail, but only shared the basics with Robbie. He sat, listening in silence. Once Drake finished, he said, 'Wow. I'm sorry, man. But I promise you. We will get him back.'

A lump in Drake's throat prevented him from replying, so he merely nodded.

'Even if it kills me, Drake, we'll get Jimmy back.'

| twenty-eight |

For the first time in days, a waiver appeared on the screen.

Do not enter without prior permission.

More of a warning than a waiver, really. Drake watched as Robbie dismissed it.

'Rut told me he has permission for us to be here. So, I think we should be fine.'

Robbie smiled unconvincingly at Drake.

'Should we maybe wake him and ask? I'm not overly keen on getting shot at, Robbie.'

'Sure, but—' Robbie glanced back, before whispering, 'he can be a bit cranky when he wakes.'

Drake wondered what an even moodier Rut would look like.

Cresting a hill, they saw a man-made silhouette on the horizon. Long straight lines, reaching into the sky. Not solid buildings, but frameworks. An industrial zone maybe?

'Almost there,' Robbie announced.

'Good.'

Both Drake and Robbie were surprised to hear Rut's voice behind them.

'Hey, boss. We're almost there,' Robbie repeated himself.

The waiver filled the screen again.

'We're good, right boss?'

Rut leaned forward and dismissed the waiver. 'Yes.'

As they approached the silhouettes, they changed from black outlines to detailed structures. Enormous towers, with gigantic wheels on them dominated the skyline.

'Is that Rakad? What are those structures?'

'Elevators. The mines here used to go kilometers into the ground.'

'Is that where the people live now?'

'No,' Robbie laughed. 'These mines aren't like that. The tunnels are barely high enough to stand in. They stretch for kilometers beneath the surface but are pretty useless for living. Some tribes just took over the mines for the prestige and to have an impressive base, I think. Most people live in Rakad, a few kilometers further north.'

Even closer to the mine now, Drake could see the buildings surrounding the two massive elevator towers. So much infrastructure was up for grabs when Shangcorp left, it didn't surprise Drake that it became a symbol of power for the local leaders and warlords.

'Do you have weapons on you?' Rut asked.

Drake had been asked this question multiple times in his life and never liked where it led.

'Of course, I do.'

'We need to lock them in the truck. If Nandi's men find anything on us, we're done.'

Every part of Drake's being shouted not to relinquish his weapons, but he could not screw up this opportunity to find Jimmy.

Reluctantly, Drake handed Rut his pulse pistol.

Rut explained, 'When we get there, let me do the talking. I've made a contact and I think I can get us in with Nandi.'

Drake nodded.

'Good.'

Two armored hydrocars came rushing towards them. Instead of forming a roadblock, they swerved to the left and right of the truck, before making a U-turn. One fell in behind them and the other sped up and passed them. It swerved and went in front. An incoming call appeared on the windscreen.

'Please provide authorization code or prepare to be boarded.'

These guys were not the normal run-of-the-mill Bulanalke bandits. They operated more like trained professionals. A lot like Nandella's elephant squad. Shangcorp might have left the territory, but a few opportunistic missionaries still lingered.

Rut accessed his HIC and swiped it at the windscreen.

'Thank you,' the person on the screen said once he validated Rut's code. 'Please stay in the convoy and follow our directions.'

In a Penta territory, they would have locked onto the truck and forced them to follow the convoy, but that technology was not present here. Robbie looked at Rut for confirmation and received a nod. Robbie nodded back and focused on driving.

'Seems we're in,' Drake said.

No reply.

Not having a weapon left Drake very vulnerable. Rut had taken control, and Robbie looked relaxed, but Drake had a feeling of great trepidation. Something was off.

The hydrocar in front stopped, a door swung open, and a guard instructed Robbie to park next to them. The other hydrocar swung around and stopped on the other side of the truck, boxing them in. The same guard ordered them to exit the truck. Everyone did.

'Follow us,' one of the guards instructed.

They used the same formation as they did with the vehicles. Two men walked in front of them and two men behind. Everyone carried a SA74. The way they walked and carried themselves reminded Drake so much of Dina and Ziggy. He would have given anything to have Dina here to help.

'This way.'

Everyone followed the guards as they entered a large building.

Inside, it was clear that this group was readying themselves for a fight. Hydrocars sat parked, shoulder to shoulder, most of them with a flatbed on the back. Half of them had massive pulse rifles mounted on them. Some of the hydros were bigger vans, and suitable for personnel carrying. Next to the vehicles were work benches and above them space to hang up rifles. It was only a quarter full.

They made their way past the vehicles and into another room.

This room was much smaller and crammed full of armed guards. As they entered, the sea of people closed in behind them, encircling them. Everyone, except the three of them, was armed. Unsettlingly, half the faces had a familiar tense grin on them. It was a show of force since shooting them in these confined spaces would lead to catastrophic collateral damage. Shooting across the room at targets standing in the middle would take out most of the people in here. Still, they had weapons and Drake had none. Advantage the other team.

A lean, muscular woman made her way to the front. She could have been Lerako's mother. Same intense, but mesmerizing face. Same athletic build. The only difference was their ages.

'I take it this is the man who is trying to cost me a war.'

There was nothing maternal or reassuring about her voice. It bellowed in the small room and made everyone shrink.

All eyes were on Drake.

'Um, your—' Drake had no idea how to address her. The titles and ranks here had no logic to them. Drake couldn't recall if she had a military rank or a title. Did Rut say she was a chief?

'My what?'

'I'm sorry, ma'am,' Drake tried to gauge his success, but only silence greeted him. He pushed on. 'A group of mercenaries ambushed us on our way to you, but I have been trying my best to catch up to the stolen truck and retrieve it. I believe with the help from my colleagues here, I can locate and return the cargo.'

A look of confusion set on Nandi's face. She turned her gaze to Rut.

'What is he talking about? Doesn't he know where my cargo is?'

'Your notice said you'll pay an award for the capture of Benjamin Drake. There was nothing about supplying any information. I've delivered Drake. My part is done.'

Drake couldn't believe his ears. Rut didn't offer to help out of the kindness of his heart. He was chasing a bounty. That's why he came to his assistance, and how he was able to break him out so easily. He must have bribed his way in. This had nothing to do with helping him. Rut broke every code in the unwritten hauler book.

He sold out a fellow hauler.

Adrenaline and anger flooded every part of Drake's being, and he flung himself towards Rut. For a second no one moved, and Drake swung his fist, harder than he had ever done before, connecting with Rut's face. Pain shot through his hand, but also the satisfying feeling of bone caving in on Rut's cheek. An arm grabbed at Drake, but he had already cocked his other fist and let it fly. It connected on the other side of Rut's face, slightly higher, straight on the eye, but with slightly less impact. Still, a solid hit. More arms grabbed at Drake, and he became immobile.

'Give this man his reward and get him out of here,' Nandi's voice instructed someone.

Drake was still standing, but multiple arms held him still.

'I'll find you, Rut, I swear! I'll hunt—'

'Where are my guns?' Nandi cut him off. She walked over to Drake, stopping right in front of him, their faces almost touching.

'I told you, I can fi—'

Nandi's fist crushed his diaphragm, forcing the air out of Drake's lungs. He doubled over, immobilized and gasping.

'Take your time. Get your breath back, Drake, then we'll try again.'

It took him a while, but eventually, Drake could breathe again. He did not look forward to the next few minutes.

'Okay. Welcome back. Now, where are my guns?'

Looking around, Drake couldn't find Rut or Robbie. What he saw was a bunch of excited faces, ready for his blood.

Drake didn't fancy having another rib broken. Or a nose, or an arm. He didn't want to stand here, taking punch after punch, trying to prolong the inevitable. He doubted he'd ever see the outside of this room. Hopefully, Jimmy would be able to get away from Lerako and make his way back home.

'You have plenty of guns right there. What do you bench? Must be clo—'

A high pitch sound penetrated his head and his ear felt like it was on fire. His vision doubled, then blurred and everything dimmed.

But no salvation yet.

Just before everything went dark, the light came back on, and soon his vision came back too. He was still here.

'We lack the technological marvels you are used to Drake, but I assure you, we have our methods of making people talk.'

He had no answer that would satisfy her. She was angry, and she had to save face in front of her subordinates. Nothing he said would save him now. Even if he knew where they were, he doubted it would save him. Telling her it was Lerako, would only put Jimmy in danger.

Unfortunately, this was it. In this dusty village, in the middle of Bulanalke.

Drake dropped to his knees and sat on the ground.

'You're not letting me go, even if I tell you everything I know. So, let's just get this over with.'

Drake felt calm and at peace. It had to happen sooner or later. Most hauler's lives ended violently. He always knew he would not be different. His only regret was not saying goodbye to Lily and Jimmy. He knew she would get over it and move on with her life, but he felt a cloud of sadness come over him imagining how Jimmy would take the news. That was his only regret. Leaving Jimmy by himself. Alone again.

A tear rolled down his cheek and fell into the dirt between his knees.

'I'm ready.'

He kept his gaze on the ground. No point in seeing what was about to happen. The energy in the room changed, as he heard people mumble and move about. Whatever was about to happen, it would be soon. He took a long breath and focused on the dark spot the tear left in the dirt.

Footsteps approached.

He kept his focus on the spot.

The person stopped.

He looked at the spot for the last time and closed his eyes.

'Lerako has your weapons! Chief Tjaka's daughter stole it, and she is taking it to him. You are wasting your time with this man. He has no idea who anyone is in Bulanalke. You should be chasing Lerako before she gets it to her father. Because once she does, he'll have the upper hand and he'll take you out.'

Drake opened his eyes.

Right next to Nandi, held by two guards, stood Robbie, pleading.

'Please. I beg you. Let my friend go. He had nothing to do with this, and I told you who has your weapons. Please.'

'Prove it,' Nandi responded.

'I need to retrieve a DDU in my bag,' Robbie said. Nandi nodded, and the guards let go of him.

'See, we have been tracking the truck since it arrived in Bulanalke,' Robbie said as he pulled the portable Data Display Unit from a bag. He walked a bit closer to Nandi so she could see the screen.

'Rut, you met him, my boss, had me place a tracker on their truck. He assumed they would get ambushed and killed and then we could swoop in and take the loot.'

Robbie looked at Drake and mouthed *sorry*.

Nandi grabbed the small DDU and inspected it. She called someone over and they verified the data's authenticity.

'Lerako is the one you're after. And now you can track her. She is still on her way to her father and if you act quickly, you can still get to her first. All I ask is that you release this man—'

'Be quiet!' Nandi snapped.

It had to be Nandi's decision. Drake had learned from his travels around the world, how important it was for leaders to have their followers believe they had all the answers. They had to be perceived as flawless gods, knowing every outcome, and making no mistakes. Because if they didn't, the people would shred them to pieces and find a new leader to follow.

'Taking everything I have learned today into consideration, I've made a decision.'

Everyone in the room moved forward to show they were paying attention.

'Captains, get your squads ready. We are leaving in ten minutes. Full combat protocol. We are taking our weapons back and sending a message to Tjaka. We will not be treated like children!'

A war cry roared through the room.

Nandi turned her back on Drake and Robbie and made for the exit.

'Get rid of them.'

| twenty-nine |

Two men grabbed Drake by the arms, and two grabbed Robbie. Using a different exit, they dragged them off into another room, threw them inside, and closed the door.

Drake waited a minute to make sure they were left alone.

'What the fuck, Robbie?'

'Hey, I know this is strange, but let me tell you what happened, okay?'

Drake exhaled loudly and shot him a look. *Go on!*

'Okay, so um, where to start,' Robbie bobbled his head as if to shake the words into the right order. 'The beginning, right?'

'No, you can fill in the details later. What I want to know right now, is why you did that and where is Rut? And hurry up. We need to be ready for when they return.'

Robbie nodded his head repeatedly.

'Yes, yes. Okay, so Rut is a bit of a dick. You might have noticed. I hate him, but it's better to not work alone in Bulanalke. So, I've stuck with him, even though I hate how he treats people and always stabs everyone in the back. It was true about the trackers, and I knew about them. Sorry. He never told me about the bounty on you, instead, he made it sound like we were going to help you. I should have known right away that something was wrong. Anyway, once we left you with Nandi and were back to the truck, I told him I was out. I've had enough. He didn't say anything. Just punched me and drove off.'

Only now did Drake notice the swelling under Robbie's eye. 'Why now?'

'You're my hero, man. A hauler who helped Santo take the Moon! I know! I know! You didn't do it on purpose but I've never met a hauler who has done anything spectacular. Most of them are just truck-driving thieves and scumbags. But you! You've shown me I can do anything and maybe even get out of here and go on my own adventures.'

Now was not the time to burst the kid's bubble and let him in on the secret. He was an idiot making mistakes all the time and then trying to fix them. He was nothing to look up to.

Yet, Robbie did.

'Okay. We will talk about my adventures later. But for now, we need to get out of here. What do you know of this place?'

'Um, not much. I've never been here. But it looks like most outposts. All their credits go towards weapons and nothing towards the buildings. Watch.'

Robbie crawled over to the wall behind Drake and moved a small cabinet out of the way. Then, grabbing the bottom of the wall, he peeled it back. Not much, and it took a lot of effort, but Drake watched him fold a corner of the wall up.

'What the hell? Is the whole wall just thin metal?'

'Yea! Most of the smaller towns only use tin sheets to build their houses with. Even the mines used it, as they knew they wouldn't be here forever. If you help me, I reckon we can peel it back enough to crawl through. It's rusty, see?'

Drake couldn't believe it. He had assumed that the tin sheets were merely cladding on top of concrete or some other material.

Grabbing on to the sheet of metal, he helped Robbie, and together they pulled it back high enough to scrape through.

'Now what?' Drake asked.

The hole in the wall led them straight outside and they had to quickly run for cover behind another building.

'We need a vehicle to follow Rut.'

Looking around, Drake saw two hydrocars, both in desperate need of a paint job and some serious body work, but judging by the tracks behind them, still operational.

He also saw something else lying in the spot where they parked Rut's truck. An orange lump of metal.

Seymour.

Using his HIC to boot it up, Drake placed it on hold and the little ASR sat up, ready for a command.

'Drake?'

'Yes, sorry,' Drake said, putting Seymour aside for now. 'I might have the codes to get one of those hydro's going.'

That would be the easy part. About a hundred armed soldiers walked the ground, going about their daily routines. On either side of the gate were two tall lookout towers, each with a guard operating a large, mounted pulse rifle. Getting out of here would not be easy.

Noise and dust filled the air. To his left, Drake saw a convoy of armored and civilian hydrocars heading towards the gate.

'It's Nandi! They must be heading off towards Tjaka.'

Robbie was right. In the third hydro from the front, Drake could see Nandi sitting in the passenger seat, ready to lead her force into battle.

They had to act quickly.

'Jump in. Now!' Drake yelled at Robbie. 'No, other side. You drive.'

Within seconds the convoy would pass them, and so too their chances of getting out. Drake ran in a wide arc, scooped up Seymour, and ran as quickly as he could, considering the extra weight he carried, back to one of the hydros. Everyone was focused on the convoy approaching and not paying any attention to them. Drake accessed the codes from Jimmy on his HIC and even quicker than he thought he was able to, he had the hydro running. Jimmy would be so proud of him.

'Go, go, go. Stay close to the last vehicle and blend in.'

Robbie smiled as he realized the plan. Join and follow the convoy, as if they were one of the locals.

Drake had to make one of the hardest choices of his life – allow someone else to do the driving. It pained him to let Robbie handle the driving, but he had local knowledge of the roads. Plus, it would give Drake some time to come up with the next part of their plan.

'So, do I just follow them?'

Judging by Nandi's outburst, Drake had a hunch she was shooting straight for chief Tjaka's compound. He had to assume she would take the most direct route unless she was trying to be stealthy and try to sneak up on him. He just didn't know.

'Robbie, is this the most direct route to Lerako's dad's place? Chief Tjaka?'

'I dunno. I told you. I've never been here.'

Drake looked at the old DDU mounted in the middle of the dash, hoping to learn something by accessing its navigation app. It didn't take long before he gave up. Not only was the screen cracked in multiple places, but the DDU was also outdated and barely showed any information on the navigation. It was useless.

It was Drake's turn to bobble his head around, hoping for an idea to fall out.

Robbie's driving was impeccable, keeping a close distance to the convoy, and always having full control of the hydro. The hydro never slid around the corners, and he never had to over correct any fish tailing. The kid really impressed Drake.

A vibration went through Drake's arm. A notification.

Hey Drake, thought you'd be back by now. Hope everything is going smoothly. Looking forward to my first payment. Numbers.

Slamming his fist on the dashboard, Drake let out a yell that startled Robbie.

'Whoa! You okay?'

'Yes. No, actually, you know what, Robbie? I'm not. I'm sick of this place. I'm over chasing credits thinking this time will be enough to get back on my feet, only for everything to go to shit again. I miss my friends.'

Robbie smiled uncomfortably.

'Sorry,' Drake offered. 'I don't know. I'm just tired, I guess. I just want this to be over.'

The hydro shook and bounced as it traversed the corrugated dirt roads. Robbie had soft hands, and never made any hard inputs into the yoke. If Drake had been driving, they would have been off the road, ages ago.

'Have you thought of a plan yet?' Robbie asked after a few minutes of silence.

Ahead of them, the convoy was still traveling at full speed, and there was no indication that Drake and Robbie had been spotted. Although everything was safe for now, he knew it wouldn't last forever. Nandi would not have set off, charging towards her enemy, if it was days away. If that were the case, there would have been a bit more preparation. Jumping in and leaving within minutes told Drake it had to be relatively close. How close, he couldn't tell.

'No, Robbie. No plan. But man, I wish we could get there before Nandi. She strikes me as a shoot first, ask questions later type.'

'If we can find an alternative route, then maybe we can beat them.'

Drake accessed his HIC, but it had no signal. He tried the hydro's DDU again but gave up almost immediately.

'This thing's nav is useless.'

Dust enveloped them, as the convoy kept marching forward. With the lack of data from the hydrocar's DDU and no visibility, Drake could not decide. If they stopped, someone in the convoy might notice and also stop to offer assistance. Once they figured out there was no problem, they would have the upper hand in weapons and overpower Drake and Robbie. If they kept going, they might drive straight into an ambush or at least a gun fight, for which they would also not be prepared.

Two bad options.

The only two options.

Time to pick.

'What weapons do you have?' Drake asked.

'Um, my pulse pistol, why?'

He hoped for a surprise arsenal hidden somewhere but figured he would only have something small on him.

'Do you trust me?' Drake asked.

Robbie looked confused but nodded.

'Okay, give me your pistol' Drake held out his hand. 'This is the plan.'

| **thirty** |

Seymour had seen better days. Not that he was in tip-top shape when Jimmy found him, but looking at the ASR, Drake could see multiple new dents and scuff marks. More than once the little ASR had proved helpful and more than once Drake had not hesitated to put it in the line of fire.

This was another such occasion.

'Hold it steady, Robbie. This is a one-shot type of deal, OK?'

Hanging outside the hydro's window, Drake flinched every time a branch came swooping past. A few smaller ones had already smacked him, and he feared a bigger one that wouldn't snap.

Up ahead, the convoy kept moving at full speed, and the hydro right in front of them had not noticed a man hanging on for dear life behind them.

'You need to get closer. A bit more!'

Visibility was poor. Not only from the dust but Drake's eyes were filled with tears from the rushing wind. Reaching into the cabin with one hand, he grabbed hold of Seymour.

'Just a bit more, Robbie.'

Taking a long slow bend, Drake dropped Seymour to get a better grip and to prevent them skidding off the road into the scrub.

'Sorry!' Robbie yelled from the inside, once they were on a slightly straighter path.

'All good. Try and catch up again.'

Robbie's driving was impeccable. Within seconds they were right behind the hydro, keeping a constant distance between them.

'Okay. Here goes!'

Once more Drake grabbed Seymour and pulled him out of the window.

'Keep it steady,' he instructed Robbie.

Swinging Seymour backward, Drake braced himself, and once the ASR reached the peak of the arc, swung him forward. As he let go, he watched it sail through the air before landing on the flatbed of the hydro in front. Slipping back into the cabin, Drake accessed his HIC and pulled up Seymour's app. He had to act fast, as a sharp corner would send Seymour flying off the back.

'Okay, Robbie, fall back.'

Immediately the vehicle lost speed and the distance increased between the two vehicles. Making sure they were out of the blast radius, Drake pressed the blue button on his HIC. The one marked EMP.

At first it was like nothing had happened until the hydro in front started to lose speed.

'Keep your distance, Robbie. Slow down with them.'

Robbie kept the distance between the two vehicles constant until both hydros came to a stop. Climbing out of their hydro, Robbie approached the stranded one.

'Hey guys, what happened?' Drake could barely hear him, having tumbled out a few meters before they stopped. He was now circling the stranded vehicle from the opposite side of Robbie. Their weapons in the hydro should have been disabled with the EMP blast, but they couldn't rule out some older tech weapons being carried too. Hence the reason for Drake flanking them.

'You guys need help?'

Inside the hydro, Drake could see two figures, shouting and gesturing to each other. Most likely a lot of blame going around and not a lot of situational awareness being applied.

Perfect.

One of the men climbed out. He had his pulse rifle raised at Robbie, but Drake could see there were no power lights on.

'Who are you?' the man yelled.

'Hey, it's all good, man. I saw you stop and thought you might need a hand.'

The man looked back at the hydro.

'Did you do that?'

'Do what?' Robbie asked.

The hydro rocked slightly, as the other passenger emerged.

'Shoot him,' he yelled and stomped towards Robbie.

'Hey! Hey! I'm here to help,' Robbie said, slowly backing up.

Drake had a clear view of both men. The one walking towards Robbie didn't have any weapons on him, and his friend's weapon was disabled. It was time for Drake to make his appearance.

'Stop, that's close enough,' he yelled as he walked out of the scrub. 'Put your busted ass gun down.'

'Don't do it,' the unarmed man growled as his companion was about to obey Drake's order. Fueled by adrenaline and the urge for revenge, he stood his ground. 'Keep that thing pointed at him.'

'Okay, let me break this down for you. You are going to grab all your weapons, including whatever you have in the hydro, and give them to me. Then, I'm going to shoot you. Now, it's up to you if I'm going to bother to switch this thing over to stun or not. It does have stun, doesn't it Robbie?'

'Um, I think so?'

'Mm. Well, I guess we'll find out.'

'You don't scare me—' the unarmed man muttered before Drake shot him. Point blank, in the chest. Luckily for him, the pulse pistol had a stun function.

'I'll get the other rifles,' the driver offered, showing a higher sense of self-preservation.

He threw his pulse rifle down at Robbie's feet and ran over to the hydro. Drake followed, making sure he wasn't trying to escape or surprise them. He wasn't. Reaching the hydro, he leaned in and grabbed a pulse rifle.

'Robbie, make sure our friend is not holding out on us.'

Robbie obliged and searched the hydro. Climbing out, he shook his head.

'Good,' Drake said, and another pulse round rang through the air.

* * *

After tying the men up, and disabling their hydro, Drake and Robbie gathered the rifles, as well as Seymour, and returned to their hydro. Drake told Robbie to keep driving, as he had work to do.

First thing was to reboot Seymour and plug him into the hydro to recharge. Not only did the EMP knock him out too, but it demanded a huge amount of energy and drained all his power.

Next, Drake had to reset the pulse rifles, and make them operational again. The EMP only disarmed them, and they would still be good to use, after a lengthy reset. Which was the aim of the throw-Seymour-at-them plan; to get some more firepower.

'Catch up to the convoy but keep back as far as you can.'

Robbie nodded and sped up. The road was twisty and narrow, which made it impossible to see the convoy in the distance. However, it didn't take them too long before they encountered dust lingering in the air.

'Okay, don't go too fast now. We don't want to run into them.'

Seymour was taking longer than expected to recharge, but at least Drake had one of the SA74's operational. He placed it on the back seat next to Seymour and started on the second one.

'I'm almost done. Looks like the rifles will be good to go, but Seymour is still out.'

'So, what do we do when we get there?'

Before Drake could answer, the cabin became quieter and stopped shaking. The dust disappeared as the dirt road made way for a very rare sight in Bulanalke. A sealed road. Being

Bulanalke, it was littered with potholes, but Robbie was able to avoid most of them, which meant a relatively smooth ride.

Unfortunately, it also meant there was no dust cloud to chase.

'Should I just keep going?'

'Yes. Unless we missed a turn-off in the dust, we'd have to assume they came this way too.'

'I don't think there was a turn-off, but then again, I was concentrating on the road ahead.'

If they went in the wrong direction, even only for a few minutes, they could be too late getting to Jimmy. Drake's gut told him to stay on the road. And he always trusted his gut.

'Keep going, Robbie. Let's catch up to those bastards.'

* * *

The cramp in Drake's stomach subsided when finally they spotted the convoy in the distance. He had completely misjudged the speed they were traveling at, and it took them forever to catch up. The longer it took, the more he started to doubt his decision, and the worse his stomach cramped. But the moment the convoy was in sight, his anxiety dissolved. They were back in the game.

Seconds after spotting the convoy, a waiver appeared on screen. They were now in Tjaka's territory. As with Nandi's waiver, it was more a warning than a set of rules to obey. There wasn't even an accept option, just a dismissal button. *You've been warned.* Something else popped up on the screen, a leftover from the Shangcorp era: street names, and directional arrows. Most of them pointed down run-down streets with nothing on them, mentioning buildings that didn't exist anymore.

However, as they drove they saw some of the buildings were still intact. Soon, the buildings were good enough to have people hanging around them. It looked and felt like the high numbers on the outskirts of New Franco. Unlike New Franco where the buildings and roads improved as you moved past them and into the smaller numbered neighborhoods, here they stayed the same the same dilapidated, barely habitable houses. The same rusted-out hydrocars. The same people going about their daily lives.

'I've lost them,' Robbie said and hit the steering yoke.

'It's okay, keep looking.'

'I can see some taller buildings in that direction,' Robbie pointed them out. 'Should I aim for them, maybe?'

'I guess if you were the leader of the area, that's where you would be, right?'

Robbie nodded eagerly. 'That's what I'm thinking.'

'Okay then, big buildings it is.'

Robbie turned off the road they had been on since arriving in town and took a smaller one. Traffic was light to non-existent, and Drake estimated that they would be at the tall buildings in under five minutes.

That's when he noticed the people on the sidewalks. As they drove, they saw more and more people who stood watching them go by. Not only did the numbers increase, but so did their energy. When they entered town, no one gave them more than a glance, but the further they went, and especially right now, people were staring at them. Not just staring, but glowering. They looked angry.

'Something's up,' Drake said.

'Yeah, I don't think they want us here.'

'I don't think it's only that. Listen.'

Robbie squinted his eyes, as he concentrated.

'Open your window. But only a little.'

Robbie lowered his window a fraction and tilted his head towards it. Drake could hear it loud and clear now. Not close by, but very distinct.

'Is that? It sounds like—' Robbie sounded unsure of himself.

'Pulse rifles,' Drake helped him out. 'Someone is having a big fight.'

On cue, a massive fireball lit up the sky on their left side. The fight was not in front of them at the tall buildings but to their left and only a kilometer or so away.

'Which way?' Robbie asked.

He slowed down the hydro, in anticipation of making a course correction.

On the sidewalks, people started to close in on them. One person picked up a rock and threw it at the hydro. It missed the window but made a loud clattering sound. Another one followed shortly.

'Crap, they're turning on us. Get us out of here!'

'OK, but which way?' Robbie yelled.

Drake closed his eyes and took a deep breath.

C'mon gut, tell me what to do.

'Go towards the explosion,' Drake said, and Robbie obeyed without any hesitation.

| thirty-one |

Finally, the ringing stopped, but everything was still out of focus. It was hard to judge his position, but it felt to Drake that he was on his side, held into place by something. Maybe a harness. Close to his face, a bright orange object filled most of his view. He quickly dismissed it as being a fire, as he felt no heat. The only other bright orange thing he knew of was Seymour. With his eyes still unable to focus, he gave up on identifying it.

As Drake's senses started to go back online, questions also popped up. Where was he? Why was he lying on his side? Was he trapped? Where was Jimmy?

He had no answers, and all his head was good for at the moment was to pulsate with pain.

A movement above him caught his attention. It was another person.

'Jimmy? Jimmy! You, okay?'

Drake wrestled with the safety harness and tried to get a better view.

A loud moan made him stop.

'Jimmy! Talk to me! Are you okay?'

Something felt wrong.

'Uh, yeah, I think so. But, um—'

Something was wrong.

It was not Jimmy's voice.

'Who are you? What's going on?'

Finally, Drake found the release button and freed himself from the safety harness. He bumped his head against the orange thing, as he fell a few inches. It didn't hurt too much, or at least not more than it already did, and he turned himself around to face the other person. A few things became clear. He was stuck inside a vehicle, which lay on its side and the other person was definitely not Jimmy.

'Who are you?' Drake asked again.

The person turned as much as they could and faced Drake.

'It's me, Drake. Robbie. I think you must have bumped your head pretty hard. There's a lot of blood.'

Robbie. The name sounded vaguely familiar, but Drake didn't feel any connection.

'You look confused, man. But I think we might still be in trouble. Help me down, and then I'll explain.'

Drake had no idea what this Robbie person was talking about, but being stuck in an overturned hydro did imply that something must have gone wrong. Considering Robbie was in the driving seat, and no one was in handcuffs, Drake had to assume he was a willing passenger before they ended up on their side.

'Okay, yeah, you're right. Let's see,' Drake maneuvered himself in the confined space to try and get a better position to help Robbie out of his harness and safely down to the ground. His vision had mostly returned, and he found the release button with ease.

'You are going to have to try and hold on to something, because the moment I pop this button, you're going to fall. You ready?'

Robbie nodded, and Drake pressed the release button. Awkwardly, Robbie fell on top of Drake. The two of them shuffled around, trying to create some space between them.

'Let's get out of this thing.'

The front window of the hydro was missing, and they took turns climbing through the gap. Once outside Drake studied the wreck.

Most of the rear was missing, with huge black streaks extending onto the parts that remained, streaks that were evidence that something burned. Add that to half the hydro missing, it was clear what had happened: a pulse mine. Drake did not doubt they had driven over a pulse mine, which would have been activated as the front wheels went over it. It should have exploded soon after, taking out the middle part of the hydro, but Robbie must have been going at high speed when they hit it and the explosion was delayed enough for them to survive.

Next to the wreckage, Robbie stood nervously surveying the area. Robbie, who came to his rescue for some reason and drove him to this town. Things were falling into place, slowly, and Drake knew in time he would remember everything. It wasn't his first big crash or concussion.

Robbie was right to look so nervous. If they triggered a pulse mine, it meant that they were in a hostile area and that whoever planted it would most likely come looking at what triggered it. They had to get out of there.

In the distance, pulse rifles were going off. Drake couldn't recall if they had been going off this whole time, but now that he was aware of them, he realized it was nonstop. Somewhere, not too far away, a huge skirmish was happening.

Voices startled Drake, as a group of people closed in on them. He couldn't see them, but they were close enough to hear.

'Robbie,' he yelled under his breath. 'Do we have weapons?'

Robbie disappeared back into the wrecked hydro and reappeared with two SA74s. He gave one to Drake and kept one for himself. Drake tilted his pulse rifle to check on its power status.

'What the hell, man? These things are dead!'

'Yes, remember? We used Seymour to deactivate the hydro we were chasing and then we stole their guns. They should be working soon.'

Drake closed his eyes and tried to recall the events as described by Robbie, but nothing came to him.

'Did we use an EMP?'

'Yes!' Robbie excitedly.

'Don't get your hopes up. I was guessing. Can you grab Seymour?'

Robbie was still standing right next to the wreck. He reached into the cabin, via the missing windshield, and pulled the orange ASR out. He placed it on the ground in front of Drake.

'Thank you, Robbie.' The kid still looked like a stranger to him.

Accessing Seymour's protocols on his HIC, Drake ran some basic tests. The ASR had enough charge to power up, and he switched it on. Lights blinked behind the dark screen housing its sensors, or what Jimmy called its face, and it slowly extended its legs to stand up.

'Drake, we need to get going.'

Drake entered a command string into Seymour that would always keep it within ten meters and alert him of any active pulse weapons.

'Okay, which way do we go?' Drake asked.

Before they could decide, the decision was made for them.

Voices, quickly followed by their owners, came running around the corner of a half-demolished building. They moved as one, aiming directly for the burned-out hydro.

'There they are! Get them!' A voice yelled from the crowd.

Shaking his pulse rifle, Drake flipped it over, hoping it was ready. An unlit power meter crushed that hope.

'That building!' Drake shouted and pointed to a building that looked slightly better than the rest.

Running at full speed, Robbie followed closely, and Seymour kept his set distance. Reaching the empty building, everyone scrambled for cover.

'They must have seen us run in here,' Robbie said, panting.

Accessing his HIC, Drake made sure Seymour was still scanning. Seymour's systems were up and running which meant the chasing mob had no pulse weapons.

Turning his rifle over, he groaned. They too had no pulse weapons, yet.

'How's your rifle? Is it online yet?' Drake asked, in case Seymour was wrong.

The voices grew louder.

'Um,' Robbie flipped his rifle over and inspected it. 'No.'

There was nothing to be done. After a hard reset, every pulse weapon had a different time frame to be operational again.

Peeking over the windowsill, Drake had a good view of the surrounding area. Unlike the buildings in the areas on the outskirts of town, these were higher and closer to each other, but the biggest difference was their condition. The buildings on the fringes, although run down, appeared to be occupied. These buildings had been abandoned and shot up. Hardly any windows were intact, and most of the doors stood open. Some still had furniture, but most were empty, most likely looted. It looked like what Drake imagined a war zone.

'What do you think happened here?'

'If I had to guess,' Robbie said, 'I would say a rebellion. Maybe a group that challenged the leader. It looks like a big fight went down, but only in this sector.'

The voices were still growing louder but at a slower pace.

Drake pointed skywards, and Robbie nodded. Slowly they moved towards a set of partially collapsed stairs and started to make their way up. They took their time, looking and listening, making sure they weren't spotted. When the stairs ended, they made their way to a window again and took cover.

The voices were right underneath them.

A blue light appeared on Robbie's SA74.

'Your gun,' Drake whispered as loud as he dared.

Robbie flipped the pulse rifle over and smiled.

'Don't do anything. Unless they saw us move up, I think we'll be safe,' Drake whispered again.

Frustratingly, his gun was still down.

'I'm going to check upstairs,' a voice said from below.

Drake shot Robbie a look and held up a finger across his lips. Robbie nodded, and Drake moved his hand away and gave him a new signal. Mimicking holding a gun, he pointed at the door. Robbie caught on, and lifted his SA74, aiming it at the door.

'You're wasting your time.'

'I'll be quick.'

'Idiot.'

The scout replied but Drake's ARP couldn't translate it.

They were five stories up, and Drake held his breath trying to imagine how far up the scout had come. He was moving quietly, making it hard to gauge. Drake tried to visualize the man climbing the stairs, as they did, and counting the steps. If he was correct, he would be on the third floor by now.

A loud crash made both Drake and Robbie jump. It sounded from further down below.

'What are you doing?' an agitated voice yelled.

'Sorry, I slipped and kicked something down.'

'Come down, right now! We need to move!'

Drake could hear a grunt, followed by receding footsteps.

'Idiot,' the agitated voice said again.

* * *

Once they were certain the mob had moved on, Drake, Robbie, and Seymour moved out. As they reached the bottom of the steps, Robbie pointed to Drake's rifle.

'It's on.'

To Drake's relief, the pale blue light confirmed that he was now armed.

'This gives us some leverage, but we still need to be careful and invisible, okay?'

Burned-out hydros littered the roads, and some were stacked to form barricades, blocking certain roads. As they moved past the wrecks and into the available streets, Drake had a feeling of being led down a certain path. Their choices of where to go were limited to where there were no burned-out vehicles. It didn't feel random but as if it was carefully planned - only one route to take. But where did it lead?

An alarm made Drake's arm vibrate. Looking at his HIC, he saw it came from Seymour.

'Robbie, we have company. And they have pulse weapons.'

Crouching and moving as slowly as possible, they moved forward cautiously, the burned-out wrecks blocking any other options.

Another vibration went through Drake's arm: whoever had weapons was close.

Before he had time to warn Robbie, or come up with a plan, a pulse round whizzed by his head and exploded into a concrete wall behind him.

'Get down!'

A few more rounds peppered the wall.

'You okay?' Drake yelled once the barrage of pulse rounds stopped.

Robbie took too long to respond.

'Robbie!'

Scrambling over to him, Drake saw why he didn't receive a reply. A piece of wall, the size of his foot, lay in Robbie's lap, smeared with blood. Looking up, Drake could see where the pulse rounds must have dislodged the piece of concrete, setting it free to fall on Robbie's head. His breathing was steady but shallow. He was out for the count.

Grabbing Robbie under the armpits, Drake dragged him backward into the nearest building. There was no time to look around and pick the best tactical location. As he grabbed Robbie, a fresh round of pulse rounds started to whizz past them. Moving as quickly as he could, he hustled into the building and leaned against a wall. The building was solid, and none of the pulse rounds penetrated the wall.

'Robbie! Wake up!' Drake yelled as he slapped him in the face a few times. The kid kept sleeping.

Pushing him aside, Drake stole a look around the open door. Things could have been way worse. Just as they were forced into a specific path to follow, so were their assailants. They too had only one way to follow to get to Drake and Robbie. And to do so, they would have to leave the safety of cover and expose themselves.

'Okay, buddy, wish me luck,' Drake said as he propped Robbie up against a wall and readied himself for a fight that he was in no position to win.

thirty-two

Robbie sat snoring, head slumped on his chest, arms hanging limply by his sides. Next to him sat Seymour, equally useless. The ASR had enough charge to move and scan, but not to trigger the EMP. Eight adversaries and only one person to hold them off. Like most haulers, Drake was a gambling man, and right now he would place a bet on the other guys.

Walking in single file, Drake judged the first person to be about a hundred meters away. The rest of the gang was spread out in roughly five-meter increments. If he shot now, thanks to the skills he picked up from Dina in Lan-noi, he would definitely drop the first person. He would back himself to take down two, maybe three, but by that time the rest would have had time to find better cover and even out the playing field. They would know where he was shooting from, and he would lose his advantage.

Unless he wasn't where they thought he was.

Flicking through his HIC he found what he needed and executed the file. Next, he grabbed Robbie's pulse weapon and ordered Seymour closer. Once the ASR was in position, he placed the pulse rifle on top of it, making sure only the tip of the barrel poked out from behind the wall.

Sixty meters and closing.

Lifting his pulse rifle, Drake lined up the first person in his sights. Keeping both eyes open, as Dina taught him, allowed him to be aware of his surroundings and more importantly, the rest of the group. Speed and accuracy were going to be key. Dina's voice whispered in Drake's ear. *Exhale, and squeeze.*

The man walking in front of the line dropped straight down, a second before the person behind him followed suit. The third person, a woman, had time to turn her head around before falling to the ground. Three for three in as many seconds. Yelling and random pulse bursts filled the air. Drake took cover, not out of fear that anyone would hit him, as their shots were way off the mark, but he needed to stay out of sight. He tapped the icon he had waiting on his HIC, and Seymour emitted a sound that mimicked a pulse round being fired. It sounded convincing enough to Drake, and he scrambled past Robbie, making his way alongside and parallel to the line of gunmen chasing them. It wasn't easy, as he had to traverse over and through broken buildings, climbing over and crawling under debris.

The people on the road were yelling instructions to each other, trying to pinpoint the shooter and slowly making their way forward. Drake was still too deep in the rubble to see them. He kept moving, hoping they did not pick up that no pulse rounds were hitting the walls around them and that the sounds from Seymour would be enough. Through a small opening, Drake could see out onto the road. Two more fighters, huddled together, presented a single target. If he shot them and someone figured out where the shot came from, he would be trapped with nowhere to hide. But if he waited, they might move, and they would go in the opposite direction. Drake would not have the opportunity again to reach Robbie; he didn't have a choice. Drake exhaled and squeezed. As he did, the other fighter popped up to fire a volley of pulse rounds toward Seymour's fake barrage. Drake could only see his legs which turned in his direction as his partner fell onto him.

Pulse rounds hit the rubble around Drake's hideout, sending pieces of concrete flying everywhere and cutting the back of his hands and face. It stung badly, but far less than a pulse round would. Drake tried to make himself as small as possible and hid his head as well as he could. The moment the pulse rounds ceased, he poked his head out.

A face filled the gap in front of him.

'Over—' the face started to say before Drake made a hole in it big enough to see through.

It was time to move.

By his count, there should only be three fighters left. Time to place a bet on himself.

Wiggling himself out from the spot he occupied, he slowly made his way further away from Seymour and Robbie. He could still hear the ASR randomly *shooting*, but he realized that Seymour was the only one making noise. They must have figured out that something was wrong. Hushed voices passed Drake, only a few meters away, but protected by tons of debris. There was no way to get to them quickly, so Drake pressed on, moving even further away. He needed to get out from under the rubble.

Electric crackles filled the air, as first a single and then multiple pulse weapons went off. Drake froze but realized nothing was exploding around him. No one was shooting at him. They were shooting at something else. And the only other things out here to shoot were Seymour and Robbie.

Panicking, Drake picked up his pace, grabbed debris, and threw it out of his way, scraping his knuckles and tearing his hands apart. It hurt, but it worked. Light came spilling in from above, and quickly Drake broke through the rubble. The sound of the pulse rifles helped him orientate as he crawled out from the debris and ran for cover.

A pulse round whizzed past his head, close enough for him to feel it.

'Dammit,' Drake cursed himself for attracting attention.

It was now a three on one battle, and Drake placed all his credits on himself.

Breaking out from his cover, Drake ran closer to where he left Robbie with Seymour, gun at eye level, ready to shoot at anything that moved. Another pulse round came flying past him and he dove behind what was left of a wall.

Breathing hard, he poked his head out to get a lay of the land. The three assailants were trapped behind a hydro wreck, hiding from Seymour's invisible pulse round. Drake almost laughed out loud, but another close flying pulse round stopped him. Who was shooting at him? All three fighters were facing the other way, and he was damn sure Seymour had not figured out how to shoot when he was away.

Which only left Robbie.

Drake poked his head out again, this time focusing on where Seymour should be. He expected to see a bit of orange, and a pulse rifle peeking out. Instead, he saw nothing. A movement to the left of where Drake was looking caught his eye. It was the thing he was looking for. The tip of a pulse rifle. Only it wasn't where it was supposed to be. It moved again, and pulse rounds went flying around the place.

Robbie must have woken up, still in a daze, and started to shoot aimlessly at the assailants. It was keeping them at bay, but shooting so wildly meant he was also keeping Drake back.

Opening the communication app on his HIC, Drake dialed Robbie. The three white dots appeared in front of him, but they never touched and kept bouncing away. The rock that fell on Robbie's head must have dislodged or damaged his Augmented Retinal Projector. Not wasting time, Drake typed him a message.

I'm down the road. Keep shooting but be careful not to hit me. I'm making my way over. BE CAREFUL.

After sending the message Drake waited for a response, but the only thing that came his way were stray pulse rounds.

'If you shoot me today, Robbie, so help me,' Drake mumbled as he sprinted towards new cover.

It didn't look like backup was on the way for the last three fighters. They were huddled together, pinned down by Robbie's pulse rounds. .

Another pulse round went flying by Drake's head. It wasn't ideal to have Robbie firing at him, but at least they were trapping the fighters. Making sure no other pulse rounds were making their way towards him, Drake made a dash to cover even closer to the fighters. This was close as he could get. Their focus was securely on the building Robbie was shooting from, so Drake took his time to figure out the best pattern. He had to allow for malfunctions, or a sudden unexpected movement from one of the fighters. Shooting them from left to right was not necessarily the best option.

The person closest to him, a female, didn't have much cover and presented him with an easy shot. But the fighter next to her was half obscured by a collapsed wall. If he somehow missed the first shot, or only injured the woman, the other person could duck down, which would also alert the third person and give them a chance to find cover. The third person was almost completely open, except for their head. Shooting them first, would be a high risk shot, and not a guaranteed kill. Injuring them would set off the same sequence of events that would lead to the other two finding better cover, and alert them to Drake's position.

Inhaling deeply, Drake finalized the order of his shots, and lined up the first one.

Exhale, and squeeze.

The woman's head rocked back as the pulse round found its intended spot, and she slumped to the ground, at the same time Drake acquired the second target. As Drake expected, the fighter with their head behind cover poked their head up to see what was happening, giving him a clear shot. Which he took. So far so good. Drake released the trigger and turned to the third target.

Which had disappeared.

Another stray pulse round reminded him Robbie was still in the game and a factor to consider. Drake took his eyes off the target zone and briefly checked his HIC for a reply from Robbie.

Nothing.

Another pulse round hit the wall next to Drake's face. But this one came from a different trajectory. This was not Robbie. Making a rough estimate, Drake had to assume it was the last fighter, shooting back. Which meant they had Drake's location. Looking around, Drake could not see any other cover that would provide a better tactical option. He knew sitting still was also not an option. Both Robbie and the last fighter stopped shooting. Drake grabbed his chance.

'I surrender. I give up. Don't shoot. I'm injured. I'm going to stand up,' Drake shouted as loud as he could.

No one replied or shot at him.

Slowly, he stood up, pulse rifle in one hand, but held in the air, as non-threatening as possible.

'Please don't shoot!' he yelled as loud as he could.

A man emerged from the rubble; pulse rifle drawn. He didn't say a word and kept walking towards Drake.

'Don't shoot,' Drake yelled again.

A movement caught his eye. He dared not look at it, for fear the armed man would see it too. It came from where he left Seymour and Robbie. Without looking, it was impossible to tell if it was Robbie getting ready to take the shot, or just more debris falling from the collapsing buildings.

The man found a spot he was comfortable with and stopped.

'Who are you fighting for?'

The question took Drake by surprise.

'Um, no one. We are here to find someone.'

'Don't lie. You attacked us. Who are you fighting with?'

Drake tried to recall who shot first.

'You chased us. We had no choice. Besides, you shot first.'

The man didn't answer.

Another movement almost made Drake look. If it was indeed Robbie, Drake wished he would hurry up and shoot already.

'Doesn't matter. Do you stand with Tjaka?'

Telling him he didn't stand with anyone didn't strike Drake as the smart call.

Giving him the wrong answer might be even worse.

'I'm trying to find a friend, that's all.'

'If you're not with Tjaka, you're against him.' Drake could tell he was about to eat a pulse round.

'My friend is traveling with Tjaka's daughter, Lerako, so I guess you could say we're standing with him?' Drake tried.

The man relaxed but kept his rifle pointed at Drake.

'Why is your friend with her? Is he helping the cause?'

Drake doubted Jimmy was helping anyone with their political cause.

'Yes. He's helping her. Do you know where she is? Or her dad, Chief Tjaka?'

The fighter studied Drake.

'Yes.'

Drake was excited. He dropped his outstretched arm holding the pulse rifle and walked towards the man.

'Please tell me!'

An electric crackle bounced off the crumbling walls of the surrounding buildings. Drake knew immediately where it came from but could do nothing to stop it. The fighter's face was surprised, then worried, before he slumped to the ground.

'No!' Drake rushed to his side.

Even if his ARP was fully functioning, he wouldn't need it to know the man was dead.

'No,' he repeated softly.

'Drake! Drake!' It was Robbie, running towards him, carrying Seymour. 'You okay? I almost missed him. I came to, and I was so disorientated, I just fired over the wall without looking. I thought you were gone or dead. Then I heard your voice and saw this guy ready to kill you. Man, that was close.'

Still kneeling next to the fallen fighter, Drake couldn't hide his disappointment and kept his gaze to the ground.

'Thanks buddy,' he said softly.

| thirty-three |

Faraway explosions and pulse fire became a constant background noise. The war for supremacy of the territory was fought in small battles and skirmishes, by groups no bigger than the one Drake came across. The fighting spread out over the whole city but was in certain areas.

None of the fighters had a Human Interface Console, and only one of them had a Human Interface Device. It hung around her neck, attached by some synthetic string. Lifting it up, Drake turned it around, only to see a big crack in the screen. It was dead. He dropped it back down on the still-grinning corpse.

'I assume it's some stimulant or drug making these people grin like idiots?'

Robbie leaned over to look at the corpse at Drakes feet.

'Yup. It's called siaquee. It's a leaf that's chewed and makes people feel invincible. Most of the so-called warlords control it and use it to control the people.'

Drake's understanding of how things worked in Bulanalke was upended again. Would he ever get a handle on how things worked here?

'What now?' Robbie asked.

Searching the bodies of the dead fighters turned up nothing useful.

'We keep moving.'

'Okay,' Robbie shrugged.

Grabbing his pulse rifle, Drake programmed Seymour to follow them and set off in the direction he hoped would lead them to Jimmy.

It didn't take long before the crumbling buildings gave way to housing units and structures that, although run down, were intact. It surprised Drake to see people going about their daily lives, only a short distance away from where they just had a battle. Surely these people would have heard it, but no one was phased. Two kids almost bumped into them, as they ran past them and into the rubble they just escaped from.

'Hey! Stop! It's not safe,' Drake yelled after them.

A laugh behind him made him turn around. It came from an old man sitting in front of a tiny housing unit. He shook his head at Drake as he continued laughing. No HIC or HID was visible, but Drake tried to talk to him regardless.

'Everything okay?'

The old man chuckled.

'I think he's, um, senile?' Robbie said.

'Is everything okay?' Drake tried once more.

The old man chuckled again but turned his head towards the demolished buildings. Drake and Robbie did the same, and saw the two kids, running back towards them.

'See, I told you it was dangerous.'

They ran past Drake and stopped at the old man, each one producing a shoe. The old man took the shoes, and taking off his worn-out pair, replaced them with the newer shoes. His smile grew even bigger. He reached into his pocket and gave the kids something. They said something Drake couldn't hear, before heading for the rubble again to loot whatever they could.

Walking away from the old man, who only had eyes for his new shoes, Drake turned to Robbie.

'We need to find someone with a HIC or HID on them. I need to speak to a local so we can figure out where to go.'

Robbie nodded.

'Also, keep an eye out for any group bigger than two. I've already seen a few people walking around carrying pulse rifles, but none of them took notice of us. But a bigger group could be a problem.'

It felt like they had stepped into a non-combat zone. Most people were minding their own business and the few who carried pulse weapons didn't seem threatening.

'There,' Robbie said, pointing to a group of people sitting outside a small building.

Using crates for chairs and an upturned cargo container for a table, they were having a meal. A woman stepped out of the building and brought some more food.

'Hi there,' Drake said hands open, and lifted up in front of his chest, his pulse rifle slung behind his back. A big smile completed the picture of not being a threat to them.

A moon-miner sized man lifted his eyes up towards Drake. His skin was as dark as most people in Bulanalke, and sweat was pouring off him in the heat, making his muscles stand out even more. Drake had no doubt the man could rip his arms off if he wanted to.

'Hi. We're looking for our friend. It's a bit of an emergency.'

Looking at the huge man's arms, Drake couldn't see an implanted HIC, and feared he would not have understood what he was saying. You could have a HIC without an ARP, but you couldn't have an ARP without a HIC. No HIC meant no chance of an ARP or that he would understand what Drake was saying.

The man pulled a HID out of his pocket and read the screen.

Drake hoped it was a translation and not a daily reminder to rip someone's arms off.

'Where is your friend?'

Unlike the giant man, Drake had a HIC and an ARP, so he could skip reading the translation on a screen.

'Well, that's the thing, I don't know.' Drake realized he couldn't mention Lerako until he knew where these peoples' loyalties were.

The man grunted and waved Drake off. 'So how can I help you then?'

A good question, Drake had to admit.

'Okay, I do know who he is with, if that helps?'

No one had any logos, insignias or uniforms that could help him determine their allegiance. Considering the people they just fought were Tjaka supporters, and their bodies were only a couple of hundred meters away, he had to assume this was a Tjaka-controlled area.

'Who?' the man grabbed a piece of whatever they were eating and stuffed it in his mouth. After he finished chewing, he lifted his hand from his lap, and wiped his face with the back of his hand.

A hand that clutched a pulse pistol.

'Nandi,' Robbie yelled past Drake's ear.

Drake slid his hand up his leg until it reached the bottom of the pulse rifle's sling. He had to be ready to shoot at any second now. Slowly he wrapped his fingers around it, trying not to draw attention to his movement.

Apparently, he failed as the other two men lifted their own weapons from underneath the table. Both had SA74's. Nobody moved.

A group, bigger than two.

'Why is your friend with Nandi?' One hand still cradled the pistol, the other grabbed more food.

'Um, its, business. That's all. We're selling her some hydro propulsion units and we lost contact with her.'

Close enough to the truth to not get confused or contradict himself later.

Wiping his hand on his pants, the man glanced at his HID.

'Okay. I'll take the toy.'

'Huh?' Drake looked at Robbie to see if he knew what the man was talking about. His face said he didn't.

'That,' the man replied pointing to Seymour.

'Oh,' Drake chuckled. 'No, that belongs to my friend who's with, uh, Nandi. Sorry.'

The man shrugged and continued eating.

It took Drake a minute to realize the conversation was over.

'I can give you credits?' Drake offered him something he hoped Robbie could supply.

Everyone laughed as they read the HID that was now lying on the table.

'There is nothing to buy here. What would I do with your credits, huh? Give me the toy, and I'll take you to Nandi.'

Jimmy was going to hate him.

'Okay. But only after we get to Nandi.'

The man shrugged again, stuffed more food in his mouth, and stood up.

'Let's go.'

* * *

The most popular vehicle in Bulanalke was a utilitarian hydro, with a cabin for two, and a large cargo area at the back. A small truck almost. Some of the hydros had pulse rifles mounted on the back, and some had two rows of seats that faced each other, enough to carry six people. Bouncing along the dirt road, Drake found himself on the back of such a hydro, with Robbie and Seymour next to him and one of the men from the small eatery across from them. He didn't say much. The man who did all the talking was sitting in the cabin up front next to the driver.

'How did you know they were loyal to Nandi?' Drake asked Robbie. Since the man sitting across from them had not shown any sign of having a HID or HIC, Drake risked talking openly in front of him.

'His hand,' Robbie replied.

Frowning, Drake turned to the man sitting across from him and studied his hand. It looked normal to Drake, and he couldn't discern any markings or unique characteristics. The hand gripping the pulse rifle by the handle was a normal, average working hand.

'I don't get?'

'The other one,' Robbie replied.

Drake turned back and looked for the other hand. The man had his other arm laying on his lap and Drake couldn't see the hand, as he assumed it was tucked in between his body and his other arm.

Drake shot Robbie a look of frustration. *Just tell me.*

Robbie lifted his eyebrows and nodded ever so slightly in the man's direction. Turning back to the man yet again, Drake saw the man repositioning himself, and unfolding his arms. He did a little stretch and placed his arm in question back on his lap, but this time he rested it on top of the pulse rifle. It allowed Drake to inspect the hand that convinced Robbie to risk their lives.

But there was no hand.

Resting on the pulse rifle, the arm ended abruptly in a stump. This did not look like something he was born with, but rather the result of an accident.

'Okay?' Drake said, hoping Robbie would elaborate.

'That's the work of Tjaka. He's known for it. If you disagree with him, steal in his territory, or he feels like it, he takes a hand. Sometimes both.'

'So, you made an assumption they had to be against him because Tjaka might have chopped off the guy's hand?'

'Yup!' Robbie looked very pleased with himself.

Drake wanted to yell at him for risking their lives like that, but he had to be honest with himself. It sounded like something he would do, and besides, Robbie seemed to be right.

There was still one issue with Robbie yelling out Nandi's name.

It wasn't the person they needed to get to.

Lerako was the target. Jimmy was last seen with her, and they needed to get to her before she reunited with her father. The chief would have massive security around him. . Their only glimmer of hope was that Nandi was in the same boat as them and wanted to intercept Lerako and her weapons before she arrived at her father's. It was going to be a delicate balancing act. If they reached Nandi too early, they might not get to Lerako in time. . If they were too late, Jimmy might not even be alive. Arriving at the same time was a mathematical improbability.

The only thing to do was wait, hope, and improvise.

A vibration in Drake's arm alerted him of a message. Hoping it was finally a message from Jimmy, he quickly accessed his HIC.

Mr. Drake

I haven't been honest with you, and I don't have the time to explain it now. The client is in trouble and needs your assistance. I know this is highly irregular, but I will triple your credits. FIND THEM ASAP.

John Simons

Drake reread the message. It didn't make any sense. It sounded more like Mr. Simons was in trouble with Nandi and trying to throw Drake under the bus.

Closing the message, Drake tried to forget about it. He was about to meet up with Nandi anyway, and he'd sort it out then.

Besides, he had way more important things to worry about right now.

| thirty-four |

Slamming into Robbie, Drake struggled to hold on, as the hydro came to an abrupt stop. Seymour had toppled over too and was maneuvering his limbs to try and get back onto his feet. The doors of the hydro flung open, and the two men spilled out.

'What's going on?' Drake shouted, standing up, only to be yanked back down by Robbie.

And just in time, too.

A flaming container whooshed by his head and exploded on impact when it hit the ground, setting everything around it on fire. Pulse fire joined the party.

'Stay down!' someone yelled.

More pulse rounds whizzed around their heads. Lying on the back of the hydro's cargo tray meant they were safe for now, but Drake knew it wouldn't last.

They had to move.

Drake grabbed Robbie by the arm. 'When I say jump, you haul ass!'

A break in the barrage of pulse rounds meant it was time to go. Drake looked for Seymour but couldn't find him.

'Now!' Drake yelled and pulled Robbie with him.

They made it to cover and readied their rifles, as a fresh barrage of pulse rounds flew over their heads.

'Where are the others?' Robbie asked.

Drake assumed he meant the driver, the man who wanted Seymour, and the man missing a hand. If so, Robbie would be glad to know that Drake had a visual on them. A visual that included the driver slumped over the hydro's yoke, blood spattered over the windscreen. It also included the man who wanted Seymour. Apparently, he really wanted Seymour, as he was spread out on the road in a pool of blood, still clutching Seymour. And lastly, the man who sat with them on the back of the hydro, was still sitting on the back. He was not going anywhere soon. Or ever.

Drake also had visual on two shooters, sitting behind a burned-out hydro wreck.

'Everyone's dead,' Drake summarized the situation. 'I have eyes on two shooters behind the wreck, under that tree.'

Robbie popped his head out for a split second to have a look.

'Okay,' Drake said once Robbie returned with his head still intact. 'We don't have time to waste. You lay down some suppressive fire and keep their attention, and I'll flank them.'

Drake didn't wait for confirmation or questions from Robbie. They had wasted so much time already, fighting random people they had no beef with. He wanted to find Jimmy and go home. He set off at once and Robbie started to fire blindly from the safety of his cover. Running as fast as he could, Drake ran past some buildings, before turning back towards the ambush. He was now in a direct line of the men shooting at Robbie. They were so focused on him, that Drake kept moving forward until he knew he couldn't miss.

And he didn't. Three shots later, and both men slumped against the wreck.

Robbie was still firing without looking, so Drake decided to run back the way he came and stay out of his way.

'You can stop now,' Drake said as he reached Robbie.

'We don't normally go to these places, Drake. We stick to the highways and towns we know are safe. Rut likes people to think he's so mean, but he never does dangerous stuff like this. I've never fired a rifle this much in my life.'

Drake couldn't tell if Robbie was about to holler for joy or break down and cry.

'How do you do it?'

The question took him by surprise. He'd never really given it any thought. Being a hauler meant he was exposed to a higher level of violence than most people, but in the last few years things had gone up a level. He didn't think twice these days of shooting someone and with the skills and techniques he picked up from Dina, he usually didn't miss either. To be fair, he hardly ever shot first, and Drake was confident that most people who shot at him didn't win citizen of the year awards.

'It's mostly out of necessity, Robbie.'

'But you make it look so easy. You never look scared. Or even nervous. You are everything I hoped you'd be.'

That made Drake feel scared and nervous.

'Robbie, in my job I run into bad guys. I've learned how to shoot a gun over the years.'

Robbie smiled and shook his head.

'Okay, we need to keep moving,' Drake spoke before Robbie could.

After retrieving Seymour from the dead man's arms, Drake inspected the hydro. It was shot up pretty badly, and it quickly became apparent that it was not going anywhere. They were going to have to do this on foot.

The three white dots before him bounced away in a random pattern. Someone was calling. But before he could see who it was, the call disconnected because of a weak signal.

Drake's arm vibrated. It was another message.

Drake,

We need to talk. Please answer my call.

John Simons

'Everything okay,' Robbie asked, as the three dots started dancing in front of Drake again.

'Yes. Just someone I need to deal with when I'm back home.' He dismissed the call.

Another vibration went through his arm.

Drake,

This is life and death. Please answer my call.

John Simons.

'I think we squeeze through there and maybe follow that road to the center of town.'

Drake barely heard what Robbie was saying, as the three white dots were back, dancing in his vision, waiting for him to accept the call and allow them to merge.

Whatever John Simons had to tell him would have to wait. They were within striking distance of Jimmy and Lerako and so was Nandi. He would talk to the old man once he had Jimmy by his side. Drake declined the call.

'Follow me,' Robbie said and set off.

Three white dots reappeared and floated in front of Drake, distracting him.

'Fuck off!' he yelled as he dismissed the call once more.

'Huh?' Robbie turned around.

'Not you, Robbie.'

As Drake reassured Robbie, John Simons called again, making the three dots appear and dance in front of Drake once more.

This time he answered.

'Not now, old man! I'm about to rescue my friend from this shit hole you sent us too, and I really don't want to talk to you right now or discuss the concerns you or your client might be having.'

Drake looked down at his HIC and extended his finger to swipe John Simons away.

'Nandi is my daughter!'

Drake's finger stopped and hovered millimeters above his HIC, leaving Mr. Simons face floating in front of him.

He looked genuinely scared.

'What?' Drake yelled. 'I thought you said she's the client?'

Confusion and anger battled it out for top emotion.

'She is the client, but she's also my daughter.'

'Drake, are we going or not?' Robbie asked.

Drake lifted a hand. *Give me a second.*

'Okay, so Nandi's your daughter. Fine, but right now none of that matters. I don't have the cargo, and Jimmy is still missing. It's a first for me, Mr. Simons, but I'm not going to complete this contract. Sorry. My only concern is to get Jimmy and get out of here.'

With the signal being so weak, the conversation was broken up a lot, and Drake hoped the old man heard all of it.

'My contract is with Mr. Something, for the record. But either way, I'm willing to forego the contract, in fact I'll sign it off as completed right now, so your record will stay clean. I'll even double the payment, Mr. Drake.'

'Why?'

Robbie was standing on top of the burned-out wreck, looking in every direction to make sure no one was approaching them. He gave Drake a thumbs up.

'Because she's pinned down. Close to your location. You are her best chance of getting out alive.'

How Mr. Simons knew his location, he could only guess. But why he was Nandi's only hope, he could not.

'Why doesn't she call in back up herself?'

'Tjaka's forces have her surrounded and outnumbered. Please Drake. She's running out of time.'

'So, the weapons were to arm her militia and take down Tjaka?'

Mr. Simons showed no surprise about Drake's knowledge of the cargo, or his guess as to the reason behind it.

'Yes.'

'This has nothing to do with me. Nandi, Tjaka, I don't care who rules. I just want out.'

Something in the old man changed. His eyes lost all softness, and the pleading look he sported till now gave way to a scowl.

'Since credits are what you people care about, I'll triple your contract. Getting rid of Tjaka and reinstating Nandi as the true ruler is all that matters.'

'Reinstating? What are you talking about?' Drake knew little of the history of the area, and no one had informed him that Nandi used to rule this area.

'We don't have time for this discussion, Drake. Save my daughter and I'll pay you handsomely.'

'I'm sorry, but—'

'Lerako is there too.'

Mr. Simons must have been keeping tabs on everyone since Drake and Jimmy landed in Bulanalke.

'You've been tracking us the whole time? You knew exactly what's been going on, didn't you? Yet you never stepped in. You didn't care if we made it back alive or not.'

'No. I'm sorry if that hurts your feelings, Drake, but all that mattered was Nandi receiving those weapons.'

The signal came and went, but Drake heard enough to follow the conversation.

'Why? Why do you want Tjaka's land so bad? Enlighten me.'

Mr. Simons did not hide his frustration at Drake, but answered him, nonetheless.

'Because that land is ours. We ruled that area for hundreds of years. It was the pride of Bulanalke. Then Shangcorp came in, started to buy up land and corrupt the people of Bulanalke, including the chiefs, especially Tjaka's dad, Chief Butha. He took all their credits and became a puppet for them, ruling the land on their behalf. When I refused to buckle under their oppressive rule, they used him to overthrow me.' Mr. Simons shoulders dropped, and his gaze drifted to the floor. 'And he did. There was a massive battle, one that cost him his life, and me my land. Before his men could capture and kill me, I escaped and fled.

But I never gave up. Neither did Nandi. She saw her mother die at the hands of Butha's men and vowed to help me. But I'm afraid her eagerness and temper took over and she went after the cargo without thinking clearly. Drake, this is not about me or you, or even Nandi. It's about the people of Bulanalke. They need to be freed, and the only person who can do that is Nandi. I beg you. Please go and help her.'

'You were the chief here, before Tjaka?'

'No,' Mr. Simons replied. 'I was the king.'

Drake didn't know what to say. Try as he might, he couldn't imagine the old man sitting in his office back in New Franco as a king in Bulanalke.

'All I ever wanted was for our land to be given back to the people. Please Drake. I'm sending you the coordinates of Nandi's position now. I'm sure Lerako and Jimmy will be there as well. If you help Nandi, you will be saving Jimmy too.'

A vibration in his arm confirmed the arrival of the coordinates.

'I'll do what I can,' Drake said and disconnected the call.

'Wow, so we are actually going to help Nandi?' Robbie shouted out from on top of the wreck.

'I don't know yet,' Drake said and set off towards Nandi's location.

| thirty-five |

The coordinates Drake received from Mr. Simons pointed to a location only a few minutes away. They were practically around the corner from Nandi.

And hopefully Jimmy.

'Okay, weapons check,' Drake said.

Both had a SA74, as well as a pulse pistol each. No grenades or heavy artillery, but all things considered, Drake felt adequately prepared. They also had Seymour, who had enough charge for one EMP blast.

By checking their weapons, Drake wanted to make sure they had enough charge and no damage. The last thing he wanted was to go in guns blazing, without guns that could blaze.

Satisfied everything was in order, they set off for what Drake hoped to be their last journey.

'I'm a bit nervous,' Robbie said as they hit the road.

'Robbie, you've been a great help so far. If you want to bail now, I get it. This is not your fight.'

'Oh, no, I'm ready to fight with you, Drake. Scared, but ready. I meant, after the fight. I'm not sure what I'm going to do. I can't go back to working with Rut. I'm pretty sure he is going to try and kill me.'

His focus had been on Jimmy, and Drake did not consider what would happen to Robbie when his mission was completed.

'What would you like to do?'

Burned-out hydros filled the street, and they had to weave their way through them. They were back in an area with no permanent residents left. In this location the people moving around were there to fight.

'Go back to a Penta territory, I guess. I haven't been home in years.'

Seymour was still scanning for pulse weapons, walking a few meters in front of them.

'I think that's a good idea, Robbie. I don't think you should stay here. You can drive back with me and Jimmy if you want.'

A big smile spread across Robbie's face.

'How can I say no to that?'

'It's settled—'

There was no warning from Seymour. One minute they were chatting, the next they were buried under a pile of concrete and metal. The explosion, from whatever source, caused a nearby building to collapse onto the road. The burned-out wrecks offered some protection, and Drake found himself pinned down against one.

Patting himself down, and feeling around for any broken bones, Drake felt satisfied he was mostly unscathed. A few minor cuts and some bleeding, but nothing major.

'Robbie! Robbie?'

No reply.

Lying on his side, back against a wreck, he saw light streaming in from his feet. He didn't have enough space to move his head and get a better look, but figured if there was light coming in, there must be some sort of a gap.

'Robbie? You okay, buddy?' Still no answer.

Drake started to wiggle his body, inching himself towards the gap at his feet. It was slow and tiring work. He was afraid of unsettling the debris and causing it to fall and crush him, so he tried his best to make small movements and not touch anything. It felt like he was making hardly any progress, but he pushed the negative self-talk out of his head and kept moving. He even repeated the phrase to himself, like a mantra – *keep moving.*

A sound made him stop moving.

It was an alarm.

A warning.

Seymour's pulse sensor.

'Robbie!'

Someone was coming. Someone with pulse weapons. Drake had to decide: play dead, or risk getting out quickly and fight. With all the debris around and the damage caused by the explosion it made sense to play dead, as anyone who came upon this scene would expect whoever they found to be dead. Play dead was the smart move.

Which meant Drake threw caution to the wind and crawled out from underneath the rubble quickly and recklessly.

Bumping his head multiple times didn't help, but also didn't slow him down too much. He would deal with the headache later. He found some cover and immediately scanned the area for the hostiles. He also used his HIC to mute the alarm from

Seymour and put him in standby mode. Drake had no idea where Seymour was and would have to look for him after he dealt with the intruders.

A man and a woman crested a pile of rubble near Drake, making them easy targets. His finger was on the trigger, slack taken up, ready to kill. But first, he had to make sure they were a threat. Dina had a list of rules as long as her arm, most of which Drake couldn't remember. The one that always stood out was to try and avoid shooting a civilian or anyone that didn't pose a threat which included wounded or unarmed enemies.

Drake scanned the two people walking towards him for weapons. Although Seymour's alarm went off, he needed to be sure. If they had any, they were a threat, and he could shoot them. As they approached him, he saw they both had pulse rifles. He now had two very easy targets to dismiss. Except they haven't posed a threat yet. Why did Dina's stupid rule pop into his head right now? Was it because of Robbie's questions?

'Stop. Don't move. Throw down your weapons or I will shoot you in the head. Do it now!'

Both people stopped but held onto their weapons.

'Do you stand with Nandi?' Drake repeated the phrase he heard earlier.

Instead of answering, they shared a quick look.

'You are about to die, so make up your minds.'

The woman shook her head and pointed to her ear. She didn't understand him, which meant no HICs or HIDs.

Keeping the rifle pointed at them, Drake moved it to his left shoulder, allowing him to use his right hand to access his HIC. He hoped they wouldn't make a run for it, because shooting left-handed was not his strong suit. Something Dina told him to work on, but he never did. He found the app to operate Seymour and used it to call him over, hoping he wasn't crushed under the debris.

He wasn't.

A small pile of rubble to the left of Drake rose and slid off an emerging orange shape. Seymour was fine.

The ASR made its way over to Drake, who switched on its speaker. He could now serve as Drake's interpreter.

'Do you stand with Nandi,' Drake tried again.

Recognition flashed over their faces, and they turned to each other. The woman nodded slightly.

'We are with the one truthful ruler, King Tjaka!'

'Long live Tjaka!'

Both dropped to their knees, closed their eyes, tilted their heads back, and raised their arms. They were ready to die for their king.

'Shit,' Drake mumbled.

He moved a bit closer to them.

'Do you know where Lerako is?'

The woman held her pose but opened one eye. She used it to study Drake.

'Are you going to shoot us?'

Drake wasn't sure yet.

'I don't want to, but also, I have no problem doing it. It's up to you. Do you know where Lerako is?'

The man next to her also opened one eye and shook his head at her.

Drake lowered his rifle.

'Listen, I'm not on anyone's team. I'm looking for my friend, who is currently with Lerako. Can you tell me where she is?'

'So why did you ask about Nandi?' asked the woman, still ready to die, judging by only having one eye open.

'I figured if you were fighting for Nandi, then you would rather shoot me than help me. I was hoping the opposite would be true, and you would help us if you were supporting Lerako.'

'So why didn't you ask if we stood with Lerako?'

'I don't know. I just had to pick one.' Drake started to regret not shooting them on sight. 'Please tell me if you can help me get to Lerako?'

The man had two eyes open now and shook his head again. Luckily, he wasn't the one in charge.

'Okay,' the woman replied. 'But it will cost you.'

Drake sighed.

'What?'

'One of your pulse rifles.'

Not a request he was willing to entertain. Glancing at their weapons lying on the ground next to him, he noticed that one was severely damaged. A pulse round or something equivalent must have hit it, and he doubted it would ever be functional again. Not having a functional rifle in this place had to be a massive handicap.

If he gave them one of theirs, he and Robbie would have that same handicap.

Everyone in Bulanalke was struggling, scraping by, trying to survive. Except for a few, like the chiefs and generals, the people were apathetic as if they held no hope for better lives. It was a daily struggle for survival. Chances were no one on either side of this conflict was good or bad, just people hoping their chosen leader would pull them out of their misery.

And like Penta and Shangcorp and any other authority that was in charge, he knew they would never help the people at the bottom. People like him and Jimmy. And the two fighters in front of him.

Which made his decision even harder.

Aiming his pulse rifle at the functioning one, lying on the ground, Drake said, 'Tell me where Lerako is, or you'll lose this one too.'

It worked. Panic set in on their faces and both waved their hands around, shaking their heads.

'No! No! Please don't. We'll die without it. We'll take you to her.'

Drake picked up the functioning rifle and threw it over his shoulder.

'Okay, let's go.'

Both nodded and turned around, ready to lead the way.

'Drake?' a faint voice said from behind.

It was Robbie. Drake had completely forgotten about his selfless helper. He felt like an idiot.

'Stop!' Drake yelled after the two fighters, who were already descending the mound of rubble. 'Find that person and get him out.'

Turning towards Robbie's voice, he said, 'Speak up Robbie. We're trying to find you.'

A rock tumbled down some debris, and Drake saw a dirty boot barely poking out.

'Can you see my foot?'

'Yes!' Drake replied and ran over to Robbie.

The two fighters arrived and, under Drake's watchful eye and pointed rifle, began to dig out Robbie. It didn't take long before he sat on top of the pile that trapped him. Dust covered him from head to toe, but his smile shined through.

'Thought I had it that time! Who are they?'

'They are going to lead us to Lerako and in exchange I'm not going to shoot them or their precious rifle,' Drake said in his most menacing voice. He really didn't want to do any of those things.

'You okay to go? Nothing hurts too much?' Drake asked Robbie.

The closer they were getting to Jimmy, the less patience he had.

'Nah, I'll live. Let's go.'

* * *

'There. That big building. That's where Lerako is fighting Nandi's forces right now.'

A massive building dominated the skyline. It wasn't extremely tall, but it was very wide. According to the woman, it was where they would find Lerako. And hopefully Jimmy.

Turning the confiscated pulse rifle on its side, Drake opened a flap and pulled out two wires. He touched them together and watched the charge indicator drop to zero. He placed the wires back into their positions and closed the flap. He handed the weapon back to the woman.

'Sorry, but I had to do that. Once you charge it, it will be fine. Thank you for helping us.'

Taking the gun, she gave Drake a look of defiance but said nothing. She nodded to the man, and they ran off quickly. Drake felt happy about not shooting them.

'Okay. You ready to do this?'

Robbie nodded.

'Thanks, man. I mean it. If it wasn't for you, I'd still be stuck in that room at Nandi's compound. You've been great, Robbie. Thanks.'

Blood rushed to Robbie's face, filling his cheeks and leaving him with a bright red blush.

'I just did what anyone would have done.'

Drake shook his head.

'Bullshit. Nobody would have done that. People only help others when it's self-serving. What you did was amazing, Robbie, and I'll never forget it.'

Somehow, he turned even more red.

Sensing his uncomfortableness, Drake punched him in the shoulder and chuckled.

'Enough of that. I would estimate the building is only three maybe four kilometers away. We better get going, because it's going to be dark soon, and I do not want to be out on these streets when it's dark.'

With the sun setting on their backs and long shadows stretching out in front, they set off to the large, squat building in the distance.

| thirty-six |

Rising high above the surrounding buildings, Drake felt a sense of déjà vu staring at the big square block of a building. No, it wasn't déjà vu but rather nostalgia. Seeing the big brand store names plastered on the outside of the structure, made him remember when he was a kid and life was simple and full of promise. He also remembered it being full of love.

A memory of going with his parents to these big buildings with hundreds of smaller shops inside floated just out of reach. If he stretched out, he would be able to grab it. Grab that feeling of being loved and secure. Instead, he allowed the memory to slowly drift off and fade away. This was no time for sentimentality. He was here for one reason only. Get Jimmy.

'You OK?' Robbie's voice stomped the memory out.

'Oh yeah. Just getting my head in the game. You good?'

Robbie nodded.

It was getting dark now, the last rays of sunlight were almost gone. Lights illuminated the building, making it stand out even more. Another thing that made it stand out was the noise. Once they were within earshot, the sound of pulse weapons never ceased. Whatever was going down inside the megalithic structure was relentless.

Drake and Robbie found a safe spot inside a building, only a few meters from their target building, and they started to observe it. From their vantage point, they saw most entrances were open, but some were better guarded than others. Hydros kept stopping by, dropping off more fighters. Some didn't even make it past their chosen entrances before they fell to the ground. Others went in straight away with no resistance. Drake made a note of the safer ones.

Next, he tried to figure out if there was a pattern to the fighters being dropped off. After a few minutes of watching them come and go, he realized it was completely random. It was hard to tell the difference between the two opposing sides as some wore uniforms, but most didn't. Same for the vehicles. Some had logos on them, but most were rundown unmarked hydros. This was not two corporations pitting their finest against each other. No, this was a brutal war of neighbor against neighbor, fighting to appease someone who promised them the world.

The longer he observed the violence and turmoil, the more he realized they would have to wing it. Strangely, it gave Drake some comfort. He was never big on planning ahead.

'See that door under the big green sign? Next to the orange one?'

Robbie turned his head to face the direction Drake pointed in. 'Yes!'

'Okay. That's our entrance. We'll make our way to it slowly, taking our time and ensuring no one sees us. If you see anything,

I mean anything, take cover, and alert me. We can't fail now. Not when we are so close.'

Robbie agreed, and Drake nodded in return.

With Seymour in tow, they set off for the door under the big green sign.

* * *

With twenty meters to go, a hydro pulled up, slamming on its brakes, and almost crashing into the building. People piled out of it, and before they could close its doors, it sped off again. Drake and Robbie saw the vehicle approaching and dove behind some abandoned hydros just in time. Watching the people run into the building, it was clear they had no leader or plan. It was every man and woman for themselves. They ran in shooting wildly, which made Drake smile.

Not because of their reckless approach to gun use, but because he could listen to their gunfire progressing into the building until it became part of the ambient noise. Hearing how they progressed into the building, Drake assumed that there wasn't too much resistance in the first half of the building. At least they would be able to get in and orientate themselves, and not get shot the moment they set foot inside the building.

With the hydro disappearing in the distance, now was as good a time as any to go in.

Drake gave Robbie the signal, and they made a beeline for the door.

Drake was there first and slammed against the building, right next to the open door. Robbie ran past him and quickly did the same on the other side. Drake opened the app for controlling

Seymour, and after making sure Robbie was in position and ready, he ordered the ASR to enter the building.

Drake had his ARP on and switched to have a small corner of his view displaying Seymour's point of view. The reception in Bulanalke was always horrendous, and the image kept disappearing and then loading again. It was frustrating but still better than nothing.

Watching the small screen in his view Drake finally saw the inside of the building.

Unlike the outside, which was still largely intact and untouched, the inside was a mess. It was hard to imagine what it would have looked like, but now everything was shot up, burned up, and overall fucked up. Ceiling panels hung down from above, exposing wires and pipes. Shelves that used to carry expensive products were now lying on the floor, empty of any goods. Multiple fires were burning everywhere. It was the stuff of nightmares.

Drake walked Seymour a little further into the building before he gave Robbie the signal to enter. Running in, they took cover, and once they confirmed everything was secure moved forward again. They repeated the process a few times. Drake moved Seymour forward, they made sure it was safe, before moving forward too.

Up ahead Drake could see a change in the building's layout. The part they were in now, most likely one of the hundreds of shops, was ending, and making way for a broad walkway. Looking down the walkway, Drake could see it leading to another space, which was much larger than the one they were in.

It was also the area where all the pulse firing was coming from.

* * *

Sending Seymour down the walkway first, Drake kept a close eye on the adjacent areas. He doubted that someone was waiting to ambush them, but he couldn't rule out the possibility. As Seymour approached the hot zone, it became harder to maneuver him around. Turned-over items, remnants from the war zone's previous life, littered the place. So did the bodies.

As Drake looked through Seymour's eyes, it filled him with dread. At least ten or maybe up to twenty bodies were visible. One thing was clear: this battle had been raging for a long time. No wonder Lerako was keen to get the weapons here and Nandi eager to get them back.

Slowly they made their way forward, trying not to be overly noisy, and trying to stay out of sight. It took them longer than it should have, as Drake kept stopping to make sure no one had arrived at the same door they had used and were coming from the rear.

Judging by the increase in the volume of the pulse fire, Drake knew they were getting close to the action. What he didn't know was if they were going to find Lerako or Nandi's forces.

Drake's leg was caught on something that made him stop.

'Robbie! Hold up.'

Without looking down, Drake tried to pull his leg forward, then shake it, but it didn't give.

'Keep an eye out.'

Looking down, he immediately saw the problem.

The problem grunted something at him, but Drake's ARP couldn't make out or translate what the dying man was saying. Awkwardly, Drake tried to shake the man off, again. Although he was missing a leg and most of his lower body, he had a vice-like grip on Drake's leg. The problem grunted at him again.

'Sorry, buddy, but I don't think I can help you. I really am sorry.'

Drake leaned down and pushed against the man's face to try and pry him off.

'What the hell are you doing?' Robbie asked right next to him.

'I can't get him to let go,' Drake said sheepishly.

'So why are you pushing on his face?'

'Just help me, okay?'

Robbie grabbed the man's arm and pulled, while Drake persisted with the face-pushing method. Somehow it worked and Drake fell free.

'Thanks.'

'That was weird.'

'Shut up. Let's just go.'

The noise was amplified now. Not only was it louder, but they could see the distinct blue flashes of pulse cartridges being discharged.

They had arrived at the battle.

In front of Drake, a walkway went around in a circle, with a massive opening in the middle. Looking up, he could see another level, with seemingly the same setup. He assumed there was a lower level with the same layout too. The two forces had barricaded themselves on opposing sides of the divide and multiple levels. Pulse rounds were flying across the gap, but also up and down to the different levels.

'What now?' Robbie asked, looking nervously at Drake.

'Shit, I don't know. It's so spread out. I don't even know which side is which.'

Accessing his HIC, Drake saw that the reception in the building was poor, but not zero. He swiped to the contacts screen and made a call.

'Drake! Did you find her?' Mr. Simons asked as soon as the three white dots merged.

'Sort of. When last did you hear from her?'

Before Mr. Simons could answer, the connection dropped out. Cursing, Drake called again.

'Listen, the service here is crap, so make it quick. Do you know where she is holding up?'

The connection held, but Mr. Simons kept freezing.

'Th…last time w…spoke she mention…ace wi…een…lephant.'

'What? I don't know what you're saying.'

Mr. Simons stared at Drake, as he realized the old man was frozen again.

'Say that again?'

'…an elephant…'

Drake's ARP went blank.

'Robbie! What is an elephant?'

It sounded familiar, and Drake knew it was another thing he heard of when he was a kid. If he had to guess, it was going to be another animal.

'An elephant is an elephant. You know? '

'Oh, of course, thanks, Robbie.'

A look of confusion confirmed that Drake was wasting time.

'I don't know what it is, and Mr. Simons said that Nandi mentioned it in her last call.'

'Shit, you really don't know. Wow. It's an animal. And it's massive. With huge ears. But I don't think they're around anymore.'

'Do you know of a shop that might have one?'

Shaking his head, Robbie said, 'No way. There is…wait a minute. Of course!'

Robbie left Drake in the dark as he crawled forward, making sure he stayed out of sight but positioning himself to get a better view of something.

'See? Over there! That shop's logo.'

Drake followed Robbie and scanned the area he was pointing to. The moment he saw the logo, another wave of nostalgia hit him as he recalled seeing pictures of it as a child.

'I forgot they used an elephant as their logo. It used to be a popular clothing brand a few years back, but when Shangcorp left, so did most companies.'

'Okay. So, if she mentioned an elephant, we assume she's there right.'

Which left him with the hardest decision to date.

Go to Lerako and hope he can convince her to hand over Jimmy or try to overpower her to get Jimmy back. The other possibility was to go to Nandi and help her defeat Lerako and hopefully not kill Jimmy in the process.

There was no time to debate the pros and cons of each plan, so Drake did what he always did.

Listened to his gut.

| thirty-seven |

Walking in, Drake and Robbie held their pulse rifles above their heads, white makeshift flags dangling off the ends. It was a risky move, but one he felt would pay off. Finding a back entrance to the store was easy, but now they faced the hard part. Trying not to be shot. Waving white flags around and holding your hands up has always been a universal sign of peace and even benevolence. Using them in the middle of a battle with adrenaline flowing and rational thinking at a low was never going to guarantee success. Yet, they had limited choices. They had to infiltrate Nandi's base, without shooting anyone or being shot. So, white flag it was.

The first fighter they encountered made Drake regret this whole plan. Clearly high on the local drug of choice, siaquee, the man stared at them with crazed wide eyes, clenched jaw, and exposed teeth. Nervous energy made his body shake and Drake knew he had little to no self-control. His eyes kept bolting to the white flag and back to Drake's face, trying to make a decision. The countdown to being shot was on.

'Don't shoot! Peace! See? Don't shoot!' Drake said, moving in front of Robbie. He doubted the man had any tech that would allow him to understand him.

'Keep your eyes on me, buddy. That's right, see, peace?' Drake kept talking to him.

Drake watched the man's finger pulling tighter on the trigger. Turning his head ever so slightly, he addressed Robbie, using the same voice and tone: 'Shoot him. We can't risk it.'

As always, Robbie obeyed without hesitation. Very cleverly, he placed his rifle's muzzle under Drake's arm, making it almost impossible for the fighter to see, and pulled the trigger. The man was down before Robbie could remove the rifle from Drake's side.

'Thanks, buddy. We're in for a treat if all the fighters are on siaquee.'

The extreme noise and commotion around them masked Robbie's pulse burst, and no one paid any attention to them. They were standing a few meters behind the next group of fighters and could easily have taken them out. They had the upper hand in position and the element of surprise. But the idea was to convince Nandi to help, not to overpower her. Not that Drake cared for her political stance, it was merely a case of the enemy of my enemy. He was also convinced that Lerako would rather shoot him on sight than negotiate.

'Remember, try not to shoot anyone.'

Robbie turned his head back to the man he just shot a minute ago.

'No one else,' Drake said.

Slowly, they approached the new group, careful to not startle them and get themselves killed. Sending Seymour ahead, he made sure the ASR would break the ice, which would allow them to follow. It worked. A handful of the fighters stopped when they saw Seymour strutting into their space, and they started to look around, trying to make sense of its presence. Drake and Robbie hung back, arms still raised, white flags visible, trying their best to look harmless. Using Seymour's inbuilt speaker, Drake addressed them.

'Please don't shoot. We were sent here for Nandi. She is expecting us. My name is Drake, and this is Robbie.'

Drake realized he didn't know if that was true. Mr. Simons, her father, did ask them, to go help, but he didn't know if Mr. Simons told her about their imminent arrival.

One of the fighters took charge of the situation and came towards them. Drake was happy to see he wasn't clenching his jaws.

'Who sent you?' the man asked.

Drake moved Seymour a bit closer to them before he replied.

'What is your name?'

'Josef.'

'Okay, Josef, I work for a man who claims to be Nandi's father. I don't know if it's true or not, but he asked us to help her. So, we're here to help. Can you tell us where she is?'

Seymour translated as Josef kept his gaze on Drake. Finally, the ASR finished, and Drake watched Josef having a seemingly conflicted inner dialogue. Drake waited it out.

'No,' came the reply, and Josef aimed his rifle point-blank at Drake's face.

'Woo, woo, woo!' Drake said, stepping backward and bumping into Robbie.

The pulse rifle was thrust in his face.

'Play him a message from Mr. Simons,' Robbie said from behind him.

It wasn't a bad idea. Except Drake wasn't sure a voicemail or some letters on a screen was going to persuade Josef.

To make things even worse, the other fighters joined Josef and aimed their pulse rifles at Drake and Robbie, too.

'Wait!' An idea came to Drake.

Making exaggerated motions with his arms and keeping his palms facing them, trying his best to show them at every turn that he was no threat, he slowly accessed his HIC.

'Drake, I hate to rush you, but I think the fighting is moving closer to us,' Robbie said.

Ignoring him, Drake found what he was looking for. Keeping an eye on Josef and his friends, Drake swiped his HIC. Three dots obscured their faces, as they bounced randomly in front of him. His heart rate increased with every second, as the white dots kept bouncing, and the pulse rounds kept flying everywhere.

'Just hang on,' Drake said, hoping the dots merged before their patience wore out.

'Drake! Is she okay?'

'Mr. Simons,' Drake sighed with relief.

The fighters shuffled around uncomfortably. Drake realized with their lack of even basic tech like Human Interface Consoles or even Human Interface Devices, they might not even know what an Augmented Retinal Projector was or how it worked.

Watching a man talking to himself might strike them as something completely unusual and could cause them to panic and even shoot. Lifting his palms, he assumed a non-threatening pose, again.

'I think so,' he addressed Mr. Simons, 'but I need some help.'

The signal was as weak as it always was in Bulanalke, but it was strong enough to get his message through.

'Have you found her?'

'Yes, but like I said, there is a small problem.' Drake tapped his HIC to make the ARP show Mr. Simons his view instead of his face.

'These guys are fighting with Nandi.'

'Is she with them?'

Drake flicked the view back to him.

'No. That is why I need your help. I need you to tell them to trust me.'

'Okay, but how are you going to patch me into them? Most people there do not have much in the way of tech, Drake.'

'I noticed. Give me a second, while you start preparing what you are going to say.'

Muting the call, Drake turned to Robbie.

'Grab Seymour, move slowly, and put him close to that wall, facing it.'

Robbie nodded, and like Drake, moved towards Seymour with palms up.

All the fighters tensed, and their eyes darted between Drake and the now-moving Robbie.

'Keep your guns on me! Please. I have something important to show you.'

By now Robbie had placed Seymour in position and he stood, waiting for Drake.

Unmuting the call, Drake said, 'Okay Mr. Simons, you're up. And make it brief. We've already wasted too much time here.'

In front of Seymour, projected against the wall, a glitchy, stuttering image of Mr. Simons appeared. .

'Greetings brothers. It is me, your king.'

The fighters' faces matched the incoherence and confusion of the whole scenario. Five minutes ago, they were fighting for their lives, and now they were standing in front of strangers, listening to their exiled king. Some looked unconvinced, while a few dropped to their knees.

'King Dinghare,' said the few on their knees.

'Yes, it is me, your beloved king, Dinghare. And these men were sent by me to help you and Nandi to reclaim what is rightly ours.'

A few more were now kneeling.

'They are not there to take over from you, but to help you. And I'm asking you, as your true king, to help them too. They bring with them marvelous machines that can help us win this war.'

Everyone was kneeling now.

'So please, listen, help, but always remain true to yourselves. Stay true to Mother Bulanalke.'

Mr. Simons, now talking and acting like the king he had once been, disconnected the call.

If not for the relentless pulse rifle firing, silence would have fallen over the group of fighters. Each one was still kneeling with their heads down. Drake gave it a few seconds before he spoke.

'Okay, you heard the king. Tell me where I can find Nandi.'

Snapping out of their submissive trance, the fighters stood up, and looked at Josef, waiting for him to lead.

'She's not with us,' Josef finally replied. 'She took a group to try and flank them and we haven't heard back from her.'

'How do you communicate with her?'

Reaching into a pocket, Josef produced a small device. He held it up for Drake and Robbie to see.

'With this.'

Drake had not seen a two-way radio for a long time, but he recognized it immediately. No one in Penta or even Shangcorp used them anymore, but he had seen one or two in his earlier hauler days.

'And she's not responding?'

'No.'

'Okay, can you show me where she went, Josef?'

After another short talk with himself, Josef nodded. He waved them over, as he walked away from them.

Drake and Robbie followed, crouching, because they were back in the firing line again.

'Over there. No one else has gone in or out.'

Drake could see why.

What might once have been a diner of sorts, was now an island, trapped between the two fighting parties. It wasn't placed right in between, but slightly off to the one side. The way it was constructed allowed for Lerako's side to have clear shots at both its entry and exit. Drake guessed Nandi used it, as no one would have expected such a crazy tactic. And now she was stuck inside, with Lerako's forces laying down suppressive fire on both sides, preventing anyone from going in or out.

It would be suicide to go after her.

'We need her,' Josef suddenly spoke. 'Look around. We're losing. If the men don't see her soon, they'll retreat. It'll be all over. We need to get her back.'

Dressed in tattered clothes, and fighting with outdated pulse rifles, Drake anticipated that morale was not high among the fighters. Either the higher-ranking fighters had already died, or there was no hierarchy, but no one was in charge here. Losing their leader could well be the end for them.

'Okay, listen up,' Drake said. 'We'll go in and try to find her. What I need you to do is get your squad to concentrate their fire on that spot.'

Both men peered over the cover and Drake pointed out the spot he wanted them to focus their firing on. It didn't make any sense for Jimmy to be on the front line, and Drake hoped he was safely hidden inside the building somewhere. The opposing force had superior numbers and firing power, but Nandi's force had a better location. The battle was on a knife's edge, and any-thing could throw it into either camp's favor.

Hopefully, he could swing that pendulum towards Nandi's team.

'Robbie, this is going to be—'

'Doesn't matter. I'm in.'

'No, listen. This is dangerous. I'm not very good at planning. I usually run in, headfirst, and see what happens. So far, I've been very lucky. But this? This feels bad. I cannot ask you to follow me. Not this time. Stay back here, and help these guys, okay?'

Nandi's men had entrenched themselves, and although pulse rounds were flying all around them, nothing penetrated their barricades. They were sitting in the eye of the storm.

'I need to know someone's got my back, okay?'

Robbie nodded, but his body language told Drake differently.

'Robbie, I'm serious. I can't go in, worrying that you might follow me. I need you here. Please.'

Nothing changed, but Drake had to move on.

After making sure Robbie and Josef were clear on the plan, Drake readied himself for what could easily be his last half-assed plan ever. A quick check to make sure his pulse rifle was ready, and that Seymour was set to follow, he glanced over at Robbie one last time and nodded.

It was go time.

* * *

The pain was not the worst part. No, the frustration of almost throwing everything away was way worse.

With ten meters to go, Drake fell forward and tumbled almost to the entrance to the diner. He was so close that it was quicker to crawl than get up again. The moment he crossed the doorway, he slid sideways and slumped against a wall. He couldn't believe he tripped over himself and almost ruined the whole operation. Seymour sat in front of him, his black eye-like sensors judging him.

'We made it, so—' Drake stopped, remembering the ASR had no emotions about what just happened.

Leaning forward to get back on his feet, a pain shot through his leg and into his spine, making him sit right back down. Grabbing his leg, Drake felt something wet and lifted his hands to inspect them.

They were covered in blood.

'What the hell?'

A little bit of relief went through Drake, as he realized he hadn't tripped over himself. The reason for his fall, and his bloodied pants, was a hole in his calf, big enough to put a finger in. It was leaking profusely. A pulse round must have blown cleanly through the muscle, missing the bone, but still delivering enough force to knock him over. Watching the blood pour out, Drake realized he had to stop admiring it and fix it.

In his true fashion, this was another rushed plan. Before he set off, he made sure his rifle was working and Seymour was operational, but he didn't think of taking any medical supplies. No blood proteins, synth skin, pain meds, or any other kits. Something that could've been fixed in a second would now be a problem, or even fatal.

Going back to basics, in true Bulanalke fashion, Drake ripped a piece of fabric off his shirt and tied it around his calf as tightly as he could. Blood soaked the material immediately, but then it slowed down. Slowly he put some weight on the leg and stood up.

It hurt. Like hell. But he was able to stand up, and even walk.

Looking around, he took stock of his surroundings. Everything was quiet inside the room. Although the pulse fire outside was still very loud, no sounds came from within the room. A few bodies lay scattered around, and there didn't appear to be any injured fighters. Nandi's chances didn't look very good.

A movement behind him made him jump around and a fresh wave of pain sent him to the ground. Pulse rifle drawn and ready he stared up into the shocked face of someone who realized they were almost shot.

'Robbie, what the hell. I told you to wait!'

'I'm sorry Drake, but when we saw you get shot and then crawl, we weren't sure you made it.'

'But I told—' Drake stopped and lowered his rifle. 'I mean, thanks, Robbie.'

'Are you okay?'

Drake flinched as he leaned forward and twisted his leg a bit so Robbie could see the impact area.

'I'll live. But it hurts like hell.'

'Well, I'm here now, so don't worry about it.'

Robbie kneeled down and pulled a small Medi-kit from a pocket. Using his teeth, he ripped the packet open and spilled the contents onto the floor. He had clearly used them before, and within seconds, he had the wound cleaned up and synth-skin applied.

'Sorry, they didn't have any blood proteins, but I don't think you lost too much blood.'

'I owe you,' Drake said sheepishly. He more than owed Robbie, but now was not the time for sentimentality.

With Robbie behind him now, Drake made his way deeper into the room, stepping over bodies, and making sure no one was still alive, by giving them a little kick as he stepped over them. No one groaned back.

Looking down at them, as he made his way through, he realized the bodies were lying closer and closer to each other and eventually started to pile up on each other. Soon he had no choice but to walk on them. The sensation made his stomach churn.

Small fragments of the wall cut into his face, as a pulse round smashed into it, right next to his head. There was no need to try and locate the origin of the pulse round, as Drake found himself staring down the barrel of a pulse rifle. Behind the barrel a pair of eyes burned through his skull. A voice, projected from further behind the murderous eyes, called out for the man to lower his weapon. Drake recognized the voice.

'What the hell are you doing here?' Nandi asked, appearing from behind the fighter.

'Risking my life to save yours so that I can save my friends'.'

Nandi did not strike him as the small talk type. He was right. 'Shoot him.'

'Wait! Wait! Please listen to me. Your father sent me.'

The fighter with the intense gaze, shot a quizzical look at Nandi.

Nandi walked up to Drake and pinned him against the wall with her forearm across his neck. She was almost as tall as he, and he recalled how hard she punched him before. He offered no resistance.

'What do you mean my father sent you?' Nandi's voice was more irritation than curiosity. 'And make it brief. I have shit to do.'

| thirty-eight |

After retelling the whole story, from them taking the contract, to him standing there, Nandi stood back and allowed Drake to breathe freely again. Even though he tried his best to keep to the facts and speak as quickly as possible, Nandi still felt the need to jab a knife in his ribs and increase the pressure every time he strayed a bit. He kept waiting for it to burst through the skin and slide into a lung, but he wrapped it up just in time.

With her team behind her still heroically defending their last stand, Nandi burst into laughter.

'And what, exactly, are you going to do? Huh?'

Her laughter made Drake feel like a child again. Small and powerless.

'I have no use for you,' she said.

Intense eyes stepped between them and raised his rifle.

'I have an EMP!'

Nandi placed a hand on intense eyes' shoulder.

'The ASR. He has an EMP built in. We can use him to penetrate Lerako's defenses.'

Nandi pushed the man aside.

'Why?'

The question caught him off guard.

'And don't tell me about my father again.'

He had nothing to lose.

'Because I'm here to find my friend. That's all I care about. But to get to him, I need help. You need your weapons. To get those, you need help. Both of these things we need are in the same spot. So, if we help each other, everyone wins.'

'I can just take your EMP and shoot you now.'

'Sure, but only I can operate it. Shoot me, and it's useless. Which would leave you stuck here, slowly losing this battle.'

'Even with an EMP, it will only take out a small number of her forces.'

'Small enough to breach her defenses and get in.'

'Then what?'

'That's up to you. Once we're in, I'm looking for my friend. The weapons and Lerako is your problem.'

Nandi stood motionless, staring right through Drake. It took every bit of self-control and courage he had, not to say anything or start rambling. It felt like he was shrinking under her gaze. Finally, turning around, Nandi called a few fighters over.

'Listen up. Here's the plan.'

* * *

Even the best-laid plans never went smoothly. And this was hardly a thought-out master plan.

Nandi used a two-way radio and told the forces outside the little island to focus their firepower on the spot where Seymour was to enter Lerako's barricade. She gave the same orders to the fighters with her. Once everyone started pelting the same spot, Drake took control of Seymour and walked him towards Lerako's forces.

He only made it halfway.

Although Nandi's side was concentrating all their firepower on one spot, Lerako's forces still shot at anything they wanted. Drake hoped they would concentrate their retaliation on the two areas where Nandi's forces were shooting from, leaving a V-shaped opening for Seymour to walk in. But like Nandi's force, there was a lack of trickle-down leadership, and the fighters on Lerako's side were shooting in every direction. Instead of splitting up into two groups and concentrating on the group targeting them, they shot across each other to whichever group they deemed necessary.

Despite his best intentions, Drake had created even more chaos. And in the process, he lost Seymour.

'Drake, I have an idea,' Robbie popped up from somewhere, right next to Drake.

'Let's have it, buddy, because right now I'm pretty sure Nandi is going to kill us.'

'Is Seymour still operational?'

Drake had already checked that but made sure, by accessing the ASR's telemetry on his HIC.

'Yup. Looks like they took out his legs, so he can't move, but the EMP is still an option. Only, he is too far away to cause any damage.'

'So, we need to move him closer?'

'Yes, you make it sound so simple.'

'I'll do it.'

'Robbie, no. I can't allow that. It's a dumb idea.'

'But I have a plan.'

Nandi looked over at Drake. He did not like the look on her face.

'Let's hear it.'

* * *

Slowly, inch by inch, Robbie made his way towards Seymour. Nandi's teams were still firing nonstop and provided some cover. Drake had also joined the fight, his pulse rifle at his shoulder, taking his time to take precision shots only. He tried his best to identify anyone who was aiming at Robbie and took them out.

Not that they would be aiming at Robbie.

Instead, they would be aiming at the two bodies slowly making their way towards the middle of the floor, towards the downed ASR. The two bodies, which should not be able to move anymore, as they were riddled with pulse rounds. Yet, they kept sliding forward. Propelled by another body, strapped underneath them, they slowly slid forward in the most unnatural way.

As long as they were moving, Robbie was alive.

Drake saw a fighter aiming at the macabre mound of flesh slithering towards the ASR and promptly disposed of them. Two more fighters met the same fate. The moving mass had finally reached Seymour. Now it was time for the risky part. The mass kept moving until it was on the far side from Drake's position and stopped. Until now, the two bodies were side by side, but pushing the one body on top of the other, Robbie revealed himself, behind a two-body high human wall. A glance at Drake, followed by a thumbs up meant he was still okay. Drake could see him take a deep breath, close his eyes for a second. Robbie grabbed Seymour and flung him towards Lerako's side. A few faces turned towards him, and Drake took out as many as he could before he saw Robbie collapse behind his cover.

Drake waited for another thumbs up, but Robbie stayed down.

For the plan to work, he had to act fast. Pushing aside any emotions about Robbie, Drake pulled up Seymour's controls and selected the EMP.

'Nandi! Nandi! We're good to go.'

'Okay, everyone. On my count.' Nandi gave Drake a nod. 'Three! Two! One…Go!'

Nandi's fighters jumped up in unison, no questions asked and showing no fear, they rushed towards Lerako's side. Drake pressed the blue icon and felt his stomach drop as he waited to see if the EMP went off successfully. There was no way to tell, no big flash or sound to let him know it was done. He could only hope that Lerako's team's pulse rifles wouldn't work.

The first line of Nandi's forces arrived at the EMP zone. Drake watched as Lerako's fighters popped up from their cover, ready to take on the enemy.

The moment of truth had arrived.

Blue streaks filled the space between the two opposing forces as pulse rounds flew through the air. It was impossible to tell if they were only flying in one direction, so Drake turned his focus on Lerako's team. What he saw gave him relief and also made him sick.

Lifting their pulse rifles, and trying to shoot them, Lerako's fighters looked on in horror as nothing happened. No pulse rounds came out to stop their enemy, instead they stood helpless as pulse round after pulse round came their way, tearing them apart. The plan worked, but it left Drake feeling empty.

But he was here for Jimmy, and now there was a way forward, and hopefully it led towards him. Drake fell in behind Nandi's fighters and followed them into Lerako's stronghold. On the way there, they ran past Robbie, and Drake saw his chest moving. He was still alive. Relieved, Drake pushed on.

Nandi's team took full advantage of their circumstances, and it didn't take long before they arrived at the inner sanctum of Lerako's operation. Lerako had the upper hand, having constructed a solid barricade using the materials lying around. Nandi's team had to break up into smaller groups to find cover, but they did, and soon the two forces were at a stalemate again.

Looking around, and observing the area, Drake could not see any other way forward. He had hoped to find an alternative route forward once they breached Lerako's front line, and to by-pass her to find Jimmy. But she had dug herself in, preparing for the inevitable onslaught from Nandi. The only way was to talk to Lerako to find out where Jimmy was.

'Nandi,' Drake had to yell, as she was entrenched a few meters away and pulse rounds were now flying in both directions again. 'I need to speak to Lerako. I can't see another way in. Please, give me one shot to talk to her.'

'Sure, but the moment she's not useful anymore she gets a pulse between the eyes.'

'Okay, okay, but just give me a chance.'

Nandi's face reluctantly agreed.

'Lerako! Can you hear me?' Drake shouted as loud as he could. 'Lerako! It's me, Drake! We need to talk!' His throat was already hurting.

'Drake?' A reply came back.

Not from Lerako. This voice was familiar but didn't belong to her. He was sure of it. A hundred percent sure. Because he knew that voice.

'Jimmy?'

'Drake?'

He found him. After spending days alone wondering if he would ever see him again, he finally found him.

'Where are you? I can't see you?' His voice was about to give up.

'Where are *you*? It's hard to tell with all this shooting, ya know. And my HIC is busted, so I can't locate you.'

'I'm here with Nandi. I'm here to save you.'

No reply. Even the pulse rounds fell silent from Jimmy's side.

'Something's going on. They've stopped shooting,' Drake yelled over to Nandi.

'Cease fire!' Nandi ordered her side.

An eerie silence fell over the battle ground.

'Jimmy? You still there?' It felt so much better not having to shout.

'Yes, but we have a problem, ya know.'

'What do you mean? Where's Lerako?' It was weird Jimmy was doing the talking and not Lerako.

Nandi must have come to the same conclusion, as she signaled her forces to move forward.

'Nandi, wait!' Drake tried, but she ignored him.

Fearing she was about to shoot Jimmy in the fierce combat about to take place, Drake broke his cover and ran towards Jimmy's side.

'Don't shoot, Jimmy! It's me!'

From behind a barricade, Drake spotted an unruly mop of red hair , followed by a face only he could love.

Jimmy.

'Buddy,' was all Drake could get out.

'Drake?' Jimmy sounded alarmed.

'What's wrong?' Drake looked around, assuming it was Nandi, but she and her fighters had taken cover again.

'You look...what happened?'

Drake shook his head. 'Nothing. I lost you and I came looking for you.'

'I can't patch into my ARP, ya know, but you are close enough now. I think you can.'

'Why? Jimmy, we need to get out of here.' This whole interaction was surreal.

'Just do it, please.'

Looking around, Drake located Nandi and made eye contact. She gave him a small nod. *Go on.*

'Okay, buddy, but we really need to get out of here.'

Being so close to Jimmy, Drake was able to hack into Jimmy's ARP and see what he was seeing. Was Jimmy trying to warn him about something? Did he just walk into a trap?

Drake made the connection and a small screen in his vision showed Jimmy's view.

In it, he saw himself and why Jimmy sounded so concerned.

What wasn't covered in dirt and bruises, was covered in blood. His one eye was half swollen shut, and he had a big gash on his forehead. His clothes were torn up, showing multiple wounds. Some bleeding, some already scabbed over. Drake had never stopped for a moment to take stock of what he was putting himself through. He only had one mission, and that mission was still not over.

He severed the connection.

'I'm all good, buddy, I promise. Now, let's go!'

All around Jimmy, fighters ran out from behind their cover.

'I'm afraid I can't, ya know.'

| thirty-nine |

It took Drake a few seconds before he could react.

'What are you talking about?'

Around him, Drake could feel Nandi and her team moving, getting themselves in the most strategically advantageous position to strike. Jimmy and the fighters stood no chance.

'Jimmy, please, we need to go. What's going on with you? Please, let's go.'

Nandi's forces were in position, and in a few seconds all hell would break lose.

Jimmy took a step closer to Drake, close enough for Drake to pull him in and hug him, but something was off. Jimmy's body language was very defensive.

'Lerako has been shot and she's dying,' Jimmy whispered. 'I promised her I would make sure Nandi didn't get her hands on the weapons.'

Every instinct was telling him to grab Jimmy and run.

'Buddy, this is not our fight. We need to go while we can.' Drake felt vulnerable and silly, standing in the middle of what was about to be a battlefield, arguing with Jimmy.

'But we can make a difference, ya know.'

He was willing to shoot Jimmy in the leg if that was what it took to get him moving.

'Buddy, I don't know what she told you, but we have no part to play in this.'

'But we do, ya know!'

Drake didn't understand what was happening.

'Jimmy—' The first pulse round flew past them, signaling the beginning of the end.

Grabbing Jimmy, Drake ran for cover and found safety behind a mound of fallen fighters. They were stuck between the two fighting forces, but in a safe enough spot to be out of harm's way for now.

'Okay, what is going on?'

A tear ran down Jimmy's cheek. 'You sure you're okay, Drake? You look horrible, ya know.'

'Yes, I promise. Now talk to me.'

Wiping the tear away, Jimmy took a deep breath.

'Remember Mr. Simons? The nice old man who gave us the contract? He's Nandi's father.' Jimmy paused for dramatic effect.

'I know.'

'Oh. Then why did you help Nandi?'

'I told you Jimmy; this is not our fight. I only helped her to get closer to you. And it worked. So can we please go now?'

'But if you know who Mr. Simons is, why wouldn't you want to stop him, ya know?'

Drake didn't follow.

'Huh?'

'He killed Lerako's grandpa and helped Shangcorp take over Bulanalke. He's responsible for thousands of deaths. Now he wants to take it all back. He's an evil man, Drake.'

It was the complete opposite of what Drake heard. Mr. Simons was the victim, not the aggressor. Even so, it changed nothing. This was not their fight. They had to move.

'Jimmy, I get it, we took a contract from a bad man. Trust me, it's not the first or last time that will happen. But right now, they are killing each other, and we need to get out while we can.'

'If we leave, Lerako and Chief Tjaka will lose everything. So will the people. Things aren't perfect under him, but at least everyone is free, ya know.'

Drake had heard of this sort of thing happening. When a victim stops fearing their kidnapper and starts sympathizing with them. Even to the extent they will choose their captors' side if rescued.

Exactly like Jimmy was behaving right now.

'Why are you fighting for Lerako, Jimmy? I mean, why did she spare your life? I'm so happy she did, but I can't figure out why.'

Jimmy shook his head as if dismissing the whole thing.

'She was about to shoot me, ya know, so I pointed out to her that I was only one with the codes to open the cargo boxes and get to the weapons. She was in a rush, so she tied me up and threw me into the Hydrostar. She also jumped in the Hydrostar when we left, and I started to chat to her and the driver. We became friends, ya know.'

Drake was reminded again that Jimmy was surviving by himself long before they met.

'But your HIC is busted. How would you open the crates?'

'Oh, I told her when you arrive, we'll use your old antique HIC to open it, ya know.'

'But what if I didn't show up?'

'Nah, I knew you would, ya know.'

Jimmy stated this as a mere fact.

They were getting sidetracked.

'Okay. I get it. But there is nothing we can do, Jimmy. Lerako's forces are pinned down and without her, there is no leadership.'

Hopefully, he would see sense now.

'Chief Tjaka is on his way. He'll be here soon. And with the weapons in the Hydrostar just outside—'

Jimmy looked at Drake with pleading eyes.

'Jimmy, I just don't—'

'Drake, these people are fighting for their lives, ya know. Their land. Their kids. Why can't we help them? What else are we going to do? Deliver packages in New Franco again?'

They were sitting in the middle of a battleground. Pulse rounds fly over their heads. People screaming in agony. Smoke and dust filled the air. Yet in the middle of the combat, Drake was arguing with his best friend about helping a group of people he had no attachment to but to whom Jimmy felt some kinship. It was totally absurd.

'I know you resent yourself for what happened on Mars. Even though you're not to blame. But this time you can make a choice to do the right thing, ya know.'

He hated Jimmy for saying that. It was a low blow. Bringing up Mars and making any comparisons was unfair. He had no idea his actions would result in a war on Mars that spilled over to Earth. How could he? And now, to make him decide if he wanted to play a part in preventing another war. Completely uncalled for.

It did, however, offer him the chance for some redemption. Even if he couldn't admit it out loud, it would lighten the burden he had been carrying for years now. If he could help the people of Bulanalke, to keep their freedoms, and prevent a civil war, he might balance out the cosmic karma a bit. Not that he believed in that crap. But still.

'How do you even know if Lerako is telling the truth? You know Nandi told me the opposite. She told me Mr. Simons is the good guy and trying to take back what is his from Tjaka.'

Nothing Nandi told Drake or anything Mr. Simons did made Drake overly loyal to them. In fact, it was almost the opposite. Mr. Simons had been destabilizing areas, not only in Bulanalke but also in Penta. Drake recalled the shipment of weapons he took to Walker and could only imagine what they would be used for. How many more towns in Penta had Mr. Simons been arming? And to what goal? He was a man hungry for power.

Drake wondered what he would do to him and Jimmy once they returned to New Franco? Surely someone so power-hungry won't let a betrayal like this go unanswered. Even if they made it out of there, they would still have to deal with him. But, if they helped Nandi defeat Tjaka, and went back to New Franco, there would be riches awaiting them. Enough credits to set them up for life. Mr. Simons did promise him three times the original amount.

Drake had always followed his gut, and it was telling him very clearly what to do.

'Jimmy,' Drake grabbed his friend by the shoulders and pulled him in. 'I'm so fucking happy I found you.'

* * *

Getting to Lerako was the easy part. Helping her was the tricky bit. Sitting against a wall, surrounded by fallen fighters, she painted a bleak picture. Her eyes were closed, but as they approached, she opened them up.

'Took your time getting here.'

She smiled, but it quickly turned into a grimace.

'Sorry. I had a ride, but they changed their mind and left me stranded.'

A small chuckle escaped from her pursed lips.

'You know you look like shit, right?'

Ignoring yet another reference to his appearance, Drake said, 'It seems you did all right by Jimmy, and he wants to help you. So, what do you need?'

Drake could feel Jimmy's smile next to him.

'My dad is almost here. He'll have medical supplies and more hands for all the weapons we have. Once he's here, it'll be over like—' Lerako tried to snap her fingers, but she was too weak. Her blood-smeared fingers just slid off each other, without a sound.

Nandi was making inroads into Lerako's defenses, and it was a race against time now, between Nandi and Tjaka. Whoever arrived first would be the victor.

They had to wait it out, and hope Nandi didn't get there first.

Just stay with Lerako and protect her as long as possible.

Do not do anything stupid.

'Did you say the Hydrostar with all the weapons was just outside?' Drake asked.

Jimmy nodded.

'Good,' Drake said. 'I have an idea.'

* * *

Jimmy clung to Drake when he told him his half-assed plan, begging him not to go. And it almost worked. Having struggled so hard to find Jimmy, he didn't want to leave him behind again, but they needed to end this battle. Nandi was almost at Lerako's door and Tjaka was still a few minutes out. If he was to redeem himself, now was the time.

Making his way back towards Nandi, Drake took stock of the two opposing forces. Both sides were running out of fighters, but Nandi had a slight advantage in numbers. If she kept pushing forward, she would easily overrun Lerako.

He was back at the mound of dead fighters, and Drake tried his best to make himself comfortable. Rearranging some of the limbs, he created a small gap, barely big enough for his rifle's muzzle and optics to fit through. In the commotion of the battle, no one would think to look over towards this pile of corpses.

Scanning the area, he found what looked like the last line of Nandi's fighters. He took a deep breath, held it, and slowly took up the slack in the trigger. He kept squeezing until a pulse round crackled out of the muzzle and straight into its target. Drake watched through the pulse rifle optic as the fighter fell to the ground. No one around him took any notice, as they were fighting their own battles. Drake moved his sights slightly to the right and repeated the process. It helped, but he had to be careful not to be spotted. Working his way from the back helped too, as it minimized the chance of someone seeing a comrade fall. He could only take out one selected fighter at a time, hoping it would even the balance a bit.

Nandi's team kept moving forward. They could smell victory. Only a few fighters stood between her and Lerako. If she captured or killed her, it would be over. Lerako's remaining people would flee as soon as their leader fell. Keeping her at bay until Tjaka arrived was crucial.

Only a few meters separated her from Lerako now. Drake had taken out a great number of fighters, but they kept crawling forward. Finger still on the trigger, he moved his rifle's optics around, trying to find the head of the spear. Until now, he hadn't been able to spot Nandi, and he had mixed feelings about what he would do if she came into his sights. If he took her out, it might be game over, but that opportunity had not presented itself. She was leading her team from the front, but she was no mindless grunt. She was as clever and opportunistic a fighter as Drake had ever encountered. He knew she was right there in front of him, but he would never be able to spot her.

But she might try to spot him.

Aiming at one of the fighters in the front, Drake took his time and made sure the shot counted. It did. The fighter fell right in front of his comrades, and in a flash, pulse rounds came flying in Drake's direction. Not only did he have their attention now, but he also slowed down their forward momentum. Instead of focusing on one area, their efforts were now split in two. Something he didn't dare do earlier, as they would have shot his cover and him to pieces. This late in the game meant he only had to survive the barrage for a little while.

That was if everything went to plan.

Pieces of human started to rain down on Drake as his cover was slowly shredded. He pulled his rifle back, not willing to risk any more shots at the opposing team. Now it was about survival. He hoped he had slowed them down enough.

A new salvo of rounds crackled through the air. Somehow, they have intensified their efforts, as the sound was louder than ever before. Yet, none of the rounds hit Drake's hideout. Slowly, and very carefully, Drake peeked through the hole he made for his rifle. The visibility was poor, and he couldn't see much. Risking it, he popped his head out to have a look. He did it so quickly that he couldn't see a thing, but he also didn't get shot at, so he tried again. This time, he lingered a bit longer.

Long enough to see his plan succeed.

| forty |

As far as plans went, it was a typical Benjamin Drake affair. Simple, to the point, and not well thought out. After he set off to ambush Nandi, Jimmy went back to the Hydrostar and sped off towards Tjaka. Nandi's forces had not been replenished in a while, so Jimmy would lead the now armed forces of Tjaka to the same entry Drake used to gain entry. This would then allow them to sneak up on Nandi from behind and overpower her.

Keeping it simple. Since Nandi reacted impulsively and chased down Lerako, she came in unprepared for a full-on attack. She could handle Lerako, but not Tjaka as well. Having two forces, from opposing sides, would be game over.

No one was paying attention to Drake's corner of the building, but he could see the whole thing playing out. Tjaka's fighters came in, pulse rifles blazing, and decimated Nandi's rear flank. Amid the chaos and confusion, some fighters even ran away, leaving the front line to defend two sides. Nandi was trapped in the middle, with no way out. Her only option was to surrender, but Drake knew that would never happen.

Being on the side, in a no-man's zone, he was able to quickly make his way back to Lerako. As planned, Jimmy was back there too. After dropping the weapons off, he gathered medical supplies from Tjaka's convoy and hurried back to attend to Lerako. He had already applied synth skin and was giving her blood proteins when Drake arrived.

'Okay. You won, Lerako. Call your dad and tell him to stop. Tell Nandi to surrender. You can still win without killing her.'

Lerako had the fire back in her eyes.

'I will grant you safe passage back to the border, and I will pay you for the weapons we took.'

It was not the answer he was looking for.

'Please. You have everything you asked for. There is no need to keep killing.'

'Drake, I know you are naïve to your own arrogance, so I'll say this as nicely as I can. Leave us alone. This is not your land. This is not your people. This is not your fight. Leave. Now.'

'But I helped you. I saved you. You owe me.'

Her smile failed to mask her irritation.

'Go now. This is not Penta or Shangcorp. This is Bulanalke. Don't dare to assume you know anything about this place. I do owe you. Therefore, I'm offering you safe passage, and credits for the weapons. Take it, before you outstay your welcome.'

People cheering and singing replaced the sound of pulse fire. It grew louder and louder until it burst into the room with them. In the middle of the singing and cheering fighters stood a tall, strong man, radiating power.

'Dad!' Lerako called out.

'Lerako! The queen of Bulanalke!'

The chanting and cheering escalated into a frenzied crescendo.

Chief Tjaka stood before his adoring warriors, basking in their adoration, patiently waiting for them to calm down.

'And this must be the man who came to my daughter's aid in her hour of need.'

Chief Tjaka stood, staring at Drake. He had no idea if he was allowed to respond or if he was supposed to bow or something. Luckily, Jimmy was back in the picture.

'That's him! Saved us all, ya know.'

'Jimmy, that's not—'

'And is this man part of your group?' Tjaka's deep voice rumbled above the chatter in the crowd.

Two men showed up, supporting a third between them.

'Yes, he definitely is,' Drake replied upon seeing Robbie.

He looked in a better state than Drake but was still a bit unsteady on his feet. Drake stepped forward and steadied him as the two men let go of him.

'Who's this?' Jimmy demanded, his face in Drake's face.

'Robbie. Don't you remember him? He worked with Rut. We met on the ship on the way here.'

Robbie lifted a hand as if to say hi. Jimmy ignored him.

'Doesn't ring a bell, ya know.'

'Jimmy, he's a friend, not an enemy. If it wasn't for him, we would never have found you.'

Jimmy snorted, and half turned his back on Robbie. Drake decided it was a conversation they could have, once they were safely back on the road.

'Sorry chief. Just some internal matters we need to clear up, later.' Drake gave Jimmy *the* look. 'Are we free to go?'

The chief looked at Lerako, before addressing Drake. 'Whatever my daughter has promised you, I will honor. You saved my daughter and delivered me, my enemy. Thank you.'

'Okay. Just one thing. What happened to Nandi?'

For the first time, Chief Tjaka's expression changed. 'Like you, we also have some internal matters to clear up.'

After all the bloodshed, and the alliances, Drake still didn't know if the right group won. He had no idea who the right group was. Did such a thing even exist?

'I can see you do not understand Bulanalke, Drake, and you never will. It's not in your blood. She is not your mother. Bulanalke is not a place for foreigners to tame. She is ours, and we are her children. It is now time for you to go.'

Things happened quickly. Lerako was swept up and carried away, the chief disappeared into the crowd, and Drake, Jimmy, and Robbie were shuffled away.

As they were ushered past the spot where Nandi's forces broke the line, Drake saw a familiar color in the mess. A color he knew would mean the world to Jimmy.

'Jimmy, look over there,' Drake pointed it out.

He saw Jimmy's eyes grow unbelievably big, as Jimmy realized what it was and ran to retrieve it. The fighters escorting them didn't give chase, as everyone was done fighting for the day. Instead, everyone watched as Jimmy retrieved the brightly, yet scuffed up, orange ASR.

'It's him, Drake! It's really him!' Jimmy yelled as he returned with Seymour. The ASR had barely any charge left and looked as if it had been dropped from a building, but Jimmy's enthusiasm for seeing his beloved ASR had no bounds.

'I hate to say it, Jimmy, but he came in very handy.'

'Of course, he did, ya know. Of course, he did.' Jimmy laughed.

Emotionally drained and physically broken, Benjamin Drake had never felt so happy in his life.

| forty-one |

The drive to the harbor was one of the longest of Drake's life.

'So, am I completely replaced now, or just partly?'

'Did he really have to come the whole way, ya know?'

'Could we maybe drop him off here?'

'Wouldn't it be better, ya know, if he stayed with Rut?'

'Do you really, I mean really know him?'

Robbie took a big hit to the head and slept most of the trip which gave Jimmy too much time to overthink things.

'So, we're dropping him off the moment, ya know, we reach the shore?'

'Jimmy, he is not replacing you. Okay.'

Jimmy glanced back at the sleeping intruder. 'Obviously, ya know.'

They were nearing the harbor, and with it came a better, stronger signal for their HICs, ARPs, and the Hydrocomet's DDU. Message notifications were going off constantly, and Drake had Jimmy mute them. Nothing that happened in their absence could be more important than what they had endured these past weeks. Whatever crisis awaited them could wait.

Drake didn't want to contemplate the shit show awaiting them back in New Franco.

Mr. Simons would surely not take the event lightly. Although Drake kept his word to the old man, his daughter still ended up killed or captured. Drake wasn't sure which but feared he knew the answer.

Numbers was surely going to try and extort more credits out of them than they made on the contract, and Drake would have to figure out a way to deal with him and his illegal military androids.

And then there was Lt. Wells. He left her, promising it would be his last dodgy job, but he was returning with even more destruction and chaos attributed to his name. It was already a risk for her to be associated with him even before he left and became involved in a civil war in another territory.

Waivers started popping up on the screen, announcing their arrival at the border crossing at the harbor. Jimmy took care of it all, creating the welcome illusion it was just a normal day. The mayhem of the last few weeks was behind them.

'Why did you help Nandi, ya know?' Jimmy had asked that question multiple times and every time Drake failed to come up with an answer that satisfied Jimmy.

'I've told you. She was a means to an end. I'm more interested in your relationship with Lerako.'

'Huh? We don't have a relationship, ya know. I just felt like she told the truth.'

A uniformed guard, dressed in a Shangcorp outfit, waved them through. It seemed the war effort made little difference this far away from the action.

'Did you think Nandi told the truth?' Jimmy asked once they passed the guard.

'I don't know, Jimmy. It felt like no matter who we helped, the people in the street were going to suffer. I don't think either one of them had the interest of the people at heart. I guess we just helped the lesser evil of the two.'

Robbie grunted from the back.

'Ugh,' Jimmy groaned back.

Another Shangcorp officer directed them, and Drake carefully maneuvered the Hydrostar onto the freight deck of the large ship. The deck was already pretty full, mostly containers, carrying who knows what back to Penta and Shangcorp. Drake found his designated spot and parked the Hydrostar.

'Should we just leave him here?'

Shaking his head, Drake said, 'For the last time, Jimmy, he is not replacing you! Okay?'

Drake and Jimmy ran the shutdown procedures and made sure the Hydrostar was put in security mode.

'I think I'll start working on Seymour, ya know? Maybe someone on the ship has some spare parts I can buy.' Jimmy grabbed the beaten-up ASR as he exited the cabin.

Drake woke Robbie up and carefully helped him out of the Hydrostar.

'And I guess I'll start working on Robbie and see if anyone has some spare parts for him,' Drake joked. Jimmy didn't laugh.

Leaving the Hydrostar behind, they made their way to the same cabin number they had on their journey to Bulanalke. As they approached the cabin, Drake felt another vibration in his arm. Somehow a message came through, unmuted. Glancing down at his arm, he was about to swipe the message away, when the name at the top caught his eye.

It was from Lt. Wells.

She must have used some Penta tech to force the message through to his HIC, bypassing his settings to mute everything. It made Drake a bit uneasy, but his excitement to hear from her overruled everything.

Propping Robbie up against the wall in the narrow walkway, and holding him steady with his hip, Drake opened the message on his HIC.

His happy mood dissolved in seconds when he read her message.

Drake, I'm in big trouble. I need your help. WHERE ARE YOU?

FROM THE AUTHOR

Thank you for purchasing and reading my book. These days, reviews are crucial to the success of a book, so if you enjoyed what Drake, Jimmy and LT Wells got up to, please take a second and leave a review or rating. Not only would I greatly appreciate it, but it would also make a huge difference.

If you wanted to stay up to date with news and upcoming books, feel free to join me on Facebook or Instagram, and subscribing to my newsletter.

Until next time!

Eric

https://www.facebook.com/erickrugerwriter/
https://erickruger.com.au/join-us
Instagram - @erickrugerauthor

www.ingramcontent.com/pod-product-compliance
Lightning Source LLC
Chambersburg PA
CBHW030508120726
47904CB00005B/1390